Also by Claire Kingsley

Sidecar Crush

CLAIRE KINGSLEY
WITH LUCY SCORE

Bloom books

Published by Bloom Books, an imprint of Sourcebooks
P.O. Box 4410, Naperville, Illinois 60567–4410
(630) 961-3900
sourcebooks.com

Cataloging-in-Publication data is on file with the Library of Congress.

Originally published in 2018 by Claire Kingsley.

Printed and bound in the United States of America.
POD

For the lovers and artists in all of us.

Chapter One

Jameson

I didn't care what my sister said, being here tonight wasn't *good for me*.

She'd called no less than half a dozen times today, insisting I needed to get out of the house. Why? Who knew with Scarlett. Once that girl got an idea in her head, it was damn hard to get it out. And apparently Miss Scarlett Rose had decided her brother needed a drink at the Lookout.

Now that I'd been sitting here awhile, I'd decided she was wrong. I didn't need to be here. I'd have been much happier if I'd stayed in my shop. I made my living as a metal artist, and I was working on a big commission—had plenty to keep me busy. Granted, I liked a cold beer as much as the next guy, and Nicolette served 'em up good. But what I did *not* like was the fact that half the people in here were looking at me.

They thought they were being so damn sneaky. Little glances over their shoulders. Heads together to whisper.

Moving my gaze back to the table, I shifted on my stool. The noise of a dozen conversations drifted around me. I knew what people were whispering about. All us Bodines knew. They were wondering if our dad—a man who was no longer among the living—had been responsible for the disappearance, and possible murder, of Callie Kendall a dozen years ago.

Did I think he'd done it? I didn't rightly know. There'd never been a lot of love between me and my father, but that didn't mean I believed he'd been a murderer.

Hadn't been a lot of love between our father and any of his children, save Scarlett. She'd always tried the hardest with him. Maybe because she was the baby, or the only girl. Hell if I knew.

There had been good times with him, and with our mama. A lot of 'em, in fact. But Dad had made it hard. Drank too much. Blamed us kids for every problem in his life. My brother, Gibson, had taken the worst of it. Turned him into a mean son of a bitch if you weren't related to him. Sometimes even if you were. Bowie seemed to have decided he'd be Dad's opposite. Nice guy, Bowie. Upstanding sort. Our half-brother, named Jonah after our father, hadn't the pleasure—or misfortune—of growing up with Dad. That seemed to have been a blessing, far as I could tell.

Me? I'd always tried to stay out of his way. Keep my head down. Be invisible. Kinda what I did in general, and it usually worked out fine.

Wasn't working no more. Not with the whole town whispering about Jonah Bodine Sr. and Callie Kendall's damn sweater. Now eyes were on me, and I did not like it. Not one bit.

Moisture beaded on my beer bottle and the scent of garlic fries and whiskey wafted by. I took a sip and ran my thumb down the cool glass.

Bowie sat across from me, staring into his beer. He was usually a bit more talkative, but tonight he'd been quiet. I hadn't asked why. June Tucker sat next to him, reading a book. I liked Juney. I found her bewildering sometimes, but she also didn't talk too much, or expect me to. Although she did tend to ask awkward questions.

Jonah sat on her other side. We'd only found out about

Jonah's existence a couple of months ago when he showed up in town looking for us. He'd heard about Dad's death, and saw he had siblings he'd never known. Of course Scarlett had claimed him as a Bodine after about ninety seconds of knowing him. I reckoned she'd been right to do so. Jonah was a decent sort. He hadn't been sure about staying in Bootleg, and I wasn't sure if he'd wind up settling here long-term. Somehow—I wasn't quite sure how, seeing as the agreement had been made in the sixth inning of a Bootleg Cock Spurs softball game, and I'd been pretty far gone on moonshine—Jonah had recently become my roommate.

I took another sip of my beer and Scarlett flashed me a sweet smile. She was standing by another table with her beau, Devlin. My brothers and I had reluctantly agreed that Dev was all right for Scarlett. She'd made us promise we wouldn't toss him in the lake again. We got around it by promising we wouldn't *unless he deserved it*. She'd thank us later. Devlin was obviously crazy about Scar, but every man deserves to get his ass thrown in the lake once in a while. Even the good ones.

Normally I wasn't one to start a conversation where one wasn't already happening, but I glanced up at June. "Where's Cass tonight, Juney?"

She blinked at me once. "On a date."

My eyes flicked to Bowie. His jaw tightened, and his eyelid twitched. Now I knew why Bowie was playing the part of the broody Bodine tonight. He had eyes for June's sister, Cassidy Tucker, but for reasons none of us could fathom, he'd never done a thing about it.

"A date, huh?" I said. "Who's she seeing?"

"Someone she met online," June said. "I told her the probability of finding a suitable match using an appropriate online resource was high."

"*You* gave her this idea?" Bowie asked.

"It's perfectly logical," June said. "Cassidy would like to meet, and date, a man with potential for long-term commitment. Utilizing a dating application will widen her range of potential mates."

3

"Potential mates?" Jonah asked. "You make it sound like she's an animal."

"Technically speaking, we're all animals," June said. "*Homo sapiens* are classified within kingdom Animalia."

"Thanks for the science lesson, June Bug," Bowie said.

"Bowie, are you experiencing feelings of jealousy because Cassidy is having a potentially romantic encounter with another man?" June asked, her voice flat. There was no sarcasm or humor in her question. She was really just asking.

I tried to cover my smirk by taking a drink of my beer.

"No," Bowie said. "I'm good."

June shrugged and went back to her book.

Scarlett swept up next to me and elbowed me in the ribs. "See, Jame. I told you this would be good for you. Aren't you glad you came out of hiding?"

"Not especially."

"Oh, stop," she said. "Y'all are a bunch of negative Nancys over here. Bowie, quit your scowling. You look like Gibs."

"Who looks like me?" Gibson asked.

He'd come up behind Scarlett, a bottle of water in his hand. The oldest and youngest Bodines were opposites, and not just in gender. Scarlett was tiny, while Gibs was the tallest of all of us. Looked the most like Dad, too, which I was pretty sure he hated.

"Bowie," Scarlett said. "He's over there trying to turn his beer sour."

Gibson just grunted.

"Y'all are a sad-lookin' lot," Scarlett said. "And I know exactly why."

"Why is that?" Bowie asked.

I wanted to kick him under the table for encouraging her.

"Because you're single," Scarlett said. "Here I am, the youngest Bodine, and I've got this great man. And you poor things are still waiting to find someone."

"Who says we want to?" Gibson asked.

She smacked his arm. "I wasn't talking about your grumpy

ass. You find a woman who can put up with you, and I swear I'll learn to cook just so I can bake her the best pecan pie in Olamette County. She'll deserve it."

Gibson snorted and took a drink of his water.

"But y'all," she said, pointing to the rest of us sitting at the table. "You need to think about it. Finding somebody. Settling down. It'd be good for you."

"Like coming out for a beer'd be good for me?" I asked.

"Yes," she said, poking me in the shoulder. "Just like that, only better. Come on, Jame, that girl you've been seeing doesn't count if you can't even bring her around to introduce to your family."

"I ain't seein' her anymore," I said.

"What?" Scarlett asked, her voice going up several octaves. Devlin paused behind her, like he wasn't sure if he should come near or wait to see if it was safe. "Since when?"

I rolled my eyes and hunched down over my beer. Half the place was looking at us openly now. And the other half was straining to listen.

"Jesus, don't make a scene," I said. "It ended quite a while ago. It's fine."

I'd been seeing Willa Sawyer, a girl who lived over in Maryland, for a couple of years. It was an on-again, off-again type thing. Long distance. Sometimes she'd come out here and see me; other times I went to her. Wasn't ever real serious, but we had a nice time when we were together. She'd decided she wanted more commitment than I could give her. Met someone else—planned to get married soon. Kinda left me without as much to look forward to, but I was glad for her. She was a nice girl—deserved that sort of thing.

"Well, you could have told us," Scarlett said. "Here I thought you were keeping her a secret for a reason. Like maybe you were ashamed of us."

Devlin seemed to have decided it was safe to come near. He stepped up next to Scarlett and slipped his arm around her waist.

"Don't be dumb, Scar," I said. "I wasn't keeping secrets, and you know I'm not ashamed of y'all. It just wasn't a big deal."

"Too bad it's over," Gibson said. "Seemed like you had a good thing going. Got a little action when you wanted it, and none of the bullshit."

"Isn't that exactly what you have?" Scarlett asked, her disdain for Gibson's dating habits—or lack thereof—evident in her tone. "Action when you want it. No bullshit… That is, no commitment or connection to anyone."

"Scarlett, just because y'all are acting like lovesick puppies doesn't mean the rest of us need to go out and get ourselves attached," Gibson said.

Scarlett rolled her eyes and turned her back to him. "What about you, June? Got your eye on anyone special?"

June looked over the top of her book. "No."

"Jonah?" she asked.

"Sorry, Scarlett," Jonah said. "Not really."

Scarlett huffed and grabbed Devlin's arm. "Y'all are no fun. Come on, let's go play pool."

Our table quieted down considerably in the absence of Scarlett. She pranced around the pool table, shaking her backside at Devlin. The way he watched her still got my hackles up, and I had to remind myself that Scarlett was his girl now. He could look at her like that. Truth was, he *should* look at her like that.

I reckoned any guy in Scarlett's life couldn't win, not with us as her brothers. If he looked at her with those hungry eyes, we wanted to bust his face. But if he hadn't been looking at her like that, we'd have hated him for not appreciating her enough.

The TV behind me caught my attention and the noise level in the bar went down a notch. Nicolette had just changed the channel to a reality TV show, *Roughing It*.

The premise wasn't all that exciting. A bunch of minor celebrities stuck in a cabin out in the woods somewhere, expected to get by without a lot of modern conveniences. Mostly it was just a bunch of drama between the cast members while they fumbled around in the woods. Definitely not something I'd watch under normal circumstances.

But my interest—and the interest of everyone else in Bootleg—stemmed from the fact that Leah Mae Larkin was on the show.

Leah Mae was one of us. A Bootlegger. She'd lived here until she was twelve. Then her mama had divorced her daddy and moved her away. After that, she'd spent summers here for a while—at least until the rest of the world discovered how pretty she was and she became a model. She'd dropped the Mae—went by Leah Larkin now.

Back when she'd still been Leah Mae, she'd been one of my only friends. Maybe my best friend.

I hadn't seen her in a long time. And it wasn't like I was harboring any foolish unrequited feelings for her. She was basically a celebrity now. I was only interested in what she was up to because it wasn't every day that a Bootlegger was on TV.

Shifting in my seat, I looked at the screen. There was Leah Mae, standing in front of a mirror, pulling all that long blond hair up into a ponytail. She'd always wanted to be on TV. When we were kids, we'd spent more hours than I could count with her making up plays and starring in them. Playing dress-up and twirling around. Telling me how she was going to be a famous actress.

The scene cut to the cast going out to the nearby lake to fish. Maybe it was one of those challenges they were always putting them through. People got voted off the show each week, and so far, Leah Mae had made it every time.

I tried not to pay attention, but they kept showing Leah Mae struggling with her fishing pole. Kinda looked like she didn't know which end was which, but that couldn't be the case. Leah Mae could out-fish anyone, and we all knew it. Sure, with her glamorous lifestyle now, posing for pictures and walking in fashion shows, she probably didn't get out fishing much. But fishing was like riding a bike. You didn't just up and forget.

The guy in the boat with her asked if she needed help.

Brock Winston. That guitar-toting pansy-ass. His music wasn't terrible, but I'd hated him from the first minute I saw him on that show with Leah Mae. He was married to some actress, but he sure seemed to be cozying up to Leah Mae in a way a man shouldn't if he already had a girl.

Damn celebrities. One famous girl wasn't enough for that guy? He had to go flirting with another?

Brock got her pole fixed and the camera zoomed in. Her eyes caught me, held me fast. Back when we were kids, she'd always had this sparkle in her eyes when she was acting. But there was no sparkle now. They were flat. Still damn pretty, but this wasn't Leah Mae. It didn't look like her, the girl I'd once known. She looked like a girl in a cage, being made to do tricks.

Leah Mae turned her gaze to Brock and the camera panned in on him. He was giving her a look I knew all too well. A distinct *I want to fuck you tonight* look. All men had one, and we could spot them in each other if we were paying attention. And that was exactly how Brock Winston was looking at Leah Mae Larkin on Nicolette's stupid big-screen TV.

I turned back to my beer. Didn't much want to see the rest.

"I bet those two are gettin' busy in the back when the cameras are off," Rhett Ginsler said behind me.

"You think?" Trent McCulty asked.

"Sure as shit," Rhett said. "She's actin' all coy, but I'd bet ten bucks and a jar of moonshine she's spending her nights getting plowed by that Brock guy."

The muscles in my back clenched and I tightened my grip on my beer.

"Maybe she's just playing it up for the camera," Trent said.

"Could be," Rhett said. "Leah Mae's an attention whore anyway."

I rose so fast my stool fell backward behind me, crashing to the floor with a loud bang. Without much awareness of how I got there, I stood behind Rhett and Trent, my hands balled into fists.

"I reckon you need to stop talking shit about her," I said, my voice a low growl.

Before I finished speaking, Bowie and Gibs were already flanking me, ready to throw down. They probably didn't know what had me so riled, but they wouldn't care. This was how we did things. Backed each other. They might kick my ass later if I got them into something stupid—although it was usually Gibson getting the rest of us into something stupid, not me. I was prepared to deal with the consequences. No one used the word *whore* in a sentence with Leah Mae's name. Not in my hearing.

Rhett shifted on his stool, turning to face me. "What's it to you?"

"She's one of ours."

He snorted and took a swig of his beer. "I guess. How long since she's even set foot in Bootleg, though?"

"Doesn't matter," Bowie said, and Gibson growled in agreement. "Jameson's right."

"And I suppose you think you're gonna do something about it?" Rhett asked.

Eyes were on us. Lines being drawn. A couple more guys stood nearby, clearly on Rhett's side. Like I gave a shit. Jonah stood on Gibson's right. He hadn't grown up here, but he understood.

"You're damn right I'm gonna do something about it," I said.

Rhett got off the stool. He was about my height—could look me in the eyes. I stared back, my face hard, my jaw set.

"Y'all better back away from my bar if you're gettin' rough," Nicolette said.

"Well, shit." Scarlett's voice.

I saw Devlin come up next to Bowie. He was rolling up his sleeves, but he leaned closer and spoke under his breath. "Watch it, guys. You're supposed to stay out of trouble."

"Bootleg justice, Dev," Bowie said, his eyes never leaving Rhett and Trent.

"I know, I know," Devlin said.

I wasn't an idiot. Hitting first was a bad idea, if you could avoid it. But if I didn't hit first…

"What are you hanging out in here for, anyway, Rhett?" I asked. "Shouldn't you be keeping tabs on your girlfriend?"

"What's that supposed to mean?" Rhett asked.

I shrugged. "Word around town is Misty Lynn's been messin' around with Wade Zirkel. I reckon you ain't man enough, so she had to go look elsewhere."

"You son of a bitch." Rhett drew his fist back, and I let it come. Took it across the jaw.

Rhett's punch was the invitation I was looking for. I clocked him square in the nose while all hell broke loose around me. Rhett grabbed his face and hollered, blood running down his chin. Gibson and Bowie dove in, pushing and punching at anyone who dared face them. Even Dev and Jonah got in on it.

The scuffle was broken up quick, and I let someone pull me back. I'd bloodied Rhett's nose, and I was satisfied with that. Didn't seem like too many punches had landed on anyone. The only blood was Rhett's, although Trent looked like he might wind up with a shiner. Gibson flexed his fingers a few times. Everyone else gave each other a good mean glower and went back to their places.

"Jameson, what in the hell were you doing?" Scarlett asked. She touched my jaw and tipped my face see if I was hurt.

"Rhett needs to remember himself, is all," I said, jerking my chin out of her reach. "I'm going home. See y'all later."

"If you wanted to go home so bad, you could have just left. You didn't have to punch someone in the dang face," Scarlett called after me.

I walked out, ignoring the eyes that followed me. Yeah, starting a bar fight meant people would look—and talk. Although a scuffle in the Lookout was pretty typical for a Friday night. But I could not abide that good-for-nothing pond scum Rhett Ginsler talking about Leah Mae like that. She'd been my friend once, and that still meant something to me. That jackass needed to remember his manners.

After I got home, I might have scrolled through her Instagram a little bit. And that might have been a habit I'd gotten into recently. A habit that was right stupid, and I knew it. Nothing had ever happened between Leah Mae and me when she'd been a normal girl, visiting her daddy for the summer. Sure as shit wasn't any chance of something happening between us now.

Chapter Two

Leah Mae

The scenery rushed by in a blur of green and brown. I'd been looking forward to the drive—I hadn't been out here in so long—but all I could think about was last night's episode of *Roughing It*.

"How could they have done that to me?" I asked.

Kelvin had his hands on the steering wheel of our rental car, his phone in a cradle on the dashboard with a map showing the route to Bootleg Springs. He was wearing a Ralph Lauren dress shirt and gray slacks, a pair of Versace sunglasses perched on his nose. I was the one with the modeling career, but Kelvin Graham looked like one too. It was how he'd gotten his start when he was just sixteen. He had that pretty-boy Abercrombie and Fitch look. Dark hair and hazel eyes. Toned physique. Perfect bone structure.

But he liked the business side of modeling more than being in front of the camera. He wasn't a man who liked people telling him what to do. He owned his own agency now—managing my career as well as the careers of dozens of other models—and this way he could grow his stubble, or cut his hair, or put on a few extra pounds of lean muscle, and no one could tell him not to.

"Babe, you're getting excited over nothing," he said without looking at me. "We both knew they were going to make it look like you and Brock were flirting."

"But we weren't," I said. "And I'm telling you, that fishing pole was rigged to break on me. I know how to fish, and they made me look like an idiot."

"You looked great," he said, flashing me a smile.

I looked down at my phone. The gossip columns were all buzzing over whether something was going to happen between Leah Larkin and Brock Winston on *Roughing It*. Would Leah tempt Brock away from his sweet-as-apple-pie wife, Maisie Miller?

It made me want to gag. Brock had seemed like a nice guy when we were filming, but even if we'd both been single, I wouldn't have been interested in him. He was too flat. Too one-dimensional. He had a nice singing voice, but he didn't write any of his own music. He wasn't that creative. Having spent time with him filming the show, I wasn't sure if he'd ever had an original thought in his head.

And Brock was most definitely *not* single. He'd had a very public romance with Maisie Miller when they were both celebrity judges on *Talent USA*. The entire country had been enamored with their sweet little glances and whispered flirtations in front of the camera. When paparazzi had caught them kissing in an out-of-the-way bistro one night, everyone had gone crazy. People had been rooting for them to fall in love, and when it happened, it was like the happily-ever-after the world had been waiting for.

Now everyone was predicting that I'd be the vixen. The woman to break up the perfect love story.

Well, I hadn't. Filming had already wrapped on the show, and as far as I knew, Brock was back in L.A. with Maisie. They'd been quiet on social media, but all the cast members had. Our contracts stipulated what we could and couldn't reveal before all the episodes aired, so the easiest thing to do was lay low for a while.

I glanced down at the ring on my left hand. I wasn't single, either, although the world didn't know. Kelvin had insisted we keep our engagement secret until after the season finale of *Roughing It* aired. I'd left my ring at home when I went to film the show, and we had yet to tell anyone, save my mom and stepdad. And they knew to keep it under wraps.

Now we were heading to my hometown to tell my dad.

I'd grown up in Bootleg Springs, West Virginia, and after my parents' divorce, I'd spent summers there with my dad. I had so many good memories of Bootleg. Long days spent in the sun sipping lemonade and sweet tea. Jumping into the lake that was as warm as bathwater. Traipsing through the woods. Coming home at sunset, hungry, dirty, and tired.

I hadn't been in Bootleg Springs since I was sixteen. That was the summer Callie Kendall had disappeared. She'd been my age, and spent her summers in Bootleg, too. As soon as my mom had heard about her disappearance, she'd insisted I come home to Jacksonville.

Not long after that, my modeling career had taken off. There were always auditions and casting calls, photo shoots and fashion shows. Things had moved fast, and my life had changed almost overnight. It had been easier to fly my dad out to visit me, wherever I happened to be, rather than make the trip to West Virginia.

But this year, Dad hadn't been doing well. Although he'd quit smoking years ago, he had ongoing lung problems. Last winter, he'd been hospitalized with pneumonia and hadn't bothered to tell me until he'd already gone home. I was still mad at him for keeping it from me, but he'd insisted he didn't want me to worry.

He was my daddy. Of course I was going to worry.

I felt awful for not having come to see him sooner. But filming *Roughing It* had gotten in the way, and afterward

I'd had a series of photo shoots to get through. But now my schedule was clear for the foreseeable future while Kelvin and I considered my next career move. With this rare time off, and our engagement, I'd decided it was time to visit Bootleg Springs again.

Although I hadn't been here in a dozen years, the road was still familiar. And as we pulled into town, it was like stepping back in time.

"You have got to be kidding me," Kelvin said, looking around as the first buildings came into view.

"What?" I asked.

He lowered his sunglasses. "Nothing. It's just… you said it was a small town in West Virginia. I guess I hadn't realized you meant *small-town West Virginia*."

"Come on, Kelvin, don't be a snob. It's charming."

"Not the word I'd use," he said. "But okay."

I rolled my eyes and looked out the window. The route to my dad's house skirted the outside of town. I'd have to show Kelvin around later. From what I could see, Bootleg Springs looked much the same as I remembered it. Dad had told me it had grown as tourists discovered the hot springs. But so far, it still held the same charm I remembered so well.

My dad lived about five minutes outside town. Kelvin cast me a questioning glance when we turned down the gravel driveway, but he didn't comment on it. We bounced down the long drive until the house came into view.

Dad's house was a little more worn that I remembered. The wood slats were weathered and there was a slight sag to the front porch that hadn't been there before.

A grin stole over my face at the sight of my dad. He sat in his old rocking chair on the front porch, just like he always had. Kelvin brought the car to a stop and I hopped out.

"Hey, Daddy."

My heart squeezed when I saw how slowly he rose from his chair. Add to that the tube beneath his nose connected to an oxygen tank, and the sight of him almost brought me to tears.

"Leah Mae sunshine," he said, holding out his arms. His hair was more gray than blond now, and the lines at the corners of his eyes and across his forehead had deepened. He wore a faded hickory shirt and a pair of jeans that had seen better days.

I walked up the creaky steps. "Dad, you didn't tell me you were on oxygen."

"Oh, this?" he asked, tugging on the clear rubber tubing. "This is nothing. Just a little extra help. I won't need it much longer."

I stepped carefully into his hug and was surprised at how far around him my arms went. Dad had always been a big man—tall with a barrel chest and arms thick from hard work. His height hadn't gone anywhere—I was five foot ten, but at six foot four, he still made me feel a bit like a little girl. But he felt so much smaller—his thickness was diminishing with either age or his illness.

He was only fifty-four—much too young for this.

"It's so good to see you," I said, pulling away. The stairs behind me creaked beneath Kelvin's feet. "Daddy, this is Kelvin Graham. Kelvin, this is my dad, Clay Larkin."

The smile left Dad's face and he straightened. He had a good three inches on Kelvin, and apparently he intended to use them.

"Mr. Larkin," Kelvin said, his voice smooth as he held out his hand to shake.

Dad hesitated a second before shaking his hand. "Kelvin, huh?"

Kelvin's eyes flicked to me, as if he wasn't sure how to respond. "Yes, well, it's nice to finally meet you. I think the last time you visited Leah, I was away on business."

"I reckon," Dad said.

I'd expected my dad to be a little cold to Kelvin at first. That was the Bootleg father way. He'd warm up to him soon.

I hoped.

"Well, Daddy, can we come inside? It was a long drive from the airport."

Dad's smile returned. "Of course, sweetheart. Come on in."

Kelvin stood back with his hands in his pockets, eying the old house while Dad shuffled inside, wheeling his oxygen tank behind him.

The house was clean and cozy, with a wood-burning stove in the corner and a worn couch with a blanket over it. It smelled faintly of pine and cinnamon. A few pictures of me as a little girl hung on the walls in mismatched frames.

Dad went over to his old leather recliner and lowered himself down. It took him a second to get his tubes situated. Kelvin followed me in, but stayed standing while I sat on the couch.

"Place looks nice," I said. "You're still getting help from Betsy Stirling, aren't you?"

"Yeah, Betsy comes by regularly," he said. "Checks up on me and helps me keep the place in order."

Dad had balked at hiring someone to help him around the house, but after his hospitalization, I'd insisted. And Betsy Stirling was perfect. She was a part-time nurse down at the Bootleg Springs Clinic, and had been looking for a side gig to keep her busy. She helped Dad with things like grocery shopping and cleaning up the house, and she kept tabs on his health. It made me feel a lot better to have her around.

"How long do you think you'll be in town?" Dad asked.

"A few days," Kelvin said.

I glanced up at Kelvin, raising my eyebrows. Our return flight to L.A. wasn't for a week. But since he'd insisted on flying in and out of Pittsburgh—as if there was something wrong with airports in West Virginia—we'd need to leave Bootleg Springs on Friday afternoon. Still, that was more than *a few days*.

"We'll be here until Friday, actually."

Kelvin cleared his throat but didn't argue with me.

"Anyway, Dad, there's something Kelvin and I wanted to talk to you about." My heart started to thump harder and my fingers tingled. I didn't know why I was so nervous to tell him I was getting married. It hadn't been difficult to tell my mom.

But I'd been more sure of how she was going to react. Dad? He could go either way. And as frail as he seemed, I didn't want to shock him too much.

"All right," he said, resting his hands on his thighs. His gaze flicked to Kelvin for a second before coming back to me.

"Well, you know Kelvin and I have been seeing each other for a couple years," I said. "We've decided to get married."

"Huh," Dad said. "Is that so?"

"Yes," I said, trying to keep my voice bright. "We can't talk about it publicly yet, but we wanted to tell you while we were here."

Dad crossed his arms and leveled Kelvin with a hard stare. "You've already asked for her hand?"

Kelvin blinked. "Asked for her hand? We decided to get married, yes."

"Isn't there something you've forgotten, son?" Dad asked.

"I'm not sure I understand."

"I don't recall you ever coming to me to ask my permission," Dad said.

Kelvin's brow furrowed, and he cracked a little smile. "Well, no, but that's a very old-fashioned custom, don't you think?"

"'Round here, that's the way it's done," Dad said.

"Okay…" Kelvin said. "But Leah is a twenty-eight-year-old woman, not a girl being handed off with a dowry."

"Daddy," I said, putting my hand on his knee, "Kelvin didn't realize that would be so important to you. That isn't the sort of thing everybody does anymore. This is my fault; I should have told him."

Dad looked at me, his eyes boring deep into mine. "You want to marry this man?"

"Well, yeah."

He held my gaze a moment longer, scrutinizing me. I tried not to fidget. He sighed, like he was resigning himself to something unpleasant. "When's the wedding?"

"We haven't set a date yet."

"It depends on our schedules," Kelvin said. "We probably

won't have time for anything fancy. I've been thinking we'd just go to Vegas after *Roughing It* airs."

I glanced at Kelvin in surprise. He'd never mentioned getting married in Vegas before. "You don't want a wedding?"

"We could still have a wedding, babe," he said. "But this way, we could work it in when we both have a few days free. Come on, you don't want to get married by Elvis?"

My mouth dropped open. "No, I don't want to get married by Elvis."

He smiled. "You know, you're right. If we have a big wedding, we could turn it into a great PR opportunity. We could sell the rights to the wedding photos."

I gaped at him. "We're not selling the rights to our wedding photos. What are you talking about?"

"I'm glad you brought it up," Kelvin said. "We'd be crazy not to. That's a huge missed opportunity. We should get planning now if we want to capitalize on your visibility from the show."

He walked outside, pulling out his phone as he went. The screen door banged shut behind him.

"Really?" Dad asked.

I sighed. "I know, he seems… opportunistic. It's just the way he is. That's why he's so successful."

Dad raised his eyebrows. He wasn't buying it.

"He's just… not a Bootleg type of man," I said.

"No, he is not."

"But that doesn't mean he doesn't have other good qualities," I said. "He's just different from what you're used to."

"Leah Mae, I've seen the sorts of people you run with now," he said. "Slick big city folk. Smooth talkers. I admit, I've never cared much for any of it. But it's your dream and I am nothing but proud of you. And if this is what you want, I'll be happy for you."

"Thanks, Dad." I squeezed his hand. "Listen, why don't I take Kelvin into town and show him around. We'll come back here with dinner for all of us before we go check in to our cabin. Do you need any groceries?"

"No, I'm fine."

I didn't believe him. I'd pick him up a few things just in case. "We'll be back in a little while."

I got up and found Kelvin on the front porch, typing something on his phone. Probably texting his assistant, asking her to look for wedding venues. I sighed again. That was Kelvin, always going at full speed. I figured I should be happy he'd let go of that silly run-off-to-Vegas idea so easily. He wasn't always so quick to change his mind.

"Come on, let's go into town," I said. "We'll bring back dinner."

"Are we going to be able to find a place that's paleo and gluten-free?"

I stopped myself from sighing. The chances of that were very slim, but I didn't want to sour him on my hometown before he'd even seen all of it. He was just a bandwagon health nut anyway; it wasn't like he had real food intolerances. "I'm not sure. I guess we'll have to look around."

We got back in the car and headed into town.

Chapter Three

Jameson

The Pop In was crowded. That was normal this time of year, especially on a Saturday. Bootleg swelled with tourists in the summer, most of them staying in cabins around the lake. I slipped inside, planning to get in and out as quickly as possible.

My jaw felt fine today. Rhett didn't hit all that hard. Hell, I'd taken worse from my brothers on more than one occasion. Wasn't even any bruising.

I went through the store and grabbed what I needed. There wasn't a line to check out, so I put my purchases on the counter and pulled out my wallet. Opal Bodine was working the cash register.

"Hey, Jameson," she said.

"Opal."

"This all for you?"

I eyed my purchases. "I think I could use something sweet. Got anything good?"

"You bet I do," she said. "I've got two more cinnamon rolls if you'd like one."

I thought about buying both and bringing one to Jonah, but he'd only tell me we shouldn't eat so much sugar. Course, if I bought both and he didn't eat his, I'd have no choice but to eat it for him.

"I'll take both."

"Sounds good," she said. "I'll be right back."

Someone brushed against me as they passed, and I winced. I hated it when people did that. The store wasn't that small; there was no need for bumping into people. I glanced over, but it wasn't anyone I knew, and he was walking out the door anyway. I shrugged it off and looked to see if Opal was coming with my cinnamon rolls.

A girl had gotten in line behind me and I did a double take when I saw her, my jaw dropping all the way to the floor. Or it would have if my jaw had been capable of such a thing. It was Leah Mae Larkin.

She was tall and willowy, with limbs that went on for miles. Her long blond hair was down and wavy. Honey-lemon skin with a few freckles across her nose. Bright eyes that were such a surprising shade of green they made you look twice.

I swallowed hard, finding it exceedingly hard to do anything but stare.

"Jameson?"

Her voice was soft and melodic, and when she smiled, I noticed the little gap between her front teeth. She'd always had it—and hated it—but it had become her trademark as a model.

"H-hey there, Leah Mae," I said, hating how strangled my voice sounded. It was not unusual for me to get a little tongue-tied around a pretty girl, but this was something else entirely.

"Jameson Bodine?" she asked, as if she hadn't said my name already.

I noticed her accent was gone. I'd noticed it on the show, too, but hearing that northern lilt to her speech here, in Bootleg Springs, made it stand out all the more.

"Yeah," I said. *Great job, dumbass. You're really going to win her over with your charm.*

"Wow, it's been a long time," Leah Mae said, looking me up and down.

I was suddenly glad I'd let Jonah talk me into working out with him and Devlin. I kept in decent shape as a rule, but I'd put on some muscle recently.

Not that it mattered. This was Leah Mae, not some girl I was hoping to impress.

I opened my mouth to speak again, but the words weren't there. Damn it. I had this problem a lot. My mind had plenty going on, it was just that sometimes the words didn't want to make it from my brain to my mouth.

What would Gibson do? No, he wasn't the one to look to. Bowie? Nah, Bowie would just pretend like he wasn't interested. I hadn't seen Jonah with a girl enough times to know how he'd handle himself. And Dev… well, he was in love with my sister, so that just made it weird.

Damn it. I still wasn't saying anything.

"It has been a while," I said.

"How have you been?"

Well, my dad died and now he's a person of interest in the Callie Kendall case. No, don't say that. Jesus, Jameson, what in the hell is wrong with you?

"Um, I've been all right. You?"

"I've been well," she said. "I was wondering if I'd run into you while I was here."

"You must be in town visiting your dad?"

She nodded and adjusted the items she had in her arms. "Yeah, just got in today."

"Here, let me help with that." I took the loaf of bread, half-gallon of milk, and a few other items from her. Used my elbow to move my stuff over and make room on the counter for hers.

"Oh, thank you," she said.

She smiled at me and my heart stopped. I was surprised I didn't drop to the ground right there in the Pop In. Could you go on living when your heart quit on you?

"You're welcome."

I stood there another second, unable to decide whether or not I was grateful to Opal for taking her sweet time. I didn't particularly want to stop talking to Leah Mae—although *talking* was a term I'd use loosely for what was happening. But I was failing at this pretty damn hard and it would have been nice to be put out of my misery sooner rather than later.

"Been watching your show," I said.

"Really?"

I nodded. "Sure. Whole town is mighty proud of you."

"Oh, yeah, the town," she said.

"It's not every day that a Bootlegger's on TV."

She tucked her hair behind her ear. "Wow, I hadn't thought about everyone here seeing it."

"Yeah, everybody's real excited. It's on at the Lookout, and I hear a few people organized viewing parties."

Her cheeks flushed a hint of pink, and she drew her teeth over her lower lip. She always did that when she was nervous. "I guess… I hope everyone's been enjoying it."

"I'd say so." Some of the tension left my shoulders and my words came a little easier now that I was starting to relax. "Been interesting to see how you're doing, even though you're far away."

She smiled again and this time I was able to smile back.

A man came up beside her and my smile faded. He had dark hair and a strong jaw. Eyes that looked around the store with a fair amount of disdain. Reminded me of some of the rich tourists who swept through town, thinking they were better than all us locals. By his clothes, he looked like he belonged in an office somewhere, not a little convenience store in an out-of-the-way town like ours.

"Hey babe, we got everything?" he asked.

He stood close to Leah Mae and that's when I realized what I'd missed. She had a ring on her finger.

I'd been wrong about my heart stopping before. It hadn't. It had kept right on going, beating a steady rhythm. But it did stop now. Stopped dead in my chest.

I gave the guy a quick once-over. He was not wearing a ring, which meant one of two things: Either they were not yet married, or they were and he didn't wear one. If it was the latter, he was a douche. The former, and there was still a bit of hope.

Hope? For what? For me and Leah Mae to reconnect after twelve years? As if we were going to wander off together and reminisce about being kids. Or talk about those summers when we were teenagers, and I'd been too shy to make a move.

Not that I would have. Me and Leah Mae were just friends. Always had been.

Damn it, I was doing a lot of *not talking* again. Where in the hell was Opal?

"Kelvin, this is Jameson Bodine," Leah Mae said, gesturing to me. "We grew up here together."

Kelvin seemed to notice me for the first time. He looked me up and down with a quick flick of his eyes. I wasn't dressed all fancy and sophisticated like him. But I was wearing a clean t-shirt and decent jeans—nothing that I ever wore in my workshop. That stuff always wound up with burn holes all over it.

"Jameson, this is Kelvin Graham," Leah Mae said.

"Leah's fiancé," Kelvin said.

Leah Mae glanced at him like something he'd said surprised her. Kelvin tipped his chin to me.

I decided to be the bigger man and offer to shake his hand. Some things needed to be handled like a gentleman. "Nice to meet you."

Kelvin shook my hand with a firm grip just as Opal finally made an appearance. She glanced at Leah Mae and Kelvin, then back at me, and lifted one shoulder in a little shrug.

"Babe, is this the only store in this town?" Kelvin asked Leah Mae while Opal started ringing up my purchases.

I turned my back to them and focused on getting my money out. Tuned out the conversation they were having. I paid, and Opal handed me the bag.

"See you later, Jameson," she said.

I started to go without saying anything else, but my pride

got the better of me. I did have something else to say to Leah Mae, and I wasn't going out like that. Pausing, I looked back at her, and she met my eyes.

"I know the fishing pole wasn't your fault," I said. "It looked faked, if you don't mind me saying so."

She nodded slowly. "Yeah, thank you."

"Good to see you again, Leah Mae," I said. "I hope you enjoy your visit."

Her smile lit up the world. "Thanks, Jameson. It's good to see you too."

Clutching my bag, I nodded and turned for the door. Because I was a gentleman, I glanced over my shoulder and tipped my chin to her fiancé. "Kevin."

"It's Kelvin—"

The door closed behind me before I heard the rest of what he was going to say, if anything.

My pulse raced as I got in my truck and slid my groceries over to the other seat. Had I really just seen Leah Mae Larkin at the Pop In? Or was I in the middle of a strange and terrible dream where my childhood friend was the most beautiful woman I'd ever laid eyes on, and she was wearing another man's ring?

Damn it. It wasn't a dream, but the rest of it was true.

I shook my head, like I could shake loose out of my stupor. I needed to get myself together. Of course I was going to run into Leah Mae one of these days. Her dad lived here, so chances were she'd come back to visit at some point. And we were old enough that one of us being engaged or married was a distinct possibility.

Not that I'd ever been anywhere close to that with a girl. I'd dated Cheyenne Hastings for a while in high school, but she'd dumped me for Cody Wyatt. After that, I'd been out with a handful of other girls, but nothing that had lasted long. Then there was Willa Sawyer. But that hadn't been much of a relationship. She'd been someone I could turn to when I needed it, but neither of us had expected much from the other. We'd known it wasn't going to last forever.

So Leah Mae was here, and she was engaged. That was all right. I ought to be happy for her. After all, she'd been my friend. Weren't you supposed to be happy for your friends when something good happened to them?

But happy wasn't what I was feeling as I drove back out to my house.

Chapter Four

Leah Mae

The sun lit up the little kitchen in our rental cabin. I stood at the sink, gazing out at the lake. I'd been all over the world, but there was nothing quite like a mountain lake in West Virginia. Especially on a summer day. The water sparkled, and the trees fluttered in the breeze. I opened the window to let in some of the fresh, clean air, closing my eyes and breathing it in.

Kelvin was on his laptop at the kitchen table. We were supposed to be taking the week off, but he didn't know what *time off* meant. I'd been hoping he'd relax a little more, but so far, he'd been as busy as if we were back in L.A.

We'd been here a few days, and I was keenly aware that we had to leave Friday afternoon. Such a short time. It felt like we hadn't done even a quarter of the things I wanted to do. So far, we'd spent most of our time here, at the cabin. I'd been visiting my dad in the afternoons, but other than that, we hadn't been out much. Kelvin was frustrated by the lack of paleo and gluten-free options at the local restaurants, so he'd been cooking dinners here. And he'd been so busy working, we hadn't done much sightseeing.

I took the whistling kettle off the stove and poured water into my mug. Dunked the tea bag a few times. The scent of pine coming in the open window filled the air while Kelvin's fingers clicked on his keyboard.

I hadn't seen Jameson again. Not since I'd been in line behind him at the Pop In. I'd recognized him instantly, although he looked a bit different from what I remembered. Still had short dark hair and sweet blue eyes. But he'd matured—his features taking on a more rugged look, with that strong Bodine jaw covered in stubble. He no longer had the same boyish face. He was a man now.

Jameson Bodine. Next to my daddy, he'd been my favorite person when I was a little girl. I'd been friends with the other girls my age, but Jameson and I had shared a special bond. We'd spent endless hours together, walking trails, swimming in the lake, splashing in mud puddles. He'd been a quiet child around most people, but when we were together, he'd opened up. Talked to me about all kinds of things. It had made me feel so special. Like I knew a secret. I got to see something no one else did—the things he was hiding on the inside.

I'd taken that responsibility very seriously. Guarded his secrets—such as they were when we were small—with care. I'd kept them tucked away inside my heart, like little presents that were only for me. I could remember looking at him in school during class—watching as he doodled on his papers, keeping his head low—and feeling like I was the most special girl in the world, because I knew things about Jameson Bodine that no one else knew.

My heart had broken when my parents told me they were getting a divorce and my mom and I were moving away. To Florida, of all places. I'd known I'd miss my daddy, and my friends at school. Bootleg Springs had been the only place I'd ever known—my only home.

But leaving Jameson Bodine had been the worst thing

of all. The stricken look on his face when I'd told him I was moving away was still burned into my memory. His blue eyes had gone dark and stormy, his jaw clenched. He'd fought back tears, which had made me cry like a baby. Then he'd wrapped his skinny twelve-year-old-boy arms around me and hugged me tight—told me everything would be okay.

When I'd come back to stay with my dad the next summer, I'd gone straight for the Bodines' house. And it had been as if Jameson and I hadn't been apart for more than a day. We'd spent the long summer days wandering around town, down to the lake, through the woods. At first, we'd caught up on what had happened over the past school year. He'd filled me in on all the Bootleg gossip; I'd told him about life in Florida. After that, things between us had gone on like they always had. We'd spent our days together, running home at sunset like all the other kids in town.

And so it had gone for the next several years. I'd spend the school year living with my mom in Jacksonville. I had friends at school. Joined the theater club and acted in plays. Performed in talent shows. Did my homework and talked on the phone too much—normal teenage girl things.

But I lived for summers, when I'd go stay with my dad in Bootleg Springs. Jameson would be waiting for me on the front steps of his house my first day in town, and we'd pick up right where we left off, as if we hadn't been apart at all.

Everything had changed the summer Callie Kendall disappeared. My mom had heard the news and hopped the first flight she could get to West Virginia. Callie and I had been the same age, and my mom had been convinced Bootleg was suddenly dangerous. Too dangerous for her daughter to be unsupervised like I was. Telling her I was rarely alone, even with Dad working all day, hadn't helped. Because for the first time, she seemed to realize I spent my summers running around with *one of those Bodine boys*.

I'd heard Mom and Dad fighting, so I'd walked into town to find Jameson. He'd sat with me at a booth at Moonshine.

Bought me a chocolate shake to make me feel better. And the next day, I'd gone home with Mom. I hadn't been back since.

I'd thought about Jameson so many times over the years. Wondered how he was doing. What his life was like. It was a relief to find him still here. If Jameson Bodine had left Bootleg Springs, the place would have lost some of its magic. It steadied me to know that some things hadn't changed.

Wrapping my hands around my hot mug, I wandered outside. The breeze was soft on my face, and the sun sparkled on the water. It smelled like summer here, in a way no other place did. It reminded me of those magical summers I'd spent here. Reminded me of Jameson.

I wanted to see him again. Not just a brief meeting in a convenience store. I wanted to talk to him. Find out about his life now. I didn't have his number or know where he lived, but it wouldn't be too hard to find out. The cabin we were staying in belonged to Scarlett, his younger sister. I hadn't talked to her—Kelvin's assistant had made the reservation—but I was sure I could find a way to get in touch with her.

I resolved to find out where Jameson lived and go say hello. It probably wouldn't work out today, but tomorrow for sure. Kelvin was busy, anyway. Depending on when Jameson had time, I could meet him for lunch and see my dad after. Or have lunch with Dad and grab coffee with Jameson in the afternoon. I'd be back in time for dinner with Kelvin.

Satisfied with my plan, I took my tea back inside and sat down at the table across from Kelvin. "What's keeping you so busy?"

He kept his eyes on his laptop screen. "A lot of things."

"Like what?"

"Other than running a multi-million-dollar modeling agency?" he asked. "And trying to salvage your career?"

"Salvage?" I asked. "What do you mean, salvage?"

"You're at a crossroads," he said. "You're not getting any younger, and you've never reached supermodel status. It's a miracle your modeling career has lasted as long as it has."

31

"What's that supposed to mean?"

"It's not personal, Leah," he said. "You know the trajectory of a model's career as well as I do. You make it when you're young and fresh-faced. You do your best to stay relevant. A lucky few get to the top and can still get work in their late twenties. Even fewer will go beyond that. You've had a great run, but you're not at that level, babe. And every year, more and more new faces arrive on the scene. Teenagers with flawless skin. No retouching necessary."

"I'm sorry I've aged so terribly," I said, my voice thick with sarcasm. "I'm surprised you can bear to look at me."

He rolled his eyes. "Don't be like that. Why do you think I'm working my ass off to get this acting thing going for you? *Roughing It* came at the perfect time, but we need to work fast to capitalize on the attention."

"I'm not so sure the attention I'm getting is good. I think people are starting to hate me. They think I was trying to take Brock away from Maisie."

"Good."

"What?"

He sighed, like he was explaining something to a stubborn child. "Everyone loves to hate a villain. You can't buy that kind of publicity. If you're lucky, they'll fabricate an entire relationship between you and Brock on the show. Babe, you'll have offers pouring in."

I gaped at him. "I don't want the world to think I seduced Brock Winston and convinced him to cheat on his wife."

"Who cares?"

"*I* do. Because it's awful," I said. "I would never do that. It isn't me."

"You want to be an actress, right?" he asked. "If your sweet little country-bumpkin self can pull off the part of the vixen on *Roughing It*, you'll prove you can nail any role."

I let out a long breath. He had a point. Although it was supposedly a reality show, I'd definitely played a part. The producers had coached me to act a certain way, so I had. I'd been given the part of the sex kitten—the sultry single girl flirting with all the men on the show. That wasn't me, but I'd figured it was good practice. And even if the public didn't know how staged the show really was, casting directors and producers would.

It was why I'd agreed to go on the show at all. Kelvin had a point about my modeling career waning. In modeling years, I was ancient. My career in the fashion world had an expiration date, and it was fast approaching. Acting had always been what I'd wanted to do, so it was the perfect time to make that transition.

Kelvin had been trying to get me auditions, but until *Roughing It*, nothing had come through. I couldn't understand why. I wasn't some vapid model with nothing going for her but a pretty face. I'd had years of acting classes. Dialect coaching to get rid of my Appalachian twang. I'd starred in plays and musicals all through my teens.

Kelvin had assured me that being on *Roughing It* would open doors. The show was only half over, but so far, I hadn't seen any doors opening. And I was afraid more were going to keep closing.

"I'm just worried this isn't turning out the way we thought it would," I said. "If I'm the hated vixen, no one's going to want to work with me. Have we heard back from Burberry yet? About the winter line?"

"They're passing on you."

"What?" I'd been working for Burberry for ten years. "They passed on me? Why?"

"Babe, we've talked about this," he said. "It was going to happen sooner rather than later."

"You think this is about my age? Not about the show?"

"It's probably both."

I stood, the chair scraping across the wood floor. My career was starting to slip through my fingers. I could feel it happening. No matter how many times Kelvin assured me things would be fine—I'd make a seamless transition into acting—I couldn't help but worry. This was my livelihood. And seeing how my dad was struggling with his health made it all the more important that I keep working. Someone had to take care of him, and the time when he'd need it was approaching sooner than I'd thought. I'd found out from Betsy that he hadn't worked more than part-time since last Christmas. I didn't know how much longer he could support himself.

He didn't have anyone else. He'd never remarried, and I didn't have any brothers or sisters. It was up to me to take care of him.

Kelvin closed his laptop and came over to stand in front of me. He ran his hands up and down my arms. "Babe, don't worry. I have some things in the works that are really exciting. You're going to be fine."

I nodded. I'd trusted him with my career for most of the past decade. I needed to keep trusting him.

Someone knocked on the door and Kelvin groaned. The first day had been quiet, but yesterday Millie Waggle had stopped by with a plate of brownies, and Maribel Schilling had brought a tater tot casserole. I'd tried to explain that this was just the Bootleg way. Bootleggers were equal parts friendly and curious—bordering on nosy. And it wasn't my fault he refused to eat Millie's brownies. His loss. They were amazing.

"Knock, knock," a chipper woman's voice came from the front. "Y'all home? Can I come in?"

I couldn't help but smile at the petite brunette who came in wearing a tank top and cut-off shorts. "Scarlett Bodine?"

"Leah Mae," she said. "You know, I heard it was you stayin' here and I wasn't quite sure if I believed it. After all, your name wasn't anywhere on the reservation. But here you are. Look at you, Leah Mae Larkin, pretty as a picture. And famous to boot."

"It's so nice to see you. This place is yours? It looks like you're doing well for yourself."

"Can't complain." She came in and put a foil-wrapped package on the counter. "That's safe to eat, I got it from Clarabell over at Moonshine. Pepperoni roll."

I gasped. "Oh my god, I haven't had one of those in years."

Scarlett shook her head, clicking her tongue. "Honey, you've been missing out."

"Thank you. That was really sweet of you."

"Sure," she said brightly. "Cabin treating you all right?"

"Yes, it's lovely." I glanced at Kelvin to see if he had anything to add, but he was back at the table on his laptop. "Scarlett, this is Kelvin Graham."

"Nice to meet you," Scarlett said.

Kelvin looked up and nodded, then went back to his laptop.

"Well then, just let me know if there's anything you need," she said. "I won't keep you. I just felt bad that I hadn't been by yet. Not very neighborly of me, but it's been a busy week."

I walked toward the door just behind Scarlett. "Thanks, I'm glad you did." I paused for a second, suddenly nervous to bring this up. "Um, Scarlett... I was wondering about your brother, Jameson."

Scarlett froze and turned slowly on her heel. "What about my brother Jameson?"

"Well, I thought it might be nice to see him. Say hello."

A slow smile crept over Scarlett's face. "Would you like his number?"

"That would be great." I grabbed my phone out of my handbag, hanging by the door. "If you don't think he'd mind, that is."

"Oh, no, I'm quite certain Jameson won't mind one bit," she said. "I'll give you his address too, if you want."

"Yes, please." I wasn't sure why she was smiling so big, but I entered Jameson's number and address into my phone. "Thank you so much. It would be nice to catch up with him a little bit. It's been a long time."

"That it has," she said, still smiling. "Y'all take care, now. Enjoy your visit."

Scarlett left, and I went back into the kitchen. Kelvin eyed me.

"What?" I asked.

"How many people are going to show up on the doorstep with food?"

I shrugged. "Hard to say. A few more at least."

He rolled his eyes. "What is with this town?"

I ignored him and looked down at the entry in my phone. My heart fluttered a little, seeing Jameson's name there. Which was silly. He'd been my friend when we were kids, but he was basically a stranger now.

It was hard to get those blue eyes out of my head, though.

"I'm going to see my dad," I said. "I'll be back for dinner."

Kelvin mumbled something, sounding distracted. I grabbed the car keys and my handbag, and slipped on a pair of sunglasses. Maybe I'd call Jameson from Dad's house. Or wait until morning. Now that I had his number, I was suddenly nervous about using it. What if he didn't want to see me? Or he was too busy? It would be so disappointing if the only time I saw him was for a hasty few minutes in line at the Pop In.

I'd give myself a little time to work up the courage, and then I'd call. Or maybe I'd just send him a text. That seemed more Jameson's style. He'd never liked talking on the phone, and he probably wouldn't answer a strange number.

With that settled in my mind, I got in our rental car and headed over to my dad's.

Chapter Five

Jameson

The heat from the forge beat at me. Droplets of sweat beaded on my forehead and slid down my spine. The quiet of my workshop surrounded me. Nothing but the clink of metal on metal, the low roar of flames in the forge. I was at peace here, alone with my work.

I pulled the metal disk out of the heat with a heavy set of tongs and brought it over to the anvil. It had once been part of a piece of machinery, long since discarded. But with some heat, and shaping, I'd give it new life. It was what I loved to do. Take something that had been thrown out and use it to make something beautiful.

With two sets of tongs, I bent and shaped the disk as it cooled. It would take several passes through the heat to get it looking like I wanted. Working with scrap could be painstaking. I always added a tremendous amount of detail to my pieces. But that's how they existed in my head. I could see every curve and angle. It was just a matter of bringing the vision in my mind to life.

My phone buzzed on the work bench. I put the tongs down and wiped the sweat from my brow with the back of my forearm. Checked the call.

It was Deanna Silvers, my art dealer. She'd discovered my work a few years back and now she found buyers for me, especially for my larger pieces. She'd secured the commission I was working on, an installation for a brand-new building in Charlotte, North Carolina. It was the biggest thing I'd ever done, and the most expensive. The client had given me a surprising amount of creative freedom, simply asking for a piece that would look beautiful in front of his building. He liked my style, and he trusted me to come up with something amazing.

For what he was paying me for it, it needed to be spectacular.

I picked up my phone and answered. "Hey, Dee."

"Hi, Jameson." She had a slight New York accent. "How's the piece coming?"

"Just fine." I was hedging a bit, because I still wasn't quite sure what the finished piece was going to look like. Until last week, I'd had it all worked out. But there was another vision in my head that I couldn't shake. It was making it hard to stay focused on this one. I usually knew exactly what each piece was going to look like, but this time was different.

"If you're going to have trouble delivering on time, you need to let me know as soon as possible," she said. "This commission is a game-changer. The client loves your work, but I wouldn't count on him being very forgiving of a missed deadline."

"Yeah, I know. You don't need to worry about it."

"All right," she said, although I could tell she wasn't sure. "There's something else I need to run by you, and you're not going to like it."

I adjusted the phone, holding it against my ear with my shoulder. "And that is?"

"There's going to be a grand opening at the building," she said. "They'll unveil your piece then. And you need to be there."

"Ah, hell, Dee. They don't need me there."

"This is part of the deal, Jameson. You need to show your face once in a while. People like to see the genius behind the art."

"I'm no genius."

"I beg to differ," she said. "Although the fact that you don't realize it is part of your charm. Don't worry about it for now; we have time. I'll be there, too. And you can bring anyone else you'd like—your girlfriend if you want."

"Don't have a girlfriend."

"Well, maybe we need to get you one," she said. "A guy like you shouldn't be single."

"I'm not sure being my art dealer qualifies you to comment on my personal life," I said, my voice light so she'd know I was teasing her. She *always* commented on my personal life. Or lack thereof, as it were.

She laughed. "You don't know how much I hold back with you, Bodine. Boy, would I love to play matchmaker. I know a few girls who—"

"No, thanks," I said, cutting her off before she could continue. "I don't need you going to all that trouble on my account."

"Fine," she said. "But if you change your mind, let me know. My niece—"

"No, Dee." We'd had this conversation too many times already. "I'm certain your niece is lovely, but I don't need you settin' me up with someone."

"All right, back to business. Keep me posted on your progress. And pencil in a trip to Charlotte for October. You're going if I have to come out there and drag you with me."

I had no doubt she'd do just that. "Duly noted. Take care, Dee."

"Talk soon."

I hung up and put my phone down just as Jonah stuck his head through the door.

"You about ready?" he asked. "We're supposed to be at Bowie's soon."

"Yeah, sure. I'll just be a minute."

He nodded. "Sounds good."

Jayme, our family's lawyer, was calling to update us on the investigation, so we were all meeting at Bowie's. The police had taken the sweater Scarlett had found and obtained a warrant to search Dad's house. So far, we hadn't heard if they'd found anything new, nor when we might be able to get back into Dad's place. Hopefully Jayme had some good news for us.

I took off my leather apron and hung it on a hook. My workshop was housed in a re-purposed old barn next to my house. It had a forge and several work benches. I'd built heavy duty shelves to house all the scrap I collected, and there was a big open area for me to work on larger pieces. Nothing fancy, but it suited my purposes just fine. I liked it in here—liked the quiet. I was in my element when I was creating things. Sometimes the rest of life seemed like it was just a bunch of interruptions.

Jonah was in the kitchen when I came in the house. One thing I would say for having a roommate foisted on me when I'd been too drunk to say no—Jonah could cook. I was eating a damn sight better than I had been before he'd moved in with me.

"I just need to change," I said as I passed him.

My jeans had a few burn holes and I'd gotten pretty sweaty, so clean clothes were in order. I rinsed off in the shower, then put on a t-shirt and a fresh pair of jeans. My going-out jeans, not my work jeans. Work clothes always ended up with scorches and burn holes. My hands and forearms had their fair share of scars, too. Small ones, mostly—I'd never seriously injured myself, but little burns were just part of life when you worked with hot metal all the time.

Jonah and I drove the short distance to Bowie's house. He lived in a duplex in downtown Bootleg, not far from the high school. Gibson's Charger was already outside, but I didn't see Scarlett's truck. Bowie let us in and grabbed us each a beer from the fridge. I took a seat on the couch and took a swig.

Gibson sat on the other side of the couch, glowering at something on his phone. I knew better than to ask him what was wrong. He either didn't want to talk about it, and he'd tell me to shut up, or he'd let us know on his own. Wasn't much in between with Gibs.

"So, I've been thinking," Jonah said as he settled onto a chair. "I'd like to organize a 5K run through Bootleg. What do you think? Would people be into that?"

"You should make it a moonshine run," I said. "Finishers get a free drink at the end."

"Does everything have to revolve around moonshine?" Jonah asked.

Bowie and I both looked at him with furrowed brows.

"You can have a regular old 5K run anywhere," I said. "This is Bootleg Springs."

"Point taken," Jonah said.

Scarlett burst in wearing a big smile. The kind of smile that made me nervous. She was up to something.

"Hey, y'all," she said. "Guess who is in town at this very moment, staying in one of my rentals?"

I glanced up. "Leah Mae Larkin?"

Her expression fell, her mouth dropping open, and her shoulders slumped. "What? How did you know?"

"I saw her at the Pop In."

"Way to ruin a girl's fun." She crossed her arms. "I was hoping to surprise you."

"Sorry."

Scarlett's grin returned. "That's okay. Because there's more." She paused, no doubt attempting to add to the drama.

"Get on with it," Bowie said, gesturing for her to continue.

"She asked about you," she said, pointing her finger at my nose.

"Me?"

"Yes, you," she said, her eyes shining with glee. "And I gave her your number."

I blinked at my sister, my mouth partially open. I couldn't think of anything to say to that.

"There's something I'm missing here," Jonah said.

"Jameson and Leah Mae Larkin were friends when they were kids," Scarlett said. "Now she's a model and on TV."

"I knew the TV part," Jonah said. "I guess now I know why you started shit with Rhett the other night."

I hunkered down in my seat. "Just wasn't right, is all."

"Hmm," Scarlett said. "Well, you better answer your phone when she calls you."

I gave her a noncommittal grunt.

"Is Jayme calling or what?" Gibson asked.

Bowie got out his phone. "I'm calling her. I was just waiting for everyone to be here." He dialed and put his phone on speaker.

"Bodines," Jayme said when she answered. "Everyone present?"

"Yes, ma'am," Bowie said.

"All right, here's the latest," she said. "The sweater tested positive for blood. There will be more DNA testing to determine whose blood, although the chances of it not being Callie Kendall's seem slim. Still, all we can do is wait for the forensics report."

"Okay," Bowie said. "What about the house?"

"They'll be finished soon," she said. "I'm pushing to get them out of there. They've had plenty of time. If they were going to find something, they would have by now."

"So they haven't found anything else?" Bowie asked.

"If they have, I haven't been made aware of it," she said. "They certainly didn't find her body buried in the backyard, or we'd all know about it."

"Hey," Gibson barked. "No need to be so insensitive about it."

I met Gibson's eyes and nodded. He was right. Callie was a Bootleg girl, and we all cared about her. Dead or alive, we stuck up for our own.

Jayme paused before replying. "Apologies. My point is, chances are they didn't find anything new."

"What are we looking at here?" Bowie asked. "Dad can't

be charged with anything, right? You can't try a dead man for murder."

"No, you can't," Jayme said. "Even if there was overwhelming evidence, no criminal charges would be filed. But since it's a missing persons case, they'll try to reconstruct what happened to see if they can locate her body and determine if anyone else was involved. The other thing you have to be concerned about is Judge and Mrs. Kendall."

"What about them?" Scarlett asked, crossing her arms like she was uncomfortable.

"They could potentially file a civil wrongful death suit against your father's estate," Jayme said.

"Over a sweater?" Scarlett asked.

"The burden of proof in a wrongful death civil suit is different than a criminal case," Jayme said. "I don't know if finding the sweater is enough, but it's a possibility to be aware of."

Gibson scowled. "His estate. Not like he had anything worth taking."

"There's the house," Scarlett said.

"Let's not get ahead of ourselves," Jayme said. "For now, keep laying low. And quit starting bar fights."

I knew everyone was looking at me, but I kept my eyes down.

"That's it for now," Jayme said. "I'll let you know when you can get back into your father's house."

"Thanks, Jayme," Bowie said. "Appreciate the time."

"Sure," she said, and hung up without saying goodbye.

"Well ain't that some shit," Gibson growled.

"I think it's all gonna be fine," Bowie said.

Ever the optimist, my brother. I wasn't so sure things would be fine, but I kept my mouth shut. Didn't have much to add that hadn't already been said.

"We done here?" Gibson asked, already up and halfway to the door.

"Bye, Gibs," Scarlett said.

Gibson grunted on his way out.

"I guess that's about as good of news as we can hope for," Bowie said.

"Y'all want to get some dinner?" Scarlett asked.

My phone buzzed in my pocket and a hit of adrenaline surged through me. Had Scarlett really given Leah Mae my number? Or had she just said that to mess with me?

While Scarlett made dinner plans with Bowie and Jonah, I carefully pulled my phone out of my pocket and peeked at the screen. I had a text, but I didn't recognize the number. Made my hands shake a little, but I didn't want to draw any attention.

I flicked my thumb across the screen. Tapped the text.

Hey Jameson. This is Leah. Hope you don't mind me sending you a message. I thought maybe we could get together and catch up. Tomorrow? What do you think?

I closed the screen quickly so no one would glance at my phone and see it. I didn't want to answer questions about it right now.

"What about you, Jameson?" Bowie asked. "Dinner? Devlin's gonna meet us there."

I stood, pocketing my phone, and kept my eyes on the floor. "Not tonight."

"Aw, come on, Jame," Scarlett said.

"You want a ride home?" Jonah asked.

"Nah, I'm good," I said. "You guys have fun. I've been holed up in my workshop so much lately, I could use some air. Gonna walk home."

"Guess I can't argue with you getting out a little," Scarlett said. "You sure you're all right?"

"Fine, Scar," I said, smiling at her over my shoulder. "Night, y'all."

The air outside was finally starting to cool. I hadn't been making shit up. I did need the fresh air. But not because I'd been working too much. One little text from Leah Mae had my palms sweating.

It was ridiculous. She was just a girl I used to know.

That's what I was telling myself, anyway.

I reckoned she *had* asked Scarlett about me. And here I'd thought I wouldn't see her again after that encounter at the Pop In.

Taking a deep breath, and feeling mighty foolish that it was necessary, I took out my phone. Kept walking down the street in case one of my nosy siblings came out.

Me: Hey Leah Mae. Yeah, I'd like that. When are you free?
Leah Mae: Really? Oh good! How does lunch sound?
Me: Lunch sounds great. Moonshine at noon?
Leah Mae: Perfect. I'll see you then.

I found myself almost typing *it's a date*, but I stopped. It wasn't a *date*. Just two old friends catching up. I reckoned she'd be leaving town soon anyway. Her life wasn't here. It was off being famous. Marrying someone else.

Still, it would be nice to spend a little time with her. Find out how she was really doing. Maybe I could figure out why her eyes didn't sparkle the way they once had. Get that image of the girl in a cage out of my head so I could focus. Because right now, it was all I could see.

Chapter Six

Jameson

Times like this, I wished I had a little more Gibson in me. Or even Bowie. I couldn't imagine my brothers being nervous the way I was. Not over a girl, anyway. Especially one that was just a friend.

Of course, they were both older than me, and neither of them showed any signs of settling down. So maybe they weren't the ones to emulate after all.

Still, I felt foolish for the way my heart thumped and nervousness unsettled my stomach. I parked down the street from Moonshine and looked out to see if Leah Mae was here yet. A few people wandered up and down the street, but no sign of her.

I got out just as a car parked across the street. My heart sank straight to the concrete below my feet as I watched Leah Mae and her fiancé get out of the car. Damn it, he was here too?

The thought that I might be able to get back in my truck and leave without her seeing me crossed my mind. But I dismissed it as quickly as it had come. I had better manners than to stand her up, even if I'd thought it would be just the two of us. It wasn't the same, but I'd make the best of it.

I looked up and our eyes met. She smiled, and I knew I was in some trouble. Damn it, she was pretty.

Shoving my hands in my pockets, I walked down the sidewalk to meet her. Or them, as it were.

"Hi, Jameson," she said. "Thanks for meeting me."

"Sure." I glanced at Kelvin. He was glaring at me, his arms crossed over his chest.

His eyes flicked to the ground behind me. "What is that?"

Mona Lisa McNugget, Bootleg's town chicken, was pecking her way up the sidewalk. She stopped near my foot and scratched, looking for some little tidbit on the ground.

"It's a chicken," Leah Mae said, her voice amused.

"I know it's a chicken," he said. "What is it doing here?"

"It's Mona Lisa McNugget," I said.

"There's a chicken just… walking around town?" he asked.

As if she could sense his disdain, Mona Lisa charged toward Kelvin and started trying to peck his ankle. He jumped backward, like she was a giant spider or something, not a regular old chicken. Mona Lisa kept after him, her head bobbing, beak thrusting.

"What the hell?" he asked. "This chicken is trying to attack me."

Leah Mae started to laugh and covered her mouth. I just kept my hands in my pockets, watching. I'd never seen Mona Lisa go after someone like that. I probably could have coaxed her away, but I wasn't so keen on interfering.

"Hey y'all," Bowie said from behind me and smacked me on the back. "What's going on?"

"Not much," I said.

"Somebody get this chicken off me," Kelvin said, hopping from foot to foot.

"Kelvin, just move out of the way," Leah Mae said. "She'll leave you alone."

"Is that Leah Mae Larkin I see?" Bowie asked.

47

"Hi Bowie," Leah Mae said.

Gibson came from the other direction. He spared half a glance for the chicken, still trying to peck Kelvin, and stopped in front of the rest of us.

"Leah Mae," he said with a nod, as if it wasn't unusual for her to be here. Or maybe he just didn't care. Hard to tell with Gibs. He looked at me and Bowie. "So we eatin' or what?"

"What are all y'all doing here?" I asked.

Bowie shrugged. "It's lunch time."

Oh my god. Was my entire family going to show up?

"Oh hey, y'all!"

I closed my eyes and shook my head, hearing Scarlett's voice. Of course she would be here, too.

"Well, isn't this fun," Scarlett said. She walked over, arm in arm with Devlin. "It's like a reunion."

"Hi again, Scarlett. Everyone, this is Kelvin Graham." Leah Mae tried to gesture at Kelvin, but he'd hopped his way down the sidewalk, trying to get away from the relentless pecking of Mona Lisa McNugget. "Kelvin, what are you doing?"

"This fucking chicken won't leave me alone," he said.

"We'll go get a table," Bowie said. He nodded at Kelvin. "Nice to meet you, Kevin."

Kelvin stopped. "It's *Kelvin*. Ow, what the hell?"

"Don't hurt her," Leah Mae said.

I was having a very hard time not laughing, but I kept quiet. Gibson, Scarlett, and Devlin followed Bowie inside Moonshine, ignoring the chicken attack occurring on the sidewalk.

"Do you want to come in and have lunch?" Leah Mae asked Kelvin. "Or go back to the cabin and get some work done?"

Kelvin took a few quick steps toward us, leaving Mona Lisa McNugget distracted by something on the sidewalk. "Jesus, this place is crazy. I'm not eating here. I'll go back to the cabin."

Leah Mae glanced at me and gave me the tiniest of winks. "Okay, if you're sure."

Kelvin eyed the chicken. "Yeah, positive. You're just having lunch?"

"Yes, I already told you that," she said with a roll of her eyes. "And you didn't have to come into town. I could have driven myself."

He leveled me with a hard stare. I met his gaze, keeping my face blank. He had nothing to fear from me as far as Leah Mae was concerned. I wasn't the sort to mess around with another man's girl. But he didn't know that, and I saw no need to clarify. If he didn't trust Leah Mae, that was his problem, not mine.

"Call me when you're done," he said. "I'll come pick you up."

"Okay," she said.

He grabbed her by the waist and planted a kiss on her forehead. Maybe it was my imagination, but it seemed like she stiffened. With another glance at me, he turned for his car. Mona Lisa McNugget went after his ankle again, so he hurried across the street. He got in his car, and the chicken strutted on down the road.

"Does Mona Lisa McNugget always do that?" Leah Mae asked.

"Nah, she's usually a real sweetheart," I said. Leah Mae laughed, and I glanced inside Moonshine. My siblings were sitting in a booth, drinks already on the table. "Do you want to grab something to go from the Pop In? We could take it down to the lake and avoid… all that." I gestured to the table full of Bodines. And Devlin, but he was one of us now, even if he wouldn't ever have our last name. Of course, Scarlett might just make him take her name eventually.

"I was hoping you might suggest that," she said.

With a fair bit of relief, I led Leah Mae up the street to the Pop In. I bought us sandwiches and drinks. It wasn't a date, but I still insisted on paying. Then we walked down to the lake and found an open picnic table.

"It's amazing how familiar this place is," she said, settling down on the other side of the table. "Some things are a little different, but it's still Bootleg Springs. Does that even make sense?"

"Sure it does," I said. "I guess that's part of its charm."

"I miss it." She unwrapped her sandwich. "I heard your dad passed away. I'm really sorry."

"Thanks," I said. "It wasn't unexpected."

"Still, must be hard."

I nodded. Didn't much want to bring up Callie, but I wanted Leah Mae to hear it from me first if she didn't already know. "Yeah. I don't know if you've heard the talk, but there's some evidence that suggests my dad could have had something to do with Callie Kendall going missing all those years ago."

Her lips parted, and she set her sandwich down. "Oh my god."

"Scarlett found Callie's sweater in an old trunk at Dad's place." I swallowed back the sick feeling creeping up my throat. "The police have been investigating again—went through his house. You stay in town long enough, you'll hear people speculating."

"Wow. That's awful. Do you have any idea why the sweater would have been at your dad's house?" She put up a hand, as if to stop me from answering. "I'm sorry, that was a rude question. Of course you don't know why."

"I don't. It's baffling, actually. I want to believe it's a coincidence. That he wasn't involved. It's hard to say after all these years. And it's certainly not something you want to think about your father."

She offered a gentle smile, her eyes full of warmth. "No, of course not. I remember your dad, and I know he wasn't always very nice. But I don't think..." She paused, taking a deep breath. "Whatever happened, hopefully they'll find out the truth someday and everyone can have some peace."

"Thanks. That's my hope too." I resisted the urge to reach over and squeeze her hand. I didn't want to talk about my dad anymore. "How's your mom these days?"

"She's fine. Still lives in Jacksonville. She remarried not long after I graduated high school. His name's Stan Michaels. He's a nice guy—runs an insurance agency. I think they're happy."

"Does she know you're here?"

"She does," she said with a smile. "She had to get used to me traveling all over the world when I started modeling. I don't think she's so worried about Bootleg Springs anymore."

"That's good." I'd always thought her mom's hysteria over Bootleg was sorely misplaced. It was a far sight safer than most places, even with Callie Kendall's disappearance. People 'round here looked after each other. "What about you? Where do you live these days?"

"Los Angeles," she said. "Actually, Kelvin just moved us into a new place. I haven't even seen it yet. He took care of everything, but my stuff is all still in boxes. He got it while I was filming the show, and I've been traveling and living in hotels since then."

She seemed all right with that arrangement, but something about it bothered me. "Sounds like you're without any roots."

"Yeah, I guess that's true." She took a bite of her sandwich, and I did the same. "Listen, Jameson, I'm sorry I didn't do a better job of keeping in touch."

"No need for apologies. I didn't do so well at it either." Which was the truth. The way we'd drifted apart had probably been more my fault than hers. We could have kept up our friendship over email at least. But she'd gotten a boyfriend in Florida, and I'd started dating Cheyenne Hastings. I'd missed Leah Mae, but at the time it had seemed easier to just let it go. And once she'd started modeling, it had seemed like she'd moved into another world. One that was far too removed from my life in Bootleg Springs for us to ever be friends again.

"I suppose," she said. "But I could have tried harder. It seemed like every year I meant to come visit, and every year something came up."

"You've led quite the life," I said. "Far fancier than anything going on around here."

"It's not always as fancy as it seems," she said. There was that thing I'd seen in her eyes again. A dulling of her light. "It's funny, but being here makes me feel like I lost touch with something. I've been so busy for so long, I forgot what it was like to slow down and just *be*."

"Bootleg is good for that."

"It really is." She took a bite of her sandwich, then set it back down. "But what about you? I don't even know what you do for a living."

"I'm an artist," I said with a shrug.

"Really?" she asked, her smile brightening her face. "You make a living with your art?"

"Sure do."

"That's amazing," she said. "Do you have a specialty?"

"Metal sculptures. I have a workshop at home."

"Wow," she said. "I'd love to see some of your pieces."

Although I didn't keep people out of my workshop on purpose, I didn't invite people in very often, either. But I liked the idea of showing her around.

"Well, if you have time before you go, maybe you could come out to my place and have a look."

"That would be fun," she said. "I'm not sure if I'll have time before we leave. We have to drive to Pittsburgh tomorrow afternoon. Can I text you?"

I smiled at her. Smiling around Leah Mae was awfully easy. "Yeah, of course you can. Anytime."

She smiled back, her green eyes sparkling. "I'm sorry if I keep staring. It's just so good to see you again. Kind of feels like those summers when I'd come back and find you sitting on the porch steps. I always imagined you were sitting there waiting for me."

"I was."

"Really?"

"Course. I'd sit out there every day from the last day of school until you'd show up in town." I glanced away, embarrassed. I couldn't believe I'd just said that to her.

"That's really sweet."

We ate our lunch and caught up on our lives a bit. She talked about some of her experiences as a model. Sounded to me like she'd worked hard, but hadn't had much time to enjoy it. She wanted to hear all about me, but there wasn't a lot to tell. I didn't think so, anyway.

The afternoon wore on, but I barely noticed the time passing. We just kept right on talking. I could have sat there with her forever, but eventually she said she needed to get back. She said she'd call Kelvin for a ride, but I insisted on driving her back to their cabin. Wasn't far, and I didn't mind.

It had nothing to do with getting a few extra minutes with her.

I didn't walk her to the door—seemed a bit much, what with her being engaged to someone else—but I did wait until she'd gone inside before I drove off. She waved to me before closing the door. I waved back, my heart feeling heavy. We'd promised each other we'd keep in touch, and I meant to.

But I missed her already.

Chapter Seven

Leah Mae

What are you wearing?" Kelvin asked.

I glanced down. I'd put on a loose turquoise shirt that I'd modified from an old dress, and my favorite pair of skinny jeans. On a whim, I'd bought a pair of cowboy boots yesterday, and they complemented my outfit perfectly.

"I appear to be wearing clothes."

"Cowboy boots?" he asked. "Please tell me you're leaving those here."

"No way. These boots are fabulous."

He shook his head and grabbed the keys. "I guess we're going out. In boots."

"You want to wear boring shoes, be my guest. I, for one, am going to have some fun in my cute new boots."

We went out to the car, the evening air fresh and cool. After Jameson had dropped me off, Kelvin had tried to pick a fight. He'd said he'd planned to pick me up. I'd said Jameson had offered, and it was a nice thing for him to do. It was silly of him to be angry.

I couldn't understand why Kelvin had made such a big deal out of me seeing Jameson today. He'd been working until I'd told him I was meeting an old friend for lunch. Suddenly he'd been very interested in what I was doing. When I'd said it was Jameson Bodine, he'd practically flown out of his chair. He'd insisted on driving me into town, even though five minutes earlier, he'd been griping about being busy.

The whole thing was ridiculous. I was around other men all the time. Men who undressed me, down to nothing, and dressed me up again. Men who waxed my body hair, for Pete's sake—*everywhere*. Of course, most of the men in fashion were gay. But still. Kelvin had never been like this.

He'd been grumpy all through dinner, so I'd decided to go out—with or without him. When I'd told him I was heading to the Lookout to have a drink, he'd said he'd go, as if he were doing me a favor.

We drove up the hill to where the bar was perched on a bluff. I'd told him about the bootlegging history of the town, and how the Lookout was where they kept watch while moonshine and hooch were smuggled across the lake into Maryland. He'd seemed bored, then questioned whether the story was true.

I got out and smoothed down my shirt. Glanced at my boots. They were cute, I didn't care what Kelvin said. He put a hand on the small of my back and led me to the entrance.

Music spilled out into the evening air when Kelvin opened the door. I stepped inside, feeling a little burst of excitement. I'd never been in the Lookout before. The last time I'd been in Bootleg Springs, I'd been too young.

It was everything you'd imagine a small-town West Virginia bar to be—only better. Neon beer signs. Peanut shells on the floor. Gibson Bodine and two other people played music from a tiny stage. Dancers occupied the dance floor in front of them. There were tables of people, more playing pool, and all the denim and cowboy boots you could ever want.

I loved it.

Kelvin seemed less impressed. He glanced around with a grimace, almost like he was afraid to touch anything.

"Come on," I said. "Let's not stand by the door."

He leaned close so I could hear him over the music. "This is what you want to do tonight?"

"Yes. You haven't done anything except work. Let's have a drink. Live a little."

"I've *lived a little* in plenty of places," he said. "Milan, Paris, London, New York. I don't think I need to add the backwoods of West Virginia to the list."

"You're impossible."

I looked around, wondering if Jameson was here, but I didn't see him. I did see Scarlett, at a table with two other women—Cassidy and June Tucker. Scarlett smiled and waved, so I went over to their table.

"Leah Mae," Cassidy said with a smile. "Scarlett was telling us you were in town. Nice to see you again."

I introduced everyone to Kelvin. Thankfully, he was polite, despite the fact that he kept looking around with that half-horrified expression on his face.

"Is it true that you had an illicit affair with Brock Winston?" June asked. "Or was that a fabrication designed by the producers to create conflict for the sake of better ratings?"

"Oh, Juney," Scarlett said.

"It's okay," I said. "The show was definitely edited for better ratings."

"I find it fascinating that the average person believes reality shows are real in any way," June said.

I wasn't supposed to admit to the amount of coaching I'd received while filming. I'd been instructed to maintain that everything on the show was completely authentic. I didn't want to lie to anyone, so I stuck with my standard non-answer. "Filming the show was an interesting experience."

"Are you contractually obligated to give vague responses?" June asked.

I laughed, and Cassidy cut in. "Well, if she was, then we'll just leave it be."

"Well, then," Scarlett said. "How'd you get on with Mona Lisa McNugget there, Kevin?"

"It's *Kelvin*," he said. "And someone should cook that chicken for dinner."

Scarlett and Cassidy both gasped.

"Deputy Tucker, I think he just threatened the life of our beloved Mona Lisa McNugget," Scarlett said. "Surely that's an offense worthy of an arrest."

"Mona Lisa McNugget is a fine little hen," Cassidy said, crossing her arms. "If I were you, I'd be careful about making idle threats against our town chicken."

I covered my mouth to keep from laughing. June ignored all of us.

"I don't... what?" Kelvin asked.

"Maybe we should get a drink," I said, patting his arm.

"I'll go." He walked away, shaking his head.

The bar was busy; it would take him a while to get service. Cassidy pushed one of the extra stools out for me and I took a seat.

"I love your shirt," Cassidy said. "That's adorable. Where'd you get it?"

"Oh, I made it," I said. "Well, not from scratch. It used to be a dress, but I modified it."

"Dang it, I was hoping I could get one," Cassidy said.

"Same here," Scarlett said. "I'd wear the shit out of that. Although I swear you're a foot taller than I am. It'd still be a dress on me."

"That would barely cover your ass," Cassidy said.

Scarlett shrugged. "Would still be cute with a pair of boots."

"Exactly." I stuck my foot out so we could all *ooh* and *ahh* over my cowboy boots.

"So what's it like, being on TV and all that?" Cassidy asked. "Must be pretty exciting."

I opened my mouth to answer, but faltered. I wanted to tell her it was amazing. That I was finally so close to living my dream. I wanted to gush about how great my life was. But the words wouldn't come.

"It's all right," I said. "The show wasn't quite what I thought it would be. But I'm still hopeful that it'll open some new doors."

"What's Brock Winston really like?" Scarlett asked. "He's such a hunk of man candy. Is he dumb as a rock?"

I laughed. "I'm not really supposed to talk about my castmates. But off the record, kind of, yeah."

"I knew it," Scarlett said and took a swig of her beer. "He doesn't seem like he has much going on upstairs."

"I was never sure what Maisie Miller saw in him," Cassidy said. "Did you meet her, too?"

"No," I said. "She was supposed to be on the show, but she broke her leg and couldn't be there for filming."

Scarlett glanced toward the bar, then looked at me. "So, how was lunch with Jameson? We missed y'all at Moonshine."

My cheeks warmed, and I hoped the light was too dim for anyone to notice. Just the mention of Jameson's name should not have made me blush. "We decided to take our lunch down to the lake. It was nice."

"Hmm," Scarlett said and took another drink.

"Oh, stop *hmm*ing," Cassidy said.

"I think she's implying that Leah Mae had romantic intentions with regard to Jameson," June said. "Or possibly the other way around."

My cheeks flushed hotter.

"I meant nothing of the sort," Scarlett said with a grin.

"Subtle," Cassidy said.

"We were just catching up," I said.

"Good man, Jameson," Scarlett said. "He may be quiet, but he's reliable. And have you seen his art? It's absolutely amazing."

"I haven't," I said. "I was hoping to have time to see his workshop, but I'm not sure if I will."

"He invited you out to his workshop?" Scarlett asked, her eyes widening.

"Well, sure," I said. "Is that unusual?"

"I've never seen it," Cassidy said.

"I guess he just likes his privacy," Scarlett said. "I've seen him work, but I hardly count, being his sister and all. You should go visit him, Leah Mae. It's mighty sweet of him to offer."

"I'd like to, but—"

I was cut short by a sudden loud commotion near the bar. Scarlett and Cassidy turned around, and I looked over to see what was going on.

"Oh god," I said and jumped from my seat.

Kelvin was backing away from the bar while two red-faced men in t-shirts that said *Bootleg Cock Spurs* stalked toward him.

Scarlett gently grabbed my wrist. "Best to let things sort themselves out."

"What are they going to do?" I asked.

"Depends," she said.

"On what?"

"On what he did."

I pulled my arm out of Scarlett's grasp—she wasn't holding me very hard—and rushed over to Kelvin.

"Excuse me." I waved my hand to get the men's attention. "Whatever happened, I'm sure he's sorry. Can we just all get along tonight?"

"I'd stay out of the way, ma'am," one of them grumbled.

I thought I recognized him. "Otto? Otto Holt?"

He glanced at me. "Yeah."

"I thought that was you," I said. "I'm Leah Mae Larkin. Remember me? Clay Larkin's daughter."

Otto eyed me, and the other man crossed his arms over his thick chest.

"Sure, I remember," Otto said.

"He's with me," I said, patting Kelvin's arm. "Maybe we could not do… whatever you're about to do. You two go enjoy your evening, and we'll stay out of your way."

The bigger man kept his arms crossed and looked Kelvin up and down, a mean scowl on his scruffy face.

Otto narrowed his eyes. "He ain't worth the trouble anyway."

"These people are insane," Kelvin said.

I leaned closer to Kelvin. "Maybe stop talking."

Otto turned back toward the bar. His angry friend pretended to lunge at Kelvin, then laughed when Kelvin flinched. But thankfully, he backed away too.

"We're leaving," Kelvin said, his voice sharp.

I sighed. Of course we had to leave now. I didn't know what he'd done to piss those guys off, but I had a feeling they wouldn't give him a pass a second time. I waved a quick goodbye to Scarlett, Cassidy, and June, then followed Kelvin to the door.

He pushed the door open hard, and Jameson jumped out of the way. Grabbing me by the wrist, Kelvin tugged me toward the car.

"You all right, Leah Mae?" Jameson asked, stepping toward us as Kelvin dragged me into the parking lot.

"Yes, I'm fine," I said over my shoulder. I twisted out of Kelvin's grasp and paused. "Just a little trouble inside. We have to go."

"All right," he said. "If you're sure."

"Get in the car, Leah," Kelvin said.

"I'm sure," I said. "He's just being cranky."

Kelvin groaned and got in, slamming the car door behind him.

I rolled my eyes and shook my head. "I don't know what happened in there, but it dinged his pride. He'll calm down."

"You sure that's all?" Jameson took another step closer. "Or do you need help?"

"No, I'm fine," I said. "Promise."

"Okay," Jameson said, but he sounded skeptical. "You look nice, by the way. I like your boots."

I smiled and opened the passenger's side door. "Thanks. Have a good night."

"You too."

"Are you finished?" Kelvin asked as I got in.

"Finished what? He just watched you drag me to the car. Would it have been better if I'd ignored him?"

"This town is fucking crazy."

"What happened in there?"

"Nothing," he said. "I tried to order drinks."

"Well, something happened," I said. "Did you step on someone's boot?"

He scowled at me. "No."

"What did you order?"

He started the car and backed out. "I ordered a Manhattan, and the bartender asked if I was new around here. I said yes, and she asked if I wanted to try the moonshine."

"And what did you say?"

"I said if I wanted a redneck drink, I would have ordered one."

I put my hand to my forehead. "Well, that was an asshole thing to say. And those guys heard you? Is that why they were staring you down like they were about to drag you outside?"

"One of them said, 'There ain't no rednecks here,' and I pointed out that he and his buddy were wearing shirts with roosters that said *Bootleg Cock Spurs*, which would suggest otherwise."

"Why would you say something like that?"

He shrugged. "It's true."

"No, it's not," I said. "This is a nice town full of decent people. You've spent the entire week acting like you're better than everyone."

"I'm not acting like I'm better than anyone," he said. "I've spent the week working my ass off. For you, I might add. I know you needed to come out here and see your dad, and that's fine. But Jesus, I'll be glad to get back to the real world."

I leaned back in my seat and looked out the window. That was as close to an apology as I was going to get out of him—which was no apology at all. I didn't understand why he had to be such a jerk about Bootleg. So it was a little different. We'd been lots of places that were different, and he'd never acted like such a jerk.

My phone buzzed with a text, so I got it out to check.

Jameson: You sure you're ok?
Me: Yeah, promise. But thanks for checking.
Jameson: Anytime.

Kelvin didn't say anything else on the short drive to the cabin. Neither did I. When we got back, the asshole had the nerve to think he could get me naked. I told him I was taking a bath—alone—and locked myself in the bathroom. He could grumble about it all he wanted. He'd ruined my night out, and the last thing I was going to do was sleep with him.

Lying in the warm bathwater, I let my mind wander. I wished I could have stayed at the Lookout. Maybe danced to a few songs. Not that Kelvin would have danced with me, but I bet the girls would have. And Jameson had come, right when we'd been leaving. I could have talked to him for a while, if we'd stayed.

But we hadn't, and we were leaving town tomorrow. I was going over to see my dad one last time, and then we'd have to drive back to Pittsburgh so we could catch an early flight on Saturday morning back to L.A. To a home I'd never seen in a neighborhood I didn't know. To an uncertain future.

I stayed up late, long after Kelvin had gone to bed, feeling lost and wondering what exactly I was doing with my life.

Chapter Eight

Leah Mae

I pulled up outside my dad's house, a brown paper sack with our breakfast sitting on the passenger's seat. I'd left Kelvin back at the cabin. I was still mad at him about last night. Plus, things were tense between him and my dad. I'd hoped once my dad got to know Kelvin, he'd warm up to him. Now I figured keeping them apart was better. Dad didn't seem to hate him, but he wasn't all that impressed either. And I wanted my last visit with my dad to be a good one.

Truthfully, I wasn't sure how I felt about Kelvin right now. Maybe it was just because we were fighting, and I was still annoyed about last night. We'd had arguments before, but this one felt different. Like it was breaking something open inside me. I was a little bit afraid of the feeling—afraid to face what it might mean.

I owed a lot to Kelvin. We'd met when I was twenty and in need of a new agent. I'd signed with his agency, and he'd been instrumental in nurturing my career. Nothing romantic had happened between us until about two years ago. But our relationship had grown naturally, mostly due to the amount of time we spent together.

I traveled so much, moving from place to place, there were few constants in my life. Especially when it came to people. I'd had a long string of model roommates, lived in temporary rentals, always surrounded by a sea of changing faces.

Kelvin had been a constant. He'd been the one meeting me at the airport. Helping me plan everything from itineraries to my next career moves. When I was exhausted or frustrated with my schedule—when the not-so-glamorous side of being a model was too much—he'd been the one I called. The one who understood. He lived the business just like I did. It was hard to find things in common with people who didn't share the same lifestyle, and the world of modeling had provided a connection.

But how much of our relationship was based on my success? If my career went away tomorrow—if no acting gigs ever came through and I faded away into obscurity—would Kelvin still care about me? He'd always made me feel like I had someone to take care of me. But I'd also been making him a lot of money. What would happen if the money dried up? If I was no longer his star client? Would he still want me then?

And what did it say about our relationship that I didn't know the answer to that question?

I got out of the car, grabbing our breakfast. The sun was warm on my skin, and birds chirped in the trees out back. Dad's house wasn't far from town, but a soft quiet was settled over his house. My ring glinted in the sunlight, and I paused, looking down at my hand.

When I'd agreed to marry Kelvin, it had seemed like an easy decision. He hadn't really proposed, in the traditional sense. He'd brought up the idea, and we'd talked about how it made sense. Back in Los Angeles, having just returned from New York and getting ready to fly out to Wyoming to film *Roughing It*, getting married had seemed like the obvious next step. I hadn't been starry eyed and squealing over my engagement ring. The ring itself had been an afterthought, picked up while we were out shopping for other things a few days later. But it had seemed sensible to get married.

The whole thing felt like a business arrangement. Like signing on with his modeling agency, only for life.

But I was probably being dramatic because of what had happened at the Lookout last night. Kelvin was out of his element, and yes, being kind of a jerk about it. But he wasn't always that way. Bootleg Springs hadn't grown on him the way I'd hoped it would, but it wasn't his sort of place. He was an urban guy—born and raised in L.A. To him, a city of less than a million people was a *small town*. A place like Bootleg Springs was barely a neighborhood in his eyes. I'd grown up here, so I knew what it was like. He didn't have the same nostalgia for it. I couldn't expect him to fall in love with the place just because I'd lived here as a child.

I was sure that by the time we got back to L.A., everything would be back to normal. He'd figure out my next career move, we'd get married, and everything would be fine. Like he'd said, I was at a crossroads. I should be excited for what the future had in store.

In the meantime, I was going to have one last visit with my dad.

I knocked on the front door as I opened it. Of course it wasn't locked. People didn't lock their doors in Bootleg. It just wasn't done.

"Hey, Daddy," I said when I came in. "I brought breakfast."

He hadn't been on his front porch—which was strange because the weather was so nice—and he wasn't in his recliner, either. His truck was outside, so I knew he had to be home. But looking around, I didn't see him.

"Daddy?"

Betsy Stirling came out of the back bedroom. She was nearing fifty—pretty, with a bit of gray in her short blond hair. "Oh good, I was about to call you."

"Is Dad okay?"

"Well, he is, and he isn't," she said. "He's been having a bit of trouble breathing this morning. I made him call Doc Trevor.

65

Doc said it was all right for Clay to stay home as long as he rests and doesn't get worse. Otherwise, he's to go get checked out at the hospital."

"Oh, no."

"I've been having a hell of a time keeping him from getting up for every little thing," she said. "I tell you, Leah Mae, men either act like they're dying when they have nothing but a bit of a cold, or they're up and working when they're at death's door. There's no in between."

I sighed and put our food on the counter. "Thanks for checking in on him. I appreciate it."

"No trouble at all, sweetie," she said. "Now if you don't mind me, I'll get a few things done around here. You're on keep-your-daddy-in-bed duty."

"Got it," I said. "Thanks."

I let Betsy get on with her work while I unpacked our breakfast and put it on a tray I found in a cupboard. It was just muffins, but I wanted to make sure Dad didn't get up. If he was supposed to rest, I was going to see to it that he did.

Dad was in bed with his head propped up against two pillows. His oxygen tank was on the far side of the bed, the rubber tubing running over the side. His skin was pale, almost ashen, and he coughed when I came in.

"Hey, Daddy." I set the tray down on his dresser. "I brought breakfast."

He coughed again, and I didn't like the way it sounded. So raspy. "Thank you, sunshine."

"That cough doesn't sound so good."

"I'm all right," he said.

I sighed and helped him sit up a little more so he could eat.

"I think you're just saying that so I won't worry." I pulled up a chair next to the bed and sat down with my plate.

"I don't want any fuss," he said. He coughed again before he started eating.

"No fuss might mean you wind up in the hospital again," I said.

He just grunted.

"Daddy, it's okay to admit you're not feeling well."

"I just don't want you changin' your plans on account of me," he said. "I'll get on just fine."

"Now that's something I don't want *you* worrying about," I said. "I need you to do something for me."

"What's that?"

"I need you to be honest," I said. "If you're getting sick, you need to call me. If you feel worse, tell me about it. Let me help you. It's worse for me to find out later that you were sick. Even if I can't make it home, I can still call around and make sure you have the help you need. And if you don't, I'm going to bribe Betsy to spy on you and report back."

The lines in the corners of his eyes deepened when he smiled. "All right, sweetheart. I will."

"Promise?"

He laid his calloused hand on mine and squeezed. "Promise."

We finished our breakfast and I stayed a while longer. He needed to rest, so I didn't bother him, but I didn't want to leave, either. I sat out on the front porch in his rocking chair and gazed out at the trees. Listened to the breeze. It was a nice day—not too hot. Would have been perfect for a dip in the lake. Or a walk through the woods.

Where would Jameson and I have gone today, if we were still kids? Probably the woods. We'd always liked to go exploring when it wasn't too hot. Maybe he'd have shown me a new climbing tree. Or a bird's nest he'd found. He'd been so good at spotting things that other kids missed.

I ran into town to make sure my dad had plenty of groceries before I had to leave. I stocked up on things that would be easy to prepare. When I got back to my dad's house, he was sound asleep. He needed his rest, so I didn't wake him. I left him a note assuring him I'd call to check on him when I got back to L.A.

I felt heartsick over having to leave my dad. And Bootleg. I needed some comfort food, so I texted Kelvin to let him know I was going out to eat at Moonshine—with or without him. He texted back to say he'd go with me, so I drove out to the cabin to pick him up.

Moonshine was a landmark in Bootleg Springs, with some of the best food you could hope for. A smiling Clarabell, with her brassy red beehive hairdo, seated us in a booth near the window.

"My goodness, Leah Mae Larkin," Clarabell said when she came over to take our orders. "It is so lovely to see you back here in Bootleg Springs."

"Thanks," I said. "It's nice to be home."

Kelvin raised an eyebrow at me. "Home?"

"Bootleg Springs is always home," Clarabell said with a wink. "What can I get you?"

"I'll have the meatloaf and mashed potatoes," I said.

"Do you have anything that's gluten-free?" Kelvin asked, still eying the menu.

"Hmm," Clarabell said, tapping her pen against her chin. "I'm afraid here in Bootleg we're not opposed to keepin' the gluten in our food. Might I suggest a salad?"

"Just order something," I said. "Get the open-faced turkey sandwich. It's to die for."

"You know I don't eat things like that," Kelvin said.

I sighed. "It won't hurt you to cheat once in a while. It's not like you actually have a gluten intolerance."

"I get bloated," he said in a low whisper.

Clarabell looked like she was trying to smother a grin.

"Salad," he said. "Dressing on the side."

"Will do," Clarabell said and took our menus.

"Do you still need to pack, or are you ready?" Kelvin asked. "I want to get moving."

I traced a little scratch on the surface of the table. I knew what I needed to do. I'd thought about it all day. But I also knew Kelvin was going to argue.

"I've been thinking about that," I said. "I don't think I should leave yet."

"What?" Kelvin asked. "What do you mean?"

"I mean, I think I should stay a while. My dad is getting sick again. If he gets worse, he might wind up back in the hospital. I don't feel comfortable leaving him alone."

"Leah, he's been taking care of himself for how many years?"

"He wasn't sick for most of those years," I said. "I don't have any jobs coming up, so it's not like I have anywhere else to be."

"Not yet," he said, his mouth twitching in a grin.

"What's that smile for?"

"I talked to the producer over at Verity Studios," he said. "They're planning a show and they think you'd be a perfect fit."

"What kind of show? Doesn't Verity only do reality TV?"

"Imagine *The Bachelor*, only six men instead of one," he said. "Dating shows have been done to death, but this is a twist that's never been seen before."

"Wait, I'm confused. Let's come back to the fact that you just said *dating show*. What do you mean six men? You mean they each choose a woman?"

"No, I mean they all choose one," he said. "And they have to agree who it's going to be."

"Six men all with the same woman?"

"It's called a reverse harem," he said. "Very progressive. Female positive. Puts a lot of power in the woman's hands. People are going to eat it up."

I gaped at him. "You can't be serious."

"Of course I'm serious."

"Kelvin, I can't go on a dating show," I said. "Let alone a dating show with six different men. That's obscene."

"Don't be dramatic."

"I'm hardly being dramatic," I said. "I can't believe you would suggest something like this."

"The studio is thrilled with your performance on *Roughing It*," he said. "And with what's coming in the later episodes, it's going to set you up perfectly for this show."

"What's coming in later episodes?"

"I don't have any details," he said. "That's just what they told me."

"Absolutely not."

"You haven't heard what it pays."

"I don't care what it pays," I said. "The answer is no."

"You won't say that when I show you the contract," he said. "They realize this is a stretch, so they're willing to compensate you. And Leah, it's not like you have other offers coming in."

"Well, I can't imagine why that would be. Oh—maybe it's because I look like a skank on their current reality show."

Kelvin rolled his eyes. "You're blowing this way out of proportion. This show is going to be all the rage."

Clarabell brought our food, but my appetite was gone.

"I don't want to be known as a reality TV whore. A show like that isn't going to take my career in the right direction."

"Why don't you let me worry about your career," he said. "You just keep looking pretty."

I gaped at him. "I can't believe you just said that to me. Besides, why would you want me on a dating show? I thought we were engaged."

"We are," he said. "But the world doesn't need to know about it. After the show wraps, we can get married. No big deal."

"What if I decide I'd rather be with the six bachelors and have my harem?"

He raised an eyebrow at me. "I guess that's a risk I'll have to take."

"Do not book me for that show."

"We have time," he said. "They won't finalize casting until next month."

I picked at my food but didn't continue the argument. He'd only get more stubborn if I kept refusing. I'd wait a little bit and bring it up again when he wasn't as likely to be defensive. Or maybe a better offer would come in and I wouldn't have to worry about it.

"I'm serious about staying here in Bootleg. I'm not leaving today."

His jaw set in a hard line. "I don't want you staying here."

"That's not your decision. It's my *father*, Kelvin."

He stared at me for a second, and I wondered how difficult he was going to make this. I stared right back.

Finally, he shook his head and let out a long breath. "All right. Stay. But if something comes up, you need to be ready to get on a plane to L.A."

"I'll make it work. And I can stay with my dad. He doesn't have an extra bed, but I'll sleep on his couch."

Another sigh, but this one wasn't so combative. "No, let me see if you can keep the cabin."

"I'll call Scarlett," I said. "If it's not available, she might know of something else."

"Fine. But don't stay here too long. It took a lot of dialect coaching to get rid of your accent. Don't go all country on me."

"Y'all are worryin' about nothin'," I said in my best Appalachian twang.

Kelvin just shook his head.

Chapter Nine

Jameson

It was with no small amount of reluctance that I followed Jonah into Moonshine. The smell of fresh coffee and pancakes on the griddle greeted us. Normally I wouldn't mind an early Saturday family meeting. Whit cooked up the best waffles in Olamette County, and that was a fact. But even the promise of waffles for breakfast wasn't enough to lighten my mood this morning.

Leah Mae had left town yesterday.

I was doing my best to act like nothing was wrong. Wasn't about to let on that I was missing her already. How would I explain that? She wasn't mine to miss. She was going back where she belonged. Better for everyone this way.

My head sorta believed that, but there was this feeling in my chest—an ache that wouldn't go away—that said my heart disagreed.

I glanced at my phone again, wondering if she was going to say goodbye. That was probably what hurt the most. I hadn't heard a word from her. I understood her not having time to come see my shop. She'd said she wasn't sure, what with her daddy being sick lately. I wasn't bothered by that. I'd hoped she would have at least sent me a text that she was leaving. But I hadn't heard a peep.

All those thoughts of Leah Mae did not put me in the mood for socializing with my siblings. But Jayme had called Bowie to let him know we could get back into Dad's house. So it was time to make a plan.

Bowie was already in a booth with a cup of coffee. Jonah and I slid in next to him just as Scarlett and Devlin wandered in. They both looked tired. I wondered if something had kept them up late, but quickly decided I didn't want to know.

"Mornin' y'all," Scarlett said. "Clarabell, this girl needs caffeine, and lots of it."

"Comin' right up," Clarabell said.

Gibson walked in and tipped his chin to Clarabell. He pulled up a chair and sat at the end of the table. Clarabell filled our mugs, then took everyone's orders before going to check on her other customers.

I added sugar to my coffee, ignoring the look Jonah gave me. He was always giving me grief about how much sugar I ate.

"Well, let's get things settled," Bowie said. "Jayme said we can get back into Dad's place as of today. There's still a lot of stuff to sort through. Then it'll be a matter of hauling things where they need to go. The dump, thrift store, what have you."

"Sounds fair," Scarlett said. "Then me and Gibs can get it ready to flip. We'll need all y'all's help with that work, too, though. Don't forget."

"We've got you," Bowie said.

Jonah and I nodded. Gibson grunted and sipped his coffee.

"What day works for everyone to get started?" Bowie asked. "Tomorrow's a holiday, and Monday's the fifth, so that's out."

We all nodded. The fifth of July was a no-go for everyone in Bootleg. Clarabell would open Moonshine, and it was likely the Pop In and a few other places would open their doors— mostly for tourists who didn't understand how things worked.

But the day after the Fourth of July was not a day for working around these parts. Bootleg Springs took her Independence Day festivities very seriously. Which meant copious amounts of liquor and some serious post-holiday hangovers.

"Let's plan for Tuesday, then," Bowie said. "Meet here for breakfast first, then we'll tackle the house. Get through as much as we can that day, then decide from there."

Clarabell brought our breakfasts, passing out plates stacked high with food. My waffles looked tasty, but I still wasn't in much of a mood for 'em.

"Sounds good," Scarlett said.

"I'll be there to help," Jonah said.

Scarlett smiled at him. "You're a good sort, Jonah Bodine."

"Thank you, Scarlett," he said. "I appreciate that."

The door opened, and I glanced up. Felt a sense of discomfort in my gut. Judge Kendall walked in with his wife. He was a large man with a round belly. Balding with a short white beard. His eyes swept around the restaurant, pausing on our table for a moment. His wife clutched a little yellow handbag and kept her eyes on the floor. He nudged her forward, and she shuffled ahead of him to a table.

I'd always felt a bit odd seeing Judge and Mrs. Kendall. They didn't live in Bootleg Springs year-round, but spent their summers here. Even kept on after Callie had disappeared. I felt bad for them. Felt bad they had to face the place their daughter was last seen—probably where she'd died. I wasn't sure why they kept coming back to Bootleg year after year. But maybe facing it helped them, somehow. Hard to be sure.

My siblings chatted over breakfast, mostly about tomorrow. There was a lot going on in Bootleg for the Fourth, and Scarlett wanted to make sure we'd all turn out for the festivities. I'd go, but I doubted I'd be in the mood to celebrate any more than I was in the mood for my waffles this morning.

Clarabell left Judge Kendall's table, and he rose from his seat. Walked over to us, and stood next to our table.

Whatever Scarlett had been about to say died on her lips as she looked up at the judge.

"Pardon the interruption," Judge Kendall said. His voice was low and smooth—almost soft coming from the big man. "I just wanted you all to know that I don't hold your daddy responsible for what happened to my daughter. I'm aware of what was found in his home, but my wife and I harbor no ill will against your family."

"Thank you, sir," Bowie said. "We appreciate hearing that."

Judge Kendall nodded. "Truth be told, we'd like it if they stopped the investigation all together. It's so difficult on my wife. She's in a fragile state, and this has brought up painful memories."

"I'd imagine so," Bowie said.

The rest of us stayed silent, allowing Bowie to speak for us.

"My daughter was... troubled," Judge Kendall said. "I've told the police many times. It runs on her mother's side of the family, I'm afraid." He glanced back at his wife who sat staring at the table. "We tried to get her help, but even Bootleg wasn't enough to cure her."

Callie Kendall had been my age, but I hadn't known her well. Talking to girls, other than Leah Mae, hadn't been my best skill in those days. But she'd been around at the lake or wherever us kids had been hanging out during the summer. Troubled wouldn't have been a word I'd have used to describe Callie, although you never knew what people were hiding. Pensive, maybe. Anxious, sometimes. But also sweet and friendly. Her father had always maintained that she'd committed suicide, and there was something about that I couldn't quite swallow.

Of course, if the alternative was that my father had killed her, I wasn't sure which was worse. Suicide was a terrible, tragic thing. But finding out my father really had murdered a sixteen-year-old girl would have been horrifying.

"I guess we'll see what the police decide about all of it," Scarlett said.

Scarlett thought the judge was wrong about Callie. I could

see it in her eyes. She was a fireball, but smart enough not to start trouble with Judge Kendall. But I could tell she was itching to say more.

"Well, I'll let you get back to your breakfasts," Judge Kendall said. "I just didn't want to let the silence between us stretch on any longer than necessary. What Callie did was tragic, and I hope the police will let it lie so my wife and I can have some peace."

"Thank you, Judge," Bowie said. "Y'all take care."

With a tilt of his head, Judge Kendall went back to his table.

"Well, that was unexpected," Scarlett said in a low voice.

"I guess that means he won't be pushing to search Dad's property again," Bowie said.

"You should all still keep your distance," Devlin said quietly. "Just go about your business, and let the Kendalls go about theirs."

We shifted in our seats and went back to our breakfasts. But no one seemed to feel like talking. I reckoned we all felt guilty that one of our own might have cost this man so much.

Gibson was the first to leave, just a minute or two after the judge went back to his seat. His plate was still half-full but he muttered something about having to work, tossed some cash on the table, and left. Bowie finished up his breakfast and excused himself to leave. Jonah and Devlin left to help Dev's Granny Louisa with something at her place, which left me and Scarlett.

"You're quiet this morning," Scarlett said. "Course, I guess you're always quiet."

"I reckon."

"Waffles not treating you so well?" she asked.

"They're fine, I'm just not hungry."

"Are you coming out for the Fourth?" she asked. "You didn't say anything when we were talking about it before."

I shrugged. She was probably about to talk me into it, but right now, I didn't much want to. "Maybe. Do you need a solid answer, or can I just show up if it works out?"

She trailed a finger through the syrup on her plate and licked it. "I guess you can just show up if you want to. But I kinda think you'll want to."

My Scarlett-alarm went off, but I could sense it was already too late. She was up to something. There was nothing else for it but to play her game. "And why do you think that?"

"Oh, I don't know," she said, her voice light. "I invited Leah Mae Larkin and she said she'd come."

My eyebrows drew in and I gave her the side-eye. "Leah Mae left town."

Scarlett's mouth turned up in a devilish little grin. "You're certain about that?"

"Well, yeah," I said. "It's not like I drove over there to see or anything. But today was her flight. I do know that."

"Seems she had a change of heart," she said. "Called me yesterday to see if she could extend her stay. Her cabin was booked, but I had a last-minute cancellation on another one, so I set her up there yesterday afternoon."

I had no idea what Scarlett could see in my face. I was trying very hard to keep everything I was feeling from showing, but there was so much. So many emotions racing through me, quick as a lightning strike. Relief, mixed with worry, topped off with something that was awfully close to elation.

I cleared my throat. "Sounds like it worked out for both of you."

"Sure did," she said. "And since she'll be all alone for the holiday, I told her she really ought to come out and celebrate with everyone."

All alone. Did that mean her fiancé had left? I wanted to know, but I didn't want to ask. Wasn't sure if I *should* ask. I picked at what was left of my waffles.

Scarlett groaned. "Why don't you just ask me?"

"Ask you what?"

"You are such a pain in the ass," she said. "Ask me about Kevin, or whatever his name was. The guy she was with."

"Why would I ask you about him?"

She rolled her eyes. "So that's how we're playin' it? Fine. Because you're my brother and I love you even though you're stupid, I'll tell you. He's gone. He left yesterday. And you best be in town tomorrow for the Fourth of July, or I will come over and haul your ass out of that damn workshop. And if you get really stubborn, I'll sic Gibs on you."

"All right, all right. I'll be there."

"Good," Scarlett said with a self-satisfied grin and licked the last of the syrup off her finger. "Then my work here is done."

Chapter Ten

Jameson

Downtown Bootleg was awash in red, white, and blue. The decorating had started days ago, and now the entire town was decked out for Independence Day. Lake Street was closed to vehicular traffic and it had been transformed into a veritable carnival. Booths sold food and drink, and games were set up all up and down the street. Crepe paper and helium balloons—all red, white, and blue—were everywhere. More booths sold little flags, buttons, pins, and other novelties, and a fireworks stand down by the lake had a line that was already at least twenty deep.

The noise of the crowd buzzed around me. Seemed like just about everyone in Bootleg had turned out, locals and tourists alike. Wasn't often that there were this many people in one place in a town like ours. Kids darted in and out of their parents' legs while they chatted with friends and neighbors. Most people held red plastic cups—filled with sweet tea, lemonade, moonshine, or beer, depending on who was holding them.

Mine was just lemonade, although I was thinking a cup of strawberry moonshine didn't sound like a bad idea. Crowds were not my favorite thing. My dad always used to tell me I was *too damn sensitive*, and maybe that was true. But the press of people tended to get overwhelming.

"Well, hello, Jameson Bodine." Misty Lynn Prosser wandered over, swaying her hips more than was natural. Her hair was big, her makeup thick, and her boobs were practically busting out of her *I heart America* tube top.

"Hey, Misty Lynn," I said, my back stiffening. I hoped she'd go away quickly.

"Where's your brother?" she asked.

"Which one?"

She looked me up and down. "You know which one."

"I don't know where any of them are."

"All right." She smacked her gum a few times. "You tell Gibson I was askin' for him if you see him."

"You ever gonna give up on that?" I muttered under my breath. She glanced back at me, so I gave her a little smile. "Sure thing, Misty Lynn. Say, how's Rhett's nose?"

She lifted one shoulder. "Fine, I guess. You didn't break it."

I almost said *that's a shame*, but decided letting her walk away was the better choice.

A light touch on my shoulder made me spin around.

"Sorry," Leah Mae said. "I didn't mean to startle you."

Before I could stop myself, I was grinning at her like an idiot. She looked like sugar and sunshine in a yellow tank top with a few little blue flowers embroidered on the front. Cut-off jeans showed her long legs, and red toenails peeked through her sandals. Her long hair was down, and she had a white flower tucked behind one ear.

"That's all right," I said. "Didn't expect to see you still here."

"Neither did I," she said. "But my dad isn't doing so well. It didn't feel right to leave."

"Sorry to hear that."

"Thanks." She fiddled with a lock of her hair. "He seemed

better this morning. I made sure he got a good breakfast, and Betsy is spending the afternoon with him. He wanted to come into town, but I talked him into going back to bed after he had a coughing fit. I had to threaten to call Doc Trevor on him, though."

I laughed. Clay Larkin had never struck me as the sort of man who took orders well. "Hopefully with you here seein' to him, he'll be up and about in no time."

"I hope so, too," she said with a smile.

Scarlett appeared at Leah Mae's side, seemingly out of nowhere. "Y'all are here! Good. We need more people to run the obstacle course."

She grabbed Leah Mae's hand, and my wrist, and tugged us up the street after her. I tossed my cup into a garbage can on the street corner as we passed.

"What obstacle course?" Leah Mae asked.

Scarlett didn't stop, dragging us alongside her. "Haven't you done the obstacle course before?"

"I don't think so," Leah Mae said.

I had definitely never done the obstacle course. In fact, I'd always made myself scarce until it had begun because I didn't want someone—like Scarlett—trying to make me do it.

"It's been a tradition for a while, but maybe it hadn't started last you were here," Scarlett said. She turned toward Gin Rickey Park. "You need a partner, but there's two of you, so that's already settled."

And that was why I avoided the obstacle course. It didn't look difficult, in and of itself. Climbing over things, slogging through mud, and jumping in the lake were all fine. It was the partner aspect that kept me away. You didn't just go through the course with another person. You did it *tied to your partner*. Being fastened to another person with a rope was not my idea of a good time.

But if Scarlett meant for me to do the course with Leah Mae, that would mean...

"Hold on there, Scarlett—"

"This will be fun," Scarlett said.

"I don't think I'm wearing the right shoes," Leah Mae said.

"You'll be fine," Scarlett said. "Barefoot's better anyway."

We got to the edge of the field where everyone was getting ready to begin. Bernie O'Dell stood nearby wearing an American flag t-shirt. He had a megaphone in one hand and lengths of rope draped over his other arm. Bowie, Devlin, and Jonah were all there, along with Cassidy and June. Apparently Gibson was smart enough to stay away. I didn't see him anywhere.

"Kick off your shoes and empty your pockets," Scarlett said. "Hey Dev, you got the ropes for everyone?"

"Yep."

"Ropes?" Leah Mae asked as she stepped out of her sandals.

"Ah, hell." I took off my shoes and put my phone and keys on top of them. Leah Mae put her things next to mine. "Yeah, ropes."

"All right, y'all," Scarlett said, raising her voice. "Devlin's with me. Jonah, you pair up with June. Bowie, that puts you with Cassidy, and Jameson can team up with Leah Mae. Y'all know how this works. Devlin and I are gonna kick everyone's asses. Got that?"

Devlin handed out lengths of smooth, braided rope to each pair. I took one and let it drape from my hand, feeling like I couldn't quite make eye contact with Leah Mae.

Jonah and June stood facing each other and wound the rope around their waists. Bowie looked like he was having a hard time taking the last couple of steps to get close enough to Cassidy. She snatched the rope from his hand with a roll of her eyes and got in front of him.

"Come on, Jame, work with me here," Scarlett said, shoving me and Leah Mae together. "Can you get it, or do you need me to tie it for you?"

Leah Mae and I stood facing each other, just inches apart. I swallowed hard. Good lord, she smelled like citrus and sunshine. How in the hell was I going to do this?

"I, uh… I think I can…"

"Get in there," Scarlett said, giving me one final shove. "I gotta get roped in."

I practically crashed into Leah Mae and had to put my arms around her to keep from knocking her over. "Sorry."

Her body was up against mine, her face close. She laughed softly, her breath warm against my neck. "That's okay. We have to tie ourselves together?"

"Yeah." I wound the rope around our waists. Now that she was pressed against me, I didn't much want that to end. "You know how it is. Bootleggers can't do anything normal. Even an obstacle course."

I tied the rope behind her and tried to think of something—anything—to calm down my raging hard-on. One wrong move and Leah Mae was going to rub up against it and that was liable to kill me dead on the spot. But good lord, she smelled good.

"All y'all listen up," Bernie O'Dell said into his megaphone. "Here's the rules, and I mean for you to follow them, so don't go gettin' any ideas about cheatin'. Partners must stay tied together at all times. Everybody keeps their feet on the ground. No piggybacks or carryin' each other. The course begins here and ends at the lake. Y'all gotta jump in, but don't go drownin' your partner once you're in the water. We clear?"

Whoops and hollers sounded from around the field.

"Line up, then," Bernie said.

Everyone's first attempts at moving while attached to their partners were halting at best. People stumbled, laughing. Giggled as they fell over and struggled to get up.

"I think the trick to this is walking sideways," I said.

Leah Mae and I turned our faces toward the start line. My arms hung awkwardly at my sides, but I wasn't sure what to do with them. We managed to get to the start line doing a kind of side-shuffle. Just walking wasn't so bad, but I had a feeling the rest of the course wasn't going to be so kind.

Bernie raised his megaphone again. "On your marks. Get set. And, go!"

Jonah and June fell next to us before they'd hardly gotten

started. Cassidy and Bowie got off to a better start, moving down toward the first obstacle just behind Scarlett and Devlin. Those two seemed to have the right idea. They were holding each other tight so they could move fast.

"Tell you what." I slid my arms around her waist. "I think we have to just commit. And I want to take Scarlett down."

She put her arms around my neck. "Let's do this."

With our bodies pressed close, we started side-shuffling across the field. After a few steps, we picked up the pace, and pretty soon we were going at a good clip. Leah Mae laughed and her hair blew in my face, but I didn't care. We covered the distance across the field and made up a good portion of the space between us and Scarlett and Dev.

The first obstacle was a maze of old tires. They were set right up against each other, so we had to pick our way through them. We hopped in and out, still moving more or less sideways so we could both see where we were going.

Scarlett and Dev were still in front of us, as were Cassidy and Bowie. I heard a screech behind us and risked a quick look. Sierra Hayes—a girl who still wore her hair in a pair of braids, despite being twenty-five—was paired up with Amos Sheridan, and it was not a pretty picture. He seemed to be trying to get her to walk backwards while he did the leading, but she kept tripping over the edges of the tires.

"We're pretty good at this," Leah Mae said when we hopped out of the last tire, one leg over, then the other.

"Sure are."

The next obstacle was a long beam. There were half a dozen of them, all the same length and thickness—barely big enough for two people. Cassidy and Bowie had somehow gotten up one of them faster than Scarlett and Devlin. They shimmied their way down while Scarlett and Devlin got onto the one next to it.

"This looks like it'll just take some balance," I said.

"Balance I can do," Leah Mae said.

We stepped onto the beam, and she wound her arms tighter around my neck, pressing her cheek to mine. It was a lot like dancing. We slid one foot down the length of the beam, far as we could go without falling. Then brought the back leg up to meet it. We got a good rhythm going and it didn't take us long to get to the end of it. Jumping off was harder, but we managed to land on our feet.

After the balance beams, the course veered to the left, and I saw why. The Bootleg Springs Fire Company had used fire hoses to turn an empty lot into a giant mess of sloppy brown mud.

"Come on, Jameson," Leah Mae said. "Let's get dirty."

Oh lord, there went my dick again. We were squished together so tight, I had to hope she was too focused on the course to notice.

A few pairs had passed us, including Cassidy and Bowie. They didn't slow down, but went barreling into the mud—and paid the price. It was thick, and Cassidy's foot got stuck. Bowie kept going and the two of them toppled over into the muck. Scarlett and Devlin went down ahead of us, laughing as they tried to get up and slipped.

"Okay, we got this," I said. "Together, now."

Leah Mae and I moved like we had on the balance beam, each moving one leg out, then bringing the back leg in to meet it. Our feet squelched through the thick mud, making sucking and smacking sounds every time we moved. Leah Mae laughed, and the feel of her body trembling with her laughter was just about the sweetest thing I could imagine.

The mud sucked at my foot as I tried to take the next step. I pulled up harder and my foot came free, but my balance faltered.

"Uh oh," I said, and Leah Mae clung harder to my neck.

I didn't want to fall on her, so I leaned backward instead. I fell straight back into the mud, sending up a spray of brown droplets. Being tied to me at the waist, Leah Mae fell smack on top of me.

"Are you okay?" she asked. She had a few drops of mud on her cheek.

"Yeah, you?"

She nodded. Her face was so close, and the weight of her body felt good on top of me. But that was not a train of thought I needed to be riding, so I focused on how to get us back on our feet.

"Now I see why this ends in the lake," she said.

"Yep," I said. "We're almost there. Let's just see if we can get up."

A few more pairs passed us, but I figured there wasn't much chance of us winning at this point, anyway. We had to roll around a bit before we found an angle that worked. God in heaven, I was rolling around in the mud with Leah Mae Larkin. By the time we got to our feet, we were covered. Judging by the state of the couples struggling around us—either still in the mud, or hauling themselves out of it—most everyone was falling in.

"Come on, we got this," Scarlett shouted, just ahead of us.

"Not happening, Scarlett Rose," I said, and Leah Mae and I made a break for the dock.

We side-galloped our way down to the water and onto the wood slats of the dock. Scarlett and Dev were right here with us. Leah Mae had the height—and leg length—advantage on Scarlett, and just as we got to the edge, we overtook them.

Without a care for how we were going to manage to avoid drowning while tied together at the waist, I launched us off the end of the dock.

We plunged into the warm water feet first. Leah Mae kept her arms around my shoulders, and we both kicked. Our heads broke the surface and we came up laughing.

"Did we win?" she asked.

"I have no idea." I wanted to hold onto her, but I had to tread water for both of us.

Water dripped down her face, glinting in the sunlight. I had to look away because what I really wanted to do was kiss her. We were wet and smiling. Breathing a little hard. It was a perfect moment for kissing. Or would have been, if things had been different.

But things weren't different. Leah Mae was someone else's girl, not mine. I wasn't the sort to violate that. She wasn't mine to kiss, no matter how much I wanted to.

"We should get over to the beach," I said.

Technically, I think we could have untied ourselves at that point, since the race was over, but it would have been tough in the water. So we swam sideways, mostly using our feet to propel us toward the shoreline. It was awkward getting out, but we managed. Once we were back on land, we got the rope undone.

Scarlett came over, dripping wet, and high-fived us. "Well done. You two make a good team. But we still won."

I was going to let her have it, but Leah Mae piped up, a smile on her lips. "Yep, y'all won second place."

Scarlett laughed and met my eyes. "I knew I liked her." She pointed at Leah Mae. "Rematch next year, Larkin."

"You're on, Bodine."

Scarlett walked up the beach with Dev while Leah Mae and I shook some of the water off our clothes. The jump in the lake had washed the mud off. Mostly I tried to keep my shirt covering my manly parts, considering my dick was trying to cause a scene. But the feel of Leah Mae's body against mine was not one I could forget.

Chapter Eleven

Leah Mae

Dusk settled over Bootleg Springs, and the bang and pop of fireworks filled the air. People had been lighting things off for most of the day, but as the darkness grew, the fireworks increased. Kids ran around the beach waving sparklers, grown-ups launched bottle rockets out of beer bottles in their hands. Bigger fireworks went off with loud bangs over the lake, the sparks reflecting on the still water.

Jameson and I sat on a blanket on the beach, watching. Our clothes had dried in the afternoon sun, and we'd gone back to the park for our shoes. Then we'd stopped for hot dogs with coleslaw. We'd bought extra for my dad and Betsy, and run the food out to his place. I'd been happy to see Dad in a good mood, despite missing out on the festivities. When I'd offered to stay, or at least come back in time for dinner, Betsy had said she'd stick around for the rest of the day. They'd be able to see some of the fireworks from the porch. I was so grateful to her for keeping him company.

We'd come back to town and gotten our first cups of

moonshine. Jameson was on his third, but he didn't seem drunk at all. I felt tipsy after just two—even sipped slow—but I didn't drink that often, and Bootleg Springs moonshine was no joke.

A big firework exploded over the lake to *ooh*s and *ahh*s of the crowd around us. A big guy with no shirt, a hairy chest, and a beer belly barely contained by his denim overalls went running by, waving an American flag. I glanced over at Jameson and he grinned at me.

"You need another drink?" he asked.

I shook my head. "I think this is plenty."

"Fair enough. Let me know if you change your mind."

Jameson's brother Gibson came over carrying a shopping bag. "Come on, Jame, it's time."

"For what?" Jameson asked.

"You know." The corner of Gibson's mouth hooked in a grin. A rare expression from the oldest Bodine, at least in my experience. Jameson's brother always seemed so surly.

Jameson smiled back. I loved his smile; his whole face lit up. When we'd come up out of the water after jumping in the lake earlier, I'd wished I had a camera to capture the moment. His smile was amazing.

"I reckon I do know." Jameson turned to me. "Come on. This'll be fun."

He got up and offered me a hand to help me stand. I only tipped a little bit, but he held onto my arms until I was sure of my feet.

"You sure you're all right?" Jameson asked.

"Yeah." I took a deep breath. The fresh air was tinged with the scent of explosives and smoke. "I'm okay."

"Good," he said, patting me on the shoulder.

He was such a gentleman. Old-fashioned, in some ways. Although that was probably from growing up in Bootleg Springs. The men here were like that. They held doors open and pulled out chairs. Put their jackets on the shoulders of chilly ladies.

I followed Jameson and Gibson down the beach. Past groups of people cooking food over fires, lighting sparklers, laughing and drinking. The mood was festive and fun. In a way, I was glad Kelvin wasn't here. He'd probably be complaining about the noise.

Jameson's arm brushed against mine as we walked, and I had the silliest urge to hold his hand. It made my cheeks warm and I was glad for the cover of darkness. I had no business blushing over thoughts of hand-holding with Jameson Bodine. I wasn't a little girl anymore. And I wasn't single. I was just a bit tipsy, and in the best mood I'd been in for quite a while. I wouldn't ruin it by making things awkward.

We kept going, and the knots of people thinned out. The darkness thickened, but neither Jameson nor Gibson pulled out a light. I started to worry I might trip over something in the dark. But just as I was about to ask how much farther we were going to walk, Gibson stopped.

With a quick glance over his shoulder, he dropped the bag. "We need to get this done quick."

"I know," Jameson said. "Where are we setting it off?"

Gibson grinned again and dragged something out from under a nearby bush. "I made a raft."

A big firework burst overhead, lighting up Jameson's face. His eyes shone with mischief as he grinned back at his brother. "Perfect."

Jameson started pulling things out of the bag. It was mostly sparklers and a few rolls of electrical tape.

"Sparklers?" I asked. "I thought you had some big fireworks or something."

"You don't know about sparkler bombs?" Jameson asked.

"Did you just say *bomb*?"

Jameson grinned at me. "You pack these in real tight, tape them secure, and add a fuse. It's loud when it goes off."

"That seems dangerous," I said.

"Yeah, if you're stupid," Jameson said with a shrug. "You have to make sure the fuse is long enough. Plus, we'll send it out on Gibson's little raft, there. That's gonna make a column of water forty feet high."

Gibson chuckled while he helped Jameson open the packages.

"Here," Jameson said and handed me the sparklers.

I held the handles while he bunched them up and started winding electrical tape around the bundle.

"Perfect," he said as he wound the tape around. "The trick to these is getting the tape nice and tight. Well, that and not getting caught."

"Hasn't happened yet," Gibson said.

"Don't jinx it, man," Jameson said. "Last year Judge Carwell almost saw us."

More fireworks went off over the lake—pops and bangs followed by cheers, whoops, and hollers.

"You want to do a little bit of it?" Jameson asked.

"Sure," I said.

He took the mostly-taped bundle of sparklers and I finished winding the tape around up to the top. He'd left a fuse sticking out of the middle. Gibson watched as we finished.

"Looks good," Gibson said. "That's gonna be a loud one."

"Sure will," Jameson said. "Let's get her launched."

Gibson's raft was made of small planks of wood. He put it in the water and held it while Jameson set the sparkler contraption on top.

"This is nice," Jameson said. "I almost hate to blow it up."

"Almost," Gibson said, grinning again.

I shook my head. What was it with guys and blowing things up? They'd been like this as boys, too. But I'd have been lying if I'd said it wasn't thrilling to be fumbling around in the dark with them, doing something that was probably illegal.

"The breeze is just right," Jameson said. He held out a lighter toward me. "Want to do the honors?"

"Okay," I said, and he handed me the lighter. "Now?"

"Go ahead and light it," Jameson said.

I crouched down and struck the lighter. The flame danced

as I moved it toward the long fuse. My hand shook, and I was ready to run as soon as the fuse caught. Jameson put a steadying hand on my shoulder.

"You're all right," he said. "We'll be well away when it blows."

I nodded and thrust the flame to the end of the fuse.

"Let's go," Gibson hissed as soon as it caught. He pushed the little raft away from shore.

Jameson grabbed my hand and next thing I knew, I was running behind him, his fingers twined with mine. We didn't go back the way we'd come, but darted down a narrow trail through the woods. Both the Bodines seemed to know exactly where to go, so I just held onto Jameson and followed along behind.

We emerged on a dirt road, the sound of fireworks behind us. The glow of the town lights weren't far ahead. A minute later, we were walking back down to the beach, like we'd just been up to the Pop In to get snacks. Nothing out of place.

Jameson was still holding my hand, and I didn't pull away. We got to the beach and he squeezed, leaning in to whisper in my ear. "Ten seconds, I reckon."

My heart raced. Gibson had stopped at a picnic table a little way down the beach and leaned his hip against it. A few more fireworks burst over the water, and I counted backward from ten in my head.

I got to two and held my breath. Waited. But nothing happened.

"Well, shit," Jameson said. "Fuse must have—"

The loudest boom I'd ever heard went off in the night. Another firework went off just in time to light up a huge column of water streaming up into the air. Some people covered their ears, others startled and flinched. Still more pumped fists in the air and cheered.

I watched the water splash down, spraying in a wide circle around what had been Gibson's homemade raft, and laughed. The explosive noise and big splash were strangely satisfying. I had a little taste of what boys seemed to enjoy about this kind of thing so much. It was fun.

Jameson shared a quick smirk with his brother, then Gibson wandered off in the other direction, his body language relaxed and casual.

Someone off to our right cleared their throat.

"Happy Fourth," Jameson said, tipping his chin to Sheriff Tucker. He still had hold of my hand.

"You wouldn't know anything about that blast out there, would you, Bodine?" Sheriff Tucker asked.

"Can't say I do, sir," Jameson said.

Sheriff Tucker hummed, a gravelly suspicious sound in his throat. "You think your brothers know anything?"

Jameson shrugged. "You'd have to ask them. I've been spending the holiday with my old friend Leah Mae, here."

The sheriff's gaze shifted to me and his expression softened. "Well, hi there, Miss Larkin. It's awfully nice to see you back in town."

I smiled. "Thank you. I've missed it."

"Course you have," he said with a nod. "Fine place to live, Bootleg Springs. All right, you two enjoy your evening."

The sheriff walked on down the beach and Jameson finally let go of my hand. It felt cold after the warmth of his skin touching mine.

"Little does he know," Jameson said, smiling at me. "You're the one who lit it."

"Only because you took me along. It wasn't my idea."

Jameson laughed. "And no one would suspect that pretty face. You look too sweet to be settin' off sparkler bombs."

Our eyes were locked, smiles fading. My heart was still racing from the anticipation of the explosion. The way Jameson looked at me made it beat harder. His gaze trailed down to my mouth. Instinctively, I licked my lips.

He blinked and looked away, rubbing the back of his neck.

I was afraid he might say he had to leave. I knew the way I'd just looked at him hadn't been right. The thoughts that had raced through my mind were not things an engaged woman should think when she was with another man. Jameson was just a friend. Running around in the dark with him after drinking a little moonshine was making me stupid.

"Should we go sit and watch the rest of the fireworks?" he asked.

I let out a breath in relief. I hadn't ruined the evening. "Yeah, sure."

We went back to the blanket and sat down. I made sure to keep plenty of space between us. But even just sitting on the beach with him, tilting our faces up to the sky, guilt washed over me. Hanging out with an old friend was fine, but my thoughts were straying to places they shouldn't.

I didn't wait long before deciding the best thing for me to do was go back to my cabin. It was late, and we'd had a fun day. The most fun I'd had in… I couldn't remember how long. But I was feeling things I didn't understand. Having thoughts about a man who wasn't the one who'd put this ring on my finger. That wasn't fair to Kelvin, and it wasn't fair to Jameson either. He'd always been a good friend to me, and I didn't want to ruin that now.

Jameson offered to walk me home, but I declined. I could see my cabin from where we were sitting, and the walk wasn't far. I glanced over my shoulder when I got to the door and saw him standing near the edge of the crowd, watching. Like he was going to wait and make sure I got inside okay.

In fact, that was probably exactly what he was doing. Ever the gentleman.

I gave him a little wave and he held up his hand. Despite the part of me that didn't want to say goodbye, I went inside and shut the door behind me.

Chapter Twelve
Leah Mae

Seeing myself on TV was stranger than I would have thought. I'd seen videos of myself walking in fashion shows. And a photo shoot I'd done had been part of a documentary on modeling. But that wasn't the same as being on a TV show. Even a so-called reality show.

It didn't feel like watching *myself*. That girl on the screen seemed like she was someone else. She looked like me, with her bony elbows and gap between her two front teeth. Sounded like me, too. But with each episode that aired, she became less and less the Leah Larkin I knew. The Leah Larkin I believed myself to be.

Some of the strangeness was probably because the show was supposed to be real, but it wasn't. I knew I'd been acting—knew about all the coaching and retakes. But most people didn't, so they believed the Leah they were seeing was true. I didn't know how to feel about that, especially with how much they'd altered the show in editing.

I sat on my dad's couch, the remote in my hand. I hadn't

seen Jameson again since the last Sunday when we'd lit off the sparkler bomb. It had been almost a week—it was Friday night—and the thought of it still made me smile. It was such a silly thing. So juvenile. But between the obstacle course, the food, the fireworks, and the little stunt with Jameson and his brother, it had been one of the best days I'd had in years.

"What are you smiling about, sweetheart?" Dad asked.

He sat in his recliner, a tray of dinner on his lap. His skin tone looked better, and although he was still hooked up to his oxygen tank, his breathing sounded much clearer. I could probably go back to L.A. soon and he'd be fine.

My heart sank at that thought.

"Aw, where'd it go?" he asked.

"What?"

"Your smile," he said.

I shrugged. "I'm okay."

He eyed me for a second, like he didn't really believe me. "This show you're on is a bit odd, don't you think?"

"It's almost all faked," I said. I had no qualms about telling my dad the unvarnished truth. "They told me a lot of what to say and coached me through all those side interviews you see. I was acting."

"Hmm."

The show came back on and I sat with my back stiff. The way they'd edited the episodes made it hard for me to predict what was going to happen. It felt strange to watch clips of myself and not know what I was going to be shown doing or saying. I could tell how they'd pieced together different moments and conversations—in the industry, they called them frankenbites—but I knew most viewers wouldn't be able to tell.

The beginning of the episode had focused on Rudy Barron, a professional basketball player who'd left the NBA last year, and Simone Prince, the daughter of a wealthy hotel mogul. They'd seemed to get along fine during filming, but from the first episode, the footage had been edited to make it appear as if they were enemies. A clip of Simone glaring at something off camera was quickly followed by a shot of Rudy.

Then I was back on screen. Everyone was in the cabin, sitting by candlelight. The episode's challenge was over, and I already knew Brock had won, earning immunity from being voted off. We'd filmed the end of this episode several different ways. In one of the versions, I was voted off, but Brock valiantly gave up his immunity so I could stay. Another had someone else being voted off, and me making a dramatic show of being relieved. I wondered which ending they were going to use.

Brock got up and looked around. The camera switched to me, glancing in what looked like Brock's direction. He tipped his head, like he was signaling someone—me, apparently, although I didn't remember that—and went into a back room.

The camera panned across the rest of the cast, showing them going about their business in the low light. Like it was important to establish that everyone was busy—no one paying attention to Brock.

I got up and slipped into the back room with him.

My stomach turned over. I remembered going in there with Brock. The producers had delivered a message from his wife, but denied his request for a phone to call her back. She'd been laid up with a broken leg, and he was worried about her. But we weren't allowed contact with the outside world during filming.

He'd told me about it earlier that day, and I'd known he was upset. So when he'd gone back there, I'd sat and talked to him for a while. I hadn't realized the crew had still been filming.

Low voices carried through the door, but it was as if the microphones couldn't pick up the words clearly. It sounded like a man and woman speaking, but there was no telling who it really was. The scene cut again to show that the other cast members were still oblivious to whatever was supposedly going on behind that door.

The camera panned to the back room, and subtitles with our names appeared on the bottom of the screen.

Leah: Are you sure you're okay?
Brock: Yeah, I'll be fine.
Leah: Good. Come here, then.
Brock: *groans* We really shouldn't.
Leah: No one will know.
Brock: Are you sure?
Leah: Positive. *sound of a zipper* Trust me.
Brock: Oh f***, Leah. Holy s***.

Anger bubbled up in my stomach. They'd actually put *sound of a zipper* on the damn screen in the middle of words I'd never said. My cheeks flushed hot and I turned it off.

"That wasn't real, Daddy," I said, suddenly keenly aware that my dad had just watched what was apparently his daughter about to give a guy a blow job in a storage room. "None of that happened. That wasn't me talking. They made all that up."

He gave me a sympathetic smile. "Ah, sweetheart."

Tears stung my eyes, but I didn't want to cry. I was angry, and tears weren't going to do me any good. I got up and went outside, bringing up Kelvin's number.

"Yeah?" he answered.

"Do you know what they did on that damn show?" I asked. "Have you seen it yet?"

"Babe, you're three hours ahead of me," he said. "It hasn't aired yet."

"They made it look like I fucking blew Brock Winston in a storage room."

"Whoa, calm down," he said. "I'm sure it's not that bad."

"Are you kidding?" I tried to lower my voice so my dad wouldn't hear, but it was hard to keep myself under control. "Kelvin, they used fake subtitles. I never unzipped his fucking pants and talked him into a fucking blow job."

"Leah, take it down a notch."

My eyes nearly bugged out of my head and my throat felt like it was closing. I gaped at the darkness, my mouth hanging open, unable to get a word out.

"Babe, listen," he said, his voice infuriatingly calm, "ratings are going to be through the roof on this episode. Hang on, I'm checking something. Oh god, Leah, this is perfect."

"What?"

"Brock saves you at the end," he said. "I'm looking at spoilers. He uses his win to keep you in the cabin."

"This is a disaster. I'm screwed, Kelvin. I'm officially Leah Larkin, slutty home-wrecker."

"You're overreacting." He sounded distracted.

"God, why do you keep saying that?" I asked. "I'm not overreacting. The world is going to hate me, and I'll never get a decent job again."

"I keep telling you, leave that to me."

"Your most recent suggestion was a dating show with six men and one woman. I'm not so sure about your judgment right now."

"By tomorrow, the whole country is going to know the name Leah Larkin. You're not going to be some dime-a-dozen pretty fashion model. You're going to be the sexy blonde who was hot enough to distract Brock Winston from Maisie Miller. People are going to eat this up. It's a great story. You can't buy this kind of attention, babe."

"It's not the right kind of attention," I said. "My reputation is shot."

"Here's what you're going to do," he said. "Lay low. Stay in Backwoods Springs or wherever you are. You're off the grid. No one knows where you are. Disable the GPS on your phone and don't post anything with your location. Post pictures of your breakfast and shit to Instagram like nothing is wrong. Let this simmer down while I work on what's next. It's going to be fine."

I let out a breath. I had no confidence that he was right, but there wasn't much else I could do. He was right that no one knew I was here. But I'd have to face the town tomorrow, knowing most of them had watched tonight's episode. I hated that more than the prospect of what all the gossip columns were going to say. I desperately didn't want my Bootleg neighbors to think the things in that episode were true. But it was no use talking to Kelvin about that. It wasn't like he'd understand.

Or care.

"I have to go," I said. "I'll call you tomorrow."

"Night, babe."

I hung up and sank down into my dad's rocking chair. Against my better judgment, I brought up the *Roughing It* fan website. The headline read, *Leah Seduces Brock!* I knew I shouldn't read the post, but I couldn't seem to stop myself.

> On tonight's episode of *Roughing It*, the moment we've all been waiting for... or dreading as we cringed in front of our screens. Leah Larkin, that lanky blonde who's been after Brock since episode one, finally got what she was after. With no respect for Brock's relationship status, or apparent care for what it's going to do to Maisie Miller, Brock's wife, Leah coaxed Brock into a supply closet for some inappropriate contact. There is little doubt that Brock was helpless against Leah's seduction. After all, what guy can resist what she was offering when he's already in a position of weakness?
>
> No doubt Leah Larkin is going to wake up tomorrow and find herself the most hated woman in America.

Tears blurred my vision, so I stopped reading. Oh my god. The most hated woman in America? They were right. Everyone loved the Brock and Maisie story. They were annoyingly sweet, gushing over each other in public every chance they got. Their wedding had been the biggest celebrity news story of the year.

I wanted to post to all my social media accounts and deny everything. Tell the truth. But I stopped myself. I'd be violating my contract if I did. The studio would blacklist me. Maybe worse. They could sue me for breach of contract. Then what would I do? I didn't have the money to fight a legal battle with a TV studio.

I'd been cast as the villain in this story, and there wasn't a thing I could do about it.

Chapter Thirteen

Jameson

Leah Mae seemed to go into hiding. I texted her a few times to see how she was doing. Asked if she wanted to get together, maybe take her mind off things. But she said she was busy taking care of her dad. I happened to know from Betsy Stirling that Clay Larkin was doing better. Leah Mae was just using him as an excuse to hide out.

Not that I blamed her. There was a lot of gossip flying about with her name attached to it, and none of it was good.

I hadn't been watching *Roughing It*. I'd stopped after my scuffle with Rhett. Felt wrong to watch it, like I was supporting something unsavory. But I'd heard the talk and knew what the show had portrayed.

All those people talking shit about her on the internet didn't know her, and they certainly didn't care about her. They wanted their juicy story. Wanted to make themselves feel better about their lives by putting someone else down. Tearing a pretty girl off her pedestal.

They'd torn her down, all right.

I'd spent the last week with my hackles up, ready to defend her. Turned out, it wasn't necessary. The entire town was outraged. The general consensus had already been that the show was a crock of shit, given how she kept being made to look like she couldn't take care of herself. No one who'd grown up in Bootleg Springs would ever be as helpless as they made her out to be.

And since she'd been back in town, people had taken to her like she'd never left. She was just Leah Mae, Clay Larkin's daughter. None of this *Leah Larkin, fashion model and reality TV star* stuff. They saw her for who she was and embraced her as their own.

Nicolette had declared she'd no longer air the show at the Lookout. The people who'd been hosting viewing parties either canceled or found other shows to follow. I'd even heard a few people talking at Moonshine about how they'd been commenting on articles online, calling out the show as being faked. Millie Waggle, who hardly ever raised her voice or said an unkind word about anyone, had gotten spitting mad when Rhett Ginsler had tried to tell her reality shows were real, this one included. She'd dumped his dinner right in his lap and walked away.

The urge to fix this for her—or at least make her feel better—was strong. But there was a line I couldn't cross, and I wasn't quite sure where it was.

Since she'd been back, things between us had felt a lot like old times—like those summers she'd spent living with her dad. I felt as comfortable with her as I ever had. Like she was my best friend again.

But I was nursing a bit of a crush, if I was being honest. I'd been reluctant to admit it, even to myself, but it was hard to deny how I felt when I was around her. She lit me up in ways no one else ever had. It wasn't right, and I certainly wasn't going to act on it. But it made what I was feeling for her now—that drive to protect her—complicated.

It wasn't my place to act like her boyfriend—to be the man

in her life. I needed to keep treating her like a friend, no matter what the rest of me wanted. So I asked myself, what would a friend do?

A friend might just have a little surprise in store for her. Something to show her she didn't have to hide out. Not from Bootleg, at least.

Scarlett was having people over tonight for a bonfire, and I decided to see if I could coax Leah Mae out of hiding. I let my sister know what I had in mind, and of course she was in. No need to convince her. We came up with an idea to make Leah Mae feel better—show her we were all on her side. All I had to do was get her there.

I didn't bother texting, or even calling. I'd tried that already. Invitations were easier to refuse over the phone. Claim you had things to see to, whether or not you really did. She wasn't at her cabin, so I drove on out to Clay Larkin's place to fetch her.

The gravel crunched beneath my tires as I pulled up to the house. Dusk was falling, but the porch light was on. I got a bit nervous, looking up at that front door—wondered if I was doing the right thing in coming. But I hated the idea of Leah Mae sitting in there afraid to come out and face the world.

I went up to the door and knocked, then rubbed the back of my neck and shoved my hands in my pockets. Nervous habit. Leah Mae answered, her eyes widening when she saw me. She was dressed in a pink short-sleeved shirt and skirt with flowers all over it.

God, she was pretty.

"Jameson," she said.

"Hey, darlin'." I shouldn't have been calling her *darlin'*, and I knew it. But it just rolled right off the tongue. "Haven't seen you in a while. Thought I'd stop by and see how you are."

"Thanks," she said. "I'm okay, I guess. Do you want to come in?"

"Sure."

I followed her inside and nodded to her dad. He was sitting in his recliner and gave me a nod in return.

"Jameson Bodine," he said. "How are you, son?"

"Can't complain, sir. I thought I might see if Leah Mae here wanted to join me down at my sister Scarlett's place. She's having a bonfire by the lake." I turned to Leah Mae. "What do you think?"

Leah Mae twisted her hands together and drew her eyebrows in. "I'm not sure."

"Be good for you to get out," Mr. Larkin said.

I met her eyes. "It'll be good. Trust me."

She favored me with a little smile and nibbled on her bottom lip. Good lord, I wanted to nibble that lip myself. I cleared my throat and resisted the urge to rub my neck again.

"All right, but just for a little while," she said. "Are you okay for tonight, Dad?"

"Course I am," he said. "You have a nice night, sweetheart. I'll see you tomorrow."

She kissed her dad on the cheek and went to get her coat. I gave Mr. Larkin another nod and left out the front door with his daughter.

We got in my truck and started toward Scarlett and Devlin's place. I could tell Leah Mae was nervous. She held her hands in her lap and watched out the window as I drove. I would have loved to touch her—hold her hand or rub her thigh—but I kept my hands on the steering wheel where they belonged.

"I know you're worried," I said. "But I'm telling you, it's okay. You don't have to be nervous about going out."

"Everyone saw," she said, her voice quiet. "And the things people are saying…"

"You should quit reading what those idiots on the internet are saying about you."

She cast me a sidelong glance. "Yeah, but half the town has been watching the show. They all saw that episode."

"I reckon it's more than half," I said. "But trust me on this, darlin', Bootleg ain't that gullible."

I pulled up to Scarlett's house and parked among the rest of the cars and trucks. Music played, and someone had built a mighty impressive bonfire. Dev stood next to it with Scarlett in his arms, her head resting against his chest. All the regulars were here. My brothers, including Jonah. Cassidy and June. There was Nash, and Buck, and Opal Bodine, and a dozen or more other Bootleggers, clutching beers or plastic cups. Talking, dancing, laughing. Just another Bootleg summer night.

Scarlett spotted us as we approached the crowd, her face lighting up. I winked, and she grinned back at me.

"Hey, y'all," she said, her voice carrying above the music, "look who's here."

Leah Mae froze in her tracks.

I put my hand on the small of her back and leaned close to speak quietly in her ear. "It's all right, darlin'."

"Hey, there!" came the shouts from the crowd. People raised their cups and bottles to us.

"I got something for all y'all," Scarlett said. "Just hang tight."

Scarlett went inside while I nudged Leah Mae toward the fire. She kept close to me and it was all I could do to keep from putting my arm around her shoulders.

"Cut the music for a minute," Scarlett said, emerging from her door with Devlin just behind. The music quieted. She and Dev had trays with shot glasses lined up in neat rows, each topped with a dollop of whipped cream. "We all know what that piece of crap show did to Leah Mae here. So, to show that we stand in solidarity with our Bootleg sister, we've got blow jobs for everyone. Shots, that is!"

The crowd cheered, the noise erupting into the night. Leah Mae laughed and the sound of it was like music.

Scarlett brought the tray to her with a smile. "You first, Miss Larkin."

Leah Mae took one of the shots and held it up, casting a quick glance at me. Her green eyes shone in the firelight.

"Bottoms up," she said, and brought the shot glass to her lips. Tilting her head back, she swallowed the shot, then raised the empty glass above her head.

Everyone cheered again, whooping and hollering. Leah Mae laughed as she put the glass back on the tray. She had some whipped cream on her lip and god, how I wished I could lick it off.

Damn it. I had to stop thinking like that.

"You're next, Jameson," Scarlett said.

I took a shot and people gathered around to get theirs. When the trays were empty, we all held them up. I wasn't one to speak up like this on most occasions, but this was different.

"To Leah Mae," I said, lifting my glass.

"Leah Mae!" everyone replied.

We all tossed back our shots. Leah Mae watched me with a smile on her face. I put the glass down and licked my lips. That whipped cream got everywhere. She still had a little bit of it on the corner of her mouth. Knowing I probably shouldn't, I reached over and rubbed her lip with my thumb to get the last of it.

She bit her lip and touched her mouth with her fingers. "Thanks. You, um… you have a little bit here." And then it was her thumb sliding across my lip. That little touch made my heart race and a rush of heat hit my groin.

The music started again, and Jonah handed us each a beer. A few couples started to dance, and someone called for another blow job, earning laughs from the people standing nearby.

Cassidy and Scarlett pulled Leah Mae over to the other side of the fire. Talking girl stuff, I reckoned. I hung back and sipped my brew. Watching.

A new song came on and I cringed. It was Brock Winston. I could tell by the look on Leah Mae's face that she'd noticed. After the first few lines, the rest of the party seemed to realize who it was, too. A chorus of boos rose up, drowning out the music. Leah Mae laughed again and met my eyes. I gave her a little wink.

By the time the boos stopped, someone had changed the song. Gibson sat near the fire and strummed along on his guitar. Bowie sat near Gibs, staring across the way at Cassidy Tucker.

As usual. I shook my head, but I wasn't one to criticize. I was the one stupidly falling for a girl who could never be anything but a friend.

Figured. I'd kinda wondered if I was too broken to love someone. Maybe I'd done such a good job keeping people out, I'd never left a space to let someone in. Too bad the first time I thought it might be worth the risk, the girl belonged to someone else.

I watched her over by the fire, a beer in her hand. The light of the flames reflected off her smooth skin. Flickered in her eyes. She smiled, and my chest felt like it might collapse in on itself. She was just so damn beautiful. It wasn't fair. I'd never had a chance with her—not really—so I shouldn't go beating myself up over not being the one who got to be with her. But staring at her across the way, watching the firelight dance in her eyes, made my soul ache something fierce.

It made me wonder, if I ever did have a chance with her, would I take it? If she told me tomorrow that her engagement was over, the ring was gone, and she was staying in Bootleg, what would I do? Would I step up and take the risk? Tell her how I felt?

I wanted to think I would. That I'd be man enough. But years of hearing my dad tell me I was too sensitive, too soft, too scared, had taken their toll. I'd retreated inside myself, and tried pretty damn hard to stay out of everyone's way. Be invisible. My art was the only place where the real me showed true. I reckoned that was one reason I hadn't turned out like Gibs— angry at the world. I had a good outlet. But it hadn't made me any better with women than he was—not really, at least.

Scarlett appeared at my side and nudged me with her elbow. "How you doing, Jame?"

"All right," I said. "Thanks for this."

"Sure," she said. "It was fun. I hope she got the message."

"I think she did. Loud and clear."

"You know, you should just go for it."

"Go for what?" I asked.

"It," she said, emphasizing the word, "with Leah Mae. Lord knows you like her, and she obviously likes you back."

I took a swig of my beer and glanced at Leah Mae again. Thought about denying how I felt. There wasn't much point in it, though. Just like there wasn't much point in having a crush on a girl I couldn't have. Didn't matter that she was here, in Bootleg Springs, standing by my sister's bonfire. She might as well have still been off in L.A. Didn't change the facts.

"Can't," I said.

"Come on," Scarlett said. "Yes, you can."

I hated saying it out loud—made the ache in my chest hurt worse. "She has a ring on her finger, Scarlett. And it ain't mine."

Suddenly, I didn't much want to be here. I wasn't going to leave Leah Mae, but I didn't want to keep talking to my sister, either. I took my beer and walked down by the water, putting distance between myself and the crowd. Felt better that way. Safer. Where no one could see the hurt that lived inside me. Where I could be alone for a spell, and just feel what I had to feel.

There was nothing else for it. Leah Mae couldn't ever be mine.

Chapter Fourteen

Leah Mae

The Lookout wasn't crowded. It was early evening, and a Wednesday. A few barflies held down stools at the bar, and a handful of people were playing pool. But other than that, it was fairly quiet.

I wasn't here to drink, necessarily, so I ordered a club soda with lime and chose a table. Scarlett had texted me earlier, asking if I'd like to meet her. I was grateful for the invitation. Not just for the excuse to get out, but because it felt good to be included. Like I was connected to more than just my dad here in Bootleg Springs.

The next episode of *Roughing It* had aired, and it had been worse than the last. I hadn't watched, but a glance at the celebrity gossip columns told me everything I needed to know. The producers had edited the footage to make it look like Brock and I had hooked up again. In a bed this time.

To make matters worse, Brock and Maisie had broken their social media silence. Brock had issued a public apology to

Maisie, and she'd been posting things like *relationships are hard work*, and *true love wins over adversity*.

Brock's apology was vague, not confirming he'd cheated with me, but not denying it either. It was ridiculous, but I knew he was trying to stay within the terms of his contract. He wanted to get paid. We were paid a portion at signing, and more at the conclusion of filming. The rest of our earnings were being held in the form of a bonus that we wouldn't get until after the last episode. It was how the producers ensured our good behavior while the show aired.

I hadn't said anything about Brock on social media. It wasn't about the money. At this point, I'd have been happy to give up my earnings from the show to get my reputation back. But I didn't think it would help. It would just give the public more content to gossip over. And if I broke my contract with this studio, I ran the risk of being blacklisted all over Hollywood. My career might be able to survive some bad press. That was all on the surface. But it wouldn't survive a blacklisting.

I took a sip of my club soda, the bite of carbonation tickling my tongue. Maybe I should have ordered something stronger. I kept hoping that if I laid low for a while, people would tire of the story and move on. I just had to get through the summer, and the show would be over.

Being in Bootleg made that easier. I wasn't exactly hiding, but I wasn't making it known I was here, either. And the town seemed to realize I needed the safety of semi-secrecy. I always ran the risk of nosy tourists recognizing me and taking my picture, and I'd taken to wearing a hat and sunglasses when I went out. But I felt protected here.

The door opened, letting in a rush of fresh air. I glanced over, but it was a young couple I didn't know—not Scarlett. I smiled down at my drink, thinking of her bonfire last week. I'd been so apprehensive about going out, but all that anxiety had melted away with those blow job shots. Jameson and Scarlett had turned the whole thing into a joke, and it was clear they—and Bootleg—were on my side.

I'd had a great time with Scarlett and Cassidy that night. Jameson, too, although he'd been quiet. But I liked his reserved nature—always had. I felt comfortable around him in a way I didn't with many other people.

When he'd taken me back to my cabin, late that night, I'd caught something in his eyes. I wasn't sure if I'd imagined it, but he'd looked sad.

Since then, I'd been spending time with my dad, helping him out around the house. Thankfully, he was starting to get better. According to Doc Trevor, he'd be off oxygen soon.

My mom had called yesterday and at first, she'd pushed for me to come stay with her in Jacksonville. I knew she was worried about me, but I'd assured her I was fine here in Bootleg. It had been a relief to hear she and Stan weren't watching the show. She was livid over how I was being portrayed, and refused to watch.

I sighed and took another sip. I felt stupid for having agreed to the show in the first place. At the time, Kelvin's insistence that it was a great opportunity had seemed to make sense. But even if the show hadn't created this stupid scandal, I didn't see how it would have led to any real acting gigs. How many reality TV stars wound up with long-term careers? There were probably a few. The rest either did more reality TV shows in an attempt to stay in the limelight, or faded into obscurity.

The truth was, I'd gone along with it because I'd *wanted* it to be a good opportunity. Not because I'd believed it was. Deep down, I'd known. But I'd been so worried that with my modeling jobs becoming fewer and further between, and no acting gigs materializing, I'd wind up out of work. Then what would I do?

It was something I was still pondering, and the questions were bigger than I really wanted to admit. Why had I wanted this so badly? I'd wanted to be famous for as long as I could remember, but why? What good was fame? Being on the brink of fame as a model for so long had been fun at times. There had been a thrill to seeing my face on advertisements, and even on a few magazine covers.

But did that momentary thrill outweigh the long hours, travel, and constant scrutiny and criticism? I hadn't felt like I was in charge of my own body since I was seventeen. I had to be careful about what I ate. Couldn't gain weight. Couldn't change my hair. My life was dictated by the brands and designers who hired me. I was hardly a person to them—just a face and body they could use to sell their products. Replaceable. Disposable.

But I'd never done anything else. What else was I qualified for? I knew how to walk a runway. How to pose. How to make myself into what the client wanted me to be. Those kinds of skills didn't exactly translate into other industries.

My phone binged with a text, so I pulled it out to check, thinking it must be Scarlett. But it was Kelvin.

Kelvin: Sending a contract. Need signature ASAP.
Me: What contract?
Kelvin: New show.

He meant the so-called reverse harem dating show. He'd been acting as if agreeing to the show was a foregone conclusion, even though I'd told him *no* every time he brought it up. He wasn't listening to me.

But did he ever? He always said he cared about my career, but was that true? It had seemed like it, when things had been going well. When he'd come to me with offers from high-end designers, and we'd celebrated with champagne. When I'd made the cover of *Vogue* a few years ago, and it had seemed like there was nowhere to go but up. I'd felt like I never would have made it that far without him.

But had he ever cared about my integrity? He certainly didn't now. With the prestigious jobs drying up like spilled water in the desert, he seemed to have no qualms about selling me to the highest bidder, no matter what they were asking me to do.

Deep down, I knew the truth. He'd always seen me as a commodity. When the buyers had been well-respected designers and famous photographers, it hadn't felt like anything was wrong. I'd wanted those jobs. But now Kelvin was willing to auction me off to anyone who'd pay for me. He saw no issue with putting me on yet another trashy reality show—and a *dating* show at that. I'd felt uncomfortable with keeping our engagement secret before *Roughing It*, but this would require straight up lies. I'd have to pose as single and pretend to want this six-men-to-one-woman scenario.

The strange thing was, looking at his text on my phone, I wasn't mad. I wasn't angry, or even hurt. I was just done. I'd been mistaking dependence for love and affection, and I felt like the world's biggest idiot for making such a colossal mistake.

The words went through my mind. *Kelvin, it's over.* I felt nothing. No rush of panic. No sense of regret or heartbreak. I didn't know what it would mean for my career, and that did send a little jolt of worry through me. But imagining my life without him in it, I felt lighter. In that moment, I knew exactly what I had to do, no matter what it would cost me professionally.

I tapped his number, hit call, and walked outside.

"Did you get the contract?" he asked. No *hello*, or *I miss you, Leah*. Just straight to business.

"I haven't checked, but I'm not going to sign it," I said. "I'm not doing the show. And we need to talk."

"I don't understand why you're making this difficult."

"Can we move on from the show?" I asked. "I have bigger things to talk to you about."

"Like what?"

"Like us." I paused, glancing at the ring on my finger. The ring that had been nothing but an afterthought. "Kelvin, I've been thinking a lot about the future—about what I want and what's best for me. And I don't think we should get married."

"That's what you're so worried about?" he asked. "Babe, that's fine."

"What?"

"I figured you needed the whole marriage thing, but if you

don't, that's great. Marriage is bullshit anyway. This is good. We'll keep things simple."

"No, I don't mean we should stay together and just never get married," I said. "I don't think we should be together at all."

He went silent for a few seconds. "Leah, you need to think very carefully about what you're saying right now."

Scarlett, Cassidy, and June approached, so I held up a finger to say I'd be right there and moved farther away from the door. They smiled at me, nodding that they understood, and went inside.

"I have thought about it," I said.

"Why?" he asked, his voice clipped.

I hesitated, taking a deep breath, the fresh country air filling my lungs. "Because I don't think we're in love. Maybe you're attracted to me, but that's not the same thing. And neither is feeling like I belong to you because you've been managing my career for so long. That's not love."

"Why do you think I work so hard for you?" he asked.

"Is it because you love me? You have a lot of clients, and you work hard for them, too. That's your business."

"Leah, you're just going through a tough spot. I know all the publicity you're getting is hard on you. But this is a good experience. It'll toughen you up. What's going on right now is temporary. You can't make irrevocable decisions during a time like this."

"This isn't about the publicity or the gossip," I said. "This is about our relationship. I'm not coming back to L.A. to be with you, and I'm definitely not marrying you."

"You're just going to throw away your career?"

"Oh my god, are you listening?" I asked. "I'm not talking about my career, I'm talking about us."

"Those aren't separate things, Leah. I'm not about to continue representing a woman who leaves me. Especially if she leaves me to be a fucking backwoods hick."

I knew he'd do this, but it still stung that he'd stoop to holding my career hostage. I decided to ignore the 'backwoods hick' remark. He wasn't going to get me riled up over that. "Then I guess I'm leaving your agency."

"Leah, this is a huge mistake," he said. "If you think you won't regret this, you couldn't be more wrong."

He was still talking about my damn career. Not once had he said anything about us. Every word out of his mouth made me more certain that I was doing the right thing.

"It's not a mistake," I said. "It's over, Kelvin."

"You're going to regret this," he said and hung up.

I lowered my phone and took in a deep breath. I wasn't sure if his last comment had been a threat, or just an expression of his anger and frustration. But it didn't matter. I wasn't in love with him and there was no way on earth I could marry him. It had been over for a long time; I just hadn't admitted it until now.

But now I was free. And it felt pretty damn good.

I kicked a little pebble into the parking lot, happy I'd worn my cute cowboy boots, and went back inside.

Scarlett, Cassidy, and June had a table near the bar. I smiled, a very silly feeling of euphoria pouring over me.

"Hey, Leah Mae," Scarlett said.

I loved how everyone here still called me by my full name, not just Leah. "Hey."

"What's up?" Scarlett asked, then took a drink of her beer.

I looked down at the ring on my finger. Pulled it off. "I just broke up with Kelvin."

Scarlett coughed, spitting beer all over the floor. Cassidy patted her on the back while June watched, one eyebrow raised.

"Is Scarlett choking?" June asked.

Cassidy laughed. "No, I think Leah Mae just surprised her a bit."

Scarlett put a hand to her chest and took a deep breath. "Did you just say you broke up with your fiancé?"

I put the ring on the table. "I did."

"Well, holy shit," Scarlett said. She called toward the bar over her shoulder. "Nicolette, we need some whiskey over here. We've got somethin' to celebrate."

"I'm confused," June said. "Don't we normally lament the end of a relationship and soothe the pain of the breakup with a lot of sympathy and sugary baked goods?"

"We do when the breakup is a bad thing," Scarlett said.

"Okay, slow down, Miss Scarlett," Cassidy said. She turned to me. "Are we celebrating this, or do you need the sympathy and cake?"

"I won't say no to cake," I said. "But I'm celebrating."

"See?" Scarlett said, a triumphant smile on her face.

Nicolette came to our table with a tray of whiskey shots. Her dark hair was in a ponytail and she had a t-shirt that said *I've got a good heart… but this mouth*. She gave me a friendly smile as she slid the shot glasses onto our table.

I picked up the whiskey. "Ladies, I might have just ruined my career. But I was in that relationship for all the wrong reasons. And now that it's over, I'm not sad. In fact, I feel great."

"That's a sign," Scarlett said. "I'm proud of you, Leah Mae. You did the right thing."

"Agreed," Cassidy said.

June picked up her shot. "I have to concur."

"Thanks," I said, feeling the prick of tears in my eyes. Not from sadness. From gratitude. The world I'd been living in for the past twelve years was so fake. Bootleg was real. These women were real. I hadn't even realized how much I'd been missing that.

"To new beginnings. And being open to the right man." Scarlett winked at me.

My cheeks warmed. I had a feeling I knew what she meant by that, but I wasn't sure what to say. I tilted my head back, swallowing the whiskey. It was strong, burning my throat as it went down.

"New beginnings," I said, putting down my glass. All I could do was smile. I'd never felt so free.

Chapter Fifteen

Jameson

Being here was odd. I was twenty-eight years old—hadn't lived in my dad's house for a decade—but it still felt familiar. Smelled familiar. Walking through the door had always made my back clench. Now it made the hairs on the back of my neck stand on end.

Didn't much like being here, but there was still a lot of work to be done. Devlin had chewed us out for dumping it all on Scarlett, and he'd been right. That hadn't been fair. We all had our own reasons for not wanting to deal with what we might find in here. But sometimes a man had to face his demons.

My brothers and Scarlett were coming over later, but I'd been up early anyway, so I'd decided to come get a head start. The air was colder inside than out. Smelled stale. We'd already done some of the cleaning out and organizing, but it looked like we'd barely made a dent. The police had left the place a mess.

Scarlett had divided up the house so we each had a section. We were supposed to box things up that were worth giving away or selling, and toss everything else. I had the kitchen to start with, and I reckoned there wasn't going to be much worth keeping in there. It had been a long time since Mama had cooked dinner or baked pie in that kitchen.

I'd brought garbage bags and picked up some empty cardboard boxes, so I got to work. Clearing out the cupboards and drawers was easy enough. Pots, pans, and the plates and glasses that were in decent shape could all go to the thrift store. Anything chipped or broken got tossed. I worked my way through each cupboard, one at a time, either throwing things out or packing them away.

I got to a cupboard with a mix of glasses and mugs. Most of them were in decent shape, so I wrapped them in newspaper and put them in a box. Way in the back, I found a mug with a chipped edge. I hadn't seen it in years, but I remembered it well. I pulled it out and turned it around. *World's Best Mom.*

Us kids had gotten that mug for our mom for Mother's Day one year. She'd used it all the time—so much the lettering had started to fade. I could still remember her, sitting with her fingers wrapped around the handle, blowing on the hot liquid before bringing it up to her lips.

I had no idea what to do with something like this. Would anyone want it? Should we just let it go? I wasn't the sentimental type, so keeping an old mug—even our mom's old mug—didn't hold much appeal. But I set it aside so Scarlett could at least see it. Even if she didn't want it, she might like to reminisce over it first.

The front door opened, and in came Jonah, followed by Bowie. Scarlett and Gibson weren't far behind. They all chatted for a few, saying hi and whatnot. I nodded to my siblings but kept working. The sooner I finished, the sooner I could get out of here.

My brothers split up. Gibson took the garage while Bowie and Jonah headed upstairs. Scarlett came into the kitchen to help. I showed her Mom's mug. She held it for a few moments, tracing her fingers across the words.

"We can let it go," she said.

"You sure?"

She nodded. "I think there's a lot of lettin' go that needs to happen."

"I reckon you're probably right."

She glanced toward our dad's bedroom door. Not the first time she'd done so. I could tell she didn't want to go in there.

"If you want to finish up in here, I'll go start on the bedroom," I said.

She nodded. "Yeah, sure."

I put an arm around her shoulders and kissed the top of her head.

"Oh, knock it off," she said, pushing me away.

I messed up her hair, then went into Dad's bedroom.

Another chill passed down my spine, worse than when I'd first come into the house. He'd died in here.

I swallowed hard, deciding to put that all aside and do what needed to be done. It was just a bedroom, and what was in here was just stuff. He was gone.

Most of his clothes were fine for the thrift store, so I packed them in big garbage bags. When the dresser drawers were empty, I decided to tackle the closet.

I groaned. It was packed, the contents bulging out. The police hadn't exactly cleaned up nicely after they'd searched the house.

Clothes hung on the rack and boxes were piled on top of one another. I spent some time going through the clothes, separating what we could donate from what was too old and worn and needed to be thrown out. Hauled bags out to my truck. By the time I finished with the clothes, Scarlett had gone out for lunch and brought it back. We took a break on the porch, but only for long enough to eat. None of us said much. Seemed we were all wrestling with being here.

But I was glad to not be here alone.

After lunch, I sorted through more stuff in the bedroom. Helped Scarlett haul boxes from the kitchen to her truck for a run to the thrift store. When her truck was full, I went back inside and started pulling stuff out of Dad's closet.

There was no telling what was in all the boxes. I opened the first one and rifled through. Seemed to be a mix of things—papers and envelopes. A handful of old photos. In one of the envelopes was a picture of the four of us, all sitting on the porch. Looked to me like I might have been five or six years old. The back said *first day of school*. I put it aside to show Scarlett.

Tucked in the envelope among some more photos was a yellowed piece of paper—looked official. It was a speeding ticket with my dad's name on it. That wasn't too odd. I reckoned my dad had probably had more than a few traffic violations in his day, although I wondered why it had been stuffed in an envelope with old pictures. What caught my eye first was the state. New York.

That was odd. When had my dad been in New York state? Then I looked at the date. Twelve years ago, almost exactly. The summer Callie Kendall had disappeared.

I knew that date. Not just because the town still talked about Callie, or that her missing persons posters still hung outside Moonshine. I knew it because that was the last summer Leah Mae had come to Bootleg.

But it wasn't just the year, or the fact that the ticket had been issued in July. Callie Kendall had gone missing on July twelfth, and this ticket was dated just three days afterward.

Given the fact that Callie's sweater had turned up here, in our dad's house, raising suspicions about his possible involvement in her alleged murder, this was probably important.

I brought it out to the living room. "Hey, y'all. Come look at this."

Scarlett and Jonah came from the kitchen, and Bowie walked down the stairs. I stuck my head in the garage and told Gibs to come on inside for a minute.

"What'd you find?" Bowie asked, gesturing to the brittle paper in my hand.

120

"It's an old speeding ticket," I said. "But there's something odd about it. It's got dad's name on it, but it's from New York state."

"When was Dad up there?" Bowie asked.

"Well, according to this, three days after Callie Kendall disappeared," I said.

A hush settled over the room, like none of us were even breathing.

"All right," Bowie said, putting his hands on his hips. "Maybe this tells us something."

"Tells us what?" Gibson asked. "That he got caught speeding? He was probably drunk."

"Stop it, Gibs," Scarlett said. "You're not helping."

"Didn't Dad leave for a few days after Callie went missing?" I asked. "Do y'all remember that?"

"He did," Bowie said. "I don't remember if Mom said why, but she told us he'd be gone a few days."

"You're right," Scarlett said. "I'd forgotten, but I remember being mad. I wanted him to stay and help look for Callie."

I thought back on what had happened in the wake of Callie's disappearance. It had been tense and confusing. Mostly I remembered trying to stay out of everyone's way. And then finding out that Leah Mae's mom was coming to fetch her home to Florida. I'd felt guilty at the time that Leah Mae leaving had hit me harder than Callie's disappearance. But I'd been crushed when she'd had to leave.

"It was something about his cousin in North Carolina," Gibson said. He shrugged, like it didn't matter. "House flooded. Dad drove out there to help them fix it so they could move back in."

I held up the ticket. "But if Dad was in North Carolina helping his cousin, how was he in New York getting a speeding ticket?"

Bowie took the ticket and looked it over. I met Gibson's eyes, and I knew we were both wondering the same thing. What if Dad had taken Callie's body somewhere to get rid of it?

"I don't know what this means," Bowie said, his eyes on the paper. "But it's not a coincidence."

"There's too much we don't know," Scarlett said. "Why he was gone. Whether Mama knew where he really went. Everyone who knew anything is dead."

"And it's not like the police are giving us any information," Bowie said.

Gibson rolled his eyes. "Y'all can play CSI West Virginia on your own time. I'm getting back to work." He stalked off to the garage, letting the door bang shut behind him.

"What do you think?" I asked Jonah, meeting his eyes.

"I don't know," he said. "I wasn't around for any of this. But looking at it from the outside, it's suspicious. The timing, and the story you were told about him going to North Carolina. This isn't just in another place, it's in the opposite direction. If he'd gone help his cousin, why would he have been hundreds of miles away?"

Scarlett groaned. "I swear, this mess keeps gettin' worse. I think I need to be done here for today."

"Fair enough," I said. "Do you think this is something we need to show to the police? For the investigation?"

"It should be on his driving record, so I'd think they'd already know," Bowie said. "But I can run it by Jayme. Want me to hang onto it?"

"Sure." I handed the ticket to Bowie.

"Y'all mind if I take some of the boxes home with me?" I asked. "That way we can get this place cleaned out faster, and I can go through more of his stuff later."

"Fine with me," Scarlett said. "I'll help you carry some."

"Yeah, if we all take some, we'll get things out of here quicker," Bowie said. "Good plan."

There were several more boxes I hadn't yet touched. Jonah and Bowie helped Scarlett and me load them in the back of my truck. Jonah was supposed to meet Devlin for a run, so he said goodbye. Bowie said he'd come back to help more tomorrow afternoon and went on his way.

Scarlett and I locked up. Her keys jingled in her hands, and she looked up at me with a little grin. "Got plans tonight?"

"No."

"Hmm," she said, and I could tell she was feigning nonchalance. I wasn't buying it. "Talked to Leah Mae recently?"

Oh lord, this again? "A bit."

"You should call her," Scarlett said.

"Any particular reason?"

She shrugged. "Oh, I don't know. She broke up with her fiancé."

My grip tightened around my keys, the hard metal digging into my palm. I tried to keep myself from choking, but it felt like my throat had closed up on me. I turned, coughing, and pounded my fist against my chest.

"You okay?" she asked, patting my back.

"Yeah," I said, my voice coming out strangled. "Fine. Just got an itch in my throat."

"Sure you did," she said, patting me again. "Anyway, just thought you'd want to know. Night, Jame."

"Night, Scar," I said, still trying to catch my breath.

She went out to her truck and drove off, leaving me standing on our dad's porch.

I was reeling. Felt as if the ground pitched beneath my feet, leaving me unstable. Before I knew it, I was sitting in my truck without so much as a glimmer of an idea as to how I'd wound up there. It was like I was in shock, my brain struggling to come to terms with what Scarlett had just told me.

Could it be true? Scarlett wouldn't lie to me, especially not about this. She saw right through me—knew I had it bad for Leah Mae.

Far from bringing me relief, the news that Leah Mae could possibly be single filled me with dread. What did it mean? Why had she done it? And what was I going to do the next time I saw her?

It wasn't as if I could suddenly confess my feelings. If she really had broken up with him, it was too fresh. The last thing

I wanted was to be a rebound fling. That was bad news all around—the kind of thing that would destroy a friendship in no time flat.

And if there was one thing that scared me more than never having a chance with Leah Mae—I'd come to terms with that for the most part—it was losing her entirely. At least this way, I could still be her friend. But if something happened between us, and it went south, then what would I do? Now that I had her back in my life—even if we were just friends—I couldn't stand the idea of losing her.

The thought of navigating this new world where Leah Mae was single again scared me to pieces. I didn't know how to handle it—didn't know what was right. I just knew I didn't want to make a mistake. Because if I lost her for good, I'd regret it for the rest of my life.

Chapter Sixteen

Leah Mae

I pulled up outside Jameson's house and turned off the engine. I'd been at my dad's place this morning and, on a whim, decided to swing by and see Jameson after I left. He'd told me more than once I could stop by anytime, and I still hadn't seen his workshop.

It was just after lunchtime on Monday, and I hadn't seen much of Jameson in the last week. We'd texted back and forth a handful of times, but that was it. I figured he was just busy. At least, I hoped that's all it was. I knew he had a lot to do on the piece he was working on. He'd told me it was for a big client in Charlotte. I wondered if he'd let me see it.

His house was set back from the road with a long gravel driveway. The house itself looked small, but tidy, with a cabin-like charm. Next to it was an old barn that looked like it must be his workshop.

I tried the front door to the house first, but no one answered. Jameson's truck was here, although I didn't see Jonah's car. I went over to the barn's side door and knocked before opening it and peeking inside.

Jameson stood with his back to me, dressed in a faded gray t-shirt and jeans with a leather apron over the top. He held a small hammer in one hand, and his other was covered with a thick glove. It didn't seem like he'd heard me knock—he didn't turn around.

His head tilted to the side, and he shifted something in front of him. The muscles in his back and arms flexed as he worked. I couldn't see what he was doing, but the way he moved was mesmerizing. The hammer clinked against metal. He paused, seeming to look at what he was working on, then hammered again a few times. Reaching up, he wiped his forehead with the back of his arm.

I knocked again, louder this time, my head sticking through the door. Jameson glanced over his shoulder, wearing safety goggles that looked like sunglasses.

"Oh, hey there," he said.

I'd been hoping to hear him call me darlin' again—it was so cute when he did—but he just licked his lips and took off his glasses.

"Hey. Sorry to drop in on you like this, but you said I could stop by sometime."

"Course," he said. "Come on in."

The air was warm inside the workshop, so I shrugged off my cardigan and draped it over my arm. I was wearing a tank top underneath with my favorite pair of cut-off jeans and low-top sneakers. Jameson's eyes drifted down, then snapped back up to my face.

There was something in his expression—a hesitance. His brow furrowed slightly and the space between us felt charged with electricity. I wasn't sure if he didn't want me here, or if he was just surprised I'd come.

"I'm sorry, I should have texted you first. I'm sure you're busy."

"No, it's all right." He put down the large pair of tongs, then slipped off the glove. "Can I show you around?"

"I'd love that."

He led me into the workshop and showed me the different

pieces of equipment, explaining a bit about what they were used for. The forge that heated pieces of scrap metal. The anvil where he shaped them. He had shelves with hunks of metal, large and small—some smooth and shiny, others pitted with rust. Boxes and bins held smaller pieces—old tools and gears.

"Is this what you're working on?" I asked, pointing to a large piece in the center of an open area.

"Sure is," he said.

I walked around it, gazing at the shape. From the back, it was difficult to tell what it was. But from the front, I could see more. It was a woman, or perhaps an angel. She had the beginnings of wings on her back, but they drooped low, hanging toward the ground. Her head was bent, and she gripped what looked like bars. She was huge, standing at least ten feet high.

"She looks like she's in a cage," I said.

"Yeah, she is," he said. "Or she will be, when she's finished."

I started to ask who she was, but stopped, biting my lower lip. I felt silly for even thinking it, but I suddenly had the craziest notion that she was me.

Of course, that was ridiculous. Jameson wouldn't make a larger than life sculpture of a woman based on me—especially one with angel wings. Who was I? Just his friend. Maybe he had someone else in his life who'd inspired this. For all I knew, she could be his mother. Or a woman he loved that I knew nothing about. As much as I hated that idea, I had to admit it could be true.

But there was something about her that felt familiar. She felt personal. Like I understood exactly what she was feeling. She wasn't finished, but I could feel the anguish of her captivity. Her desire to be free.

"It's beautiful," I said, finally.

"Thank you," he said, and exhaled a breath like he was relieved to hear me say that. "I still have a lot of work to do before she's finished."

"She looks so real," I said, moving around to look at her from another angle. "So... alive."

Jameson gazed at me. I could see him from the corner of my eye. "I hope so. That's what I'm going for. Idea is for her to look more so by the time she's done."

"I'm sure she will," I said. "She already looks amazing."

"Thanks."

The tension between us was still there, and I wondered if I should leave. After all, I'd interrupted him while he was working.

"So…" He paused and rubbed the back of his neck, then put his hands in his pockets behind the leather apron. "I was going to head out in a bit to go scrap hunting. If you aren't busy, would you like to join me?"

"Scrap hunting?"

"Sure," he said. "I mostly use scrap metal. People dump things out in the woods sometimes. I take my four-wheeler out on the trails and see what I can find."

I met his eyes and smiled. "I'd love to come. But am I dressed okay?"

His eyes flicked up and down. "Yeah, you're fine. Might get a little dirty, though."

"That's okay."

He took off his apron and hung it on a hook, then led me out to the side of the barn. He had a four-wheeler with a small trailer attached behind it.

"I don't go real fast when I'm pulling the trailer." He grabbed two helmets and handed one to me. "But we'll wear 'em anyway."

"Sounds good."

I put on the helmet. It covered my whole face, but it was lighter than I expected. Jameson got on, straddling the seat, and I climbed on behind him.

"Hold on," he said.

I put my arms around his waist while he started the engine. His body was warm. The four-wheeler lurched forward, and I held on tighter, gripping his shirt with my fists.

"You're all right," he said over his shoulder. "I've got you."

We drove forward and turned behind his house, heading for the woods. I scooted closer so I could hold on. My body pressed against his and my hands rested on the ridges of his abs. It made me wonder what he'd look like with his shirt off. Reminded me of the Fourth of July when we'd done the obstacle course. He'd come out of the lake dripping wet, his shirt plastered to his lean, muscular body.

I'd pointedly ignored the way he'd made me feel that day, reminding myself repeatedly that Jameson and I were just friends.

Things were different now—for me, at least. I was no longer engaged to someone else. But I hadn't told him about leaving Kelvin. Scarlett might have, but I wasn't sure. I'd meant to bring it up today, thinking I'd rather talk to him in person than send him a text. But now that I was with him, it felt awkward. Like it would show on my face that at least part of the reason I'd broken off my engagement was him.

Because that was the truth, and I felt it more keenly than ever, with the warmth of his body against mine. Even if Jameson and I hadn't reconnected the way we had, I wouldn't have married Kelvin. But Jameson and I *had* reconnected, and I had to admit, I had a bit of a crush on my friend.

Okay, it was more than *a bit* of a crush. I was crushing on him *hard*.

But god, how could I not? He was far and away the sweetest man I'd ever met. A perfect gentleman. Fun, and easy to talk to. And sexy—god, so sexy. I shifted my grip on his waist, just to feel the lines of his body.

Jameson was gorgeous. I'd always thought so, although I'd been very adept at stifling my attraction to him. When we were younger, I'd certainly noticed. He had those brilliant blue eyes and that shy smile that melted me inside. As a teenager, I'd secretly wished for him to like me. Maybe even kiss me. But he never had, and I'd always assumed it was because he didn't see me that way. We were just friends.

I was sure that was still the case, now. And the last thing

I wanted to do was ruin what we had together. If I said too much, or let him see what I felt, I risked our whole friendship. And that wasn't a risk I was willing to take. Not now, at least. Everything in my life was in chaos, but Jameson was solid. He was sure, and true, and I couldn't lose him.

So for now, I hugged him tight, relishing the physical contact—loving that I had an excuse to keep my arms around him. I hoped we'd drive a long way, so I wouldn't have to let go.

We crossed into the woods, bumping along the trail. It was pleasantly warm, even in the shade of the trees. Jameson leaned to the side as we turned a corner, and I moved with him, still holding his waist.

The land sloped up and we kept climbing. I didn't know if he had a destination in mind, or if he was just driving. I assumed he'd know how to get us home. He probably knew these trails like the back of his hand—certainly drove as if he did.

We came to a clearing and he slowed, finally bringing the four-wheeler to a stop.

Reluctantly, I let go and we both stood to take our helmets off, then put them on the seat. Jameson's had left his hair messy, but it looked so adorable, I didn't say anything.

"Trail gets narrow up ahead, so I reckon we should walk a bit," he said. "But there's a spot up there I've been meaning to scope out."

"Okay, let's do it."

His mouth twitched in a grin. It was so tempting to step closer to him. Maybe slip my arms around his waist again—but standing face to face. What would he do?

I looked away. He'd probably pull back and wonder what the hell I was doing. But that shy smile of his was so adorable. I wanted to kiss those sweet lips. Feel his stubble against my face.

"You comin'?" he asked.

"Yeah, sorry." I took a few quick steps to catch up with him. "Whose land is this? Does it belong to anyone?"

"Old Jefferson Waverly owns it now—been in his family

130

for generations. He doesn't mind if I come out here, especially if I'm hauling stuff people dumped."

The trail did narrow, so much that I had to walk behind him. He glanced back at me a few times, as if making sure I was still there. Each time he gave me that little grin just before turning ahead again. It made my heart want to burst.

He stopped so suddenly, I almost ran into him.

"That's what I'm talkin' about," he said.

Just past him, almost overgrown with plants, was a very old car. From what little I could see, it looked like it could have been from the fifties. Who knew how long it had been sitting out here.

Jameson pulled away some of the brush and ran his hand along the side. "Will you look at this…"

"How did this even get up here?"

"Not sure," he said, moving more plants off the hood. "I think there might have been a dirt road that came up here, long time ago. It'd be overgrown now."

I took slow steps along the old car. It was mottled with rust and dirt, but parts of it seemed to be in decent shape, considering.

"What will you do with it?" I asked.

He pulled a piece of ivy off the front fender and caressed the smooth metal. "I'll pull apart whatever I can and bring it back to my shop. It'll take a bunch of trips, but there's so much here I can use."

"You'll sculpt with it?"

"Absolutely," he said, and I couldn't help but smile at the enthusiasm in his voice. He sounded like a kid at Christmas. "This is a great find. Poor thing's been sitting up here for who knows how long, abandoned—its useful life long over. But I'll take it back with me and make it into something new. Something beautiful."

My breath caught in my throat. "That's… that's amazing."

He met my eyes. "It's my favorite thing to do—take something no one wanted and give it new life."

"Do you know what you'll make with this?"

He ran his hand along the metal again. "A lot of things, I reckon. I'll have to see what I can bring back, and what it looks like in the shop."

We started uncovering the old car—pulling back plants and vines and dusting off dirt. It was impossible to tell what its original color might have been. There was a lot of dirt and rust. Some of the metal had holes where rust had eaten through, but much of it was still smooth and strong.

Jameson stood next to me and our arms touched as we brushed dirt off the side door. It made my heart beat faster.

A branch snapped, and something rustled in the brush off to our right. Suddenly Jameson's arms were around me. He yanked me toward the back end of the car and pulled me down into the bushes.

"What—"

"Shh." He gently touched my lips.

I held my breath. We crouched low, leaves and branches all around us. Jameson was behind me, one arm locked firmly around my waist. His body was tense and with his face so close, I could feel the warmth of his breath on my cheek.

"Jonah and I saw a bear out here a while back," he whispered, his voice soft in my ear.

I gasped, a surge of adrenaline making my limbs tingle. A bear? Oh my god. That wasn't good.

The rustling got louder, and Jameson tightened his arm around me. I tried to look, but I couldn't see much from our hiding spot behind the car. I wanted to ask what we should do if the bear came close, but I was afraid to speak. Afraid to move.

Something bumped on the metal roof of the car. Instinctively, I huddled closer to Jameson. But the noise wasn't loud, like the sound of something heavy. It was more of a click.

"I'll take a look," he whispered, loosening his grip on my waist, and we both rose slowly.

I peeked over the top of the car and let out a breath that

was half-sigh, half-laugh. A fat squirrel sat on the roof, staring at us with beady black eyes.

"Well, shit." Jameson let go of me, and we both extricated ourselves from the bushes. "Jesus. A squirrel?"

I laughed and brushed some of the dirt off my legs. "It's okay. Better safe than sorry?"

He shook his head and gave the squirrel the side-eye. "Thanks for that, little buddy."

The squirrel scampered off, climbing a nearby tree, and disappeared from sight.

Jameson rubbed the back of his neck. "Sorry. Guess that was a false alarm."

He looked so cute, acting all bashful, I couldn't help but smile. "It's really fine. Are we going to bring any of this back today, or do you need to come back?"

"I'd like to get what we can." He seemed to relax at the change of subject. "Barring any more interruptions by forest creatures."

He unfastened one of the fenders and the front bumper. I helped him detach the side mirror, but we couldn't get to the other side. He took some smaller pieces of the car that he could get without too much trouble. Then we brought everything down to the trailer.

"This'll do for now," he said, stepping back to look at his haul.

"That was fun," I said. "Like treasure hunting."

"Exactly," he said with a smile.

We donned our helmets and got back on the four-wheeler. I scooted as close to him as I could and wrapped my arms around his waist. God, he felt so good. I let my hands splay across his abs. Pressed my thighs against the backs of his. Just so I could feel him while I had the chance.

All too soon, we were back at his barn, and he pulled to a stop. I got up and took off my helmet, then shook out my hair.

When I looked up, Jameson was watching me, but he quickly glanced away.

I was feeling so many things, it was hard to keep track. I'd had such a great afternoon. But I always had a great time when I was with him. And now, unencumbered by a bad relationship, it was more difficult than ever to keep my emotions contained. He took my helmet and I wanted to launch myself at him. Throw my arms around his neck and kiss him. Take the chance.

He put the helmet down and paused, his eyes on my face. For the briefest moment, I thought maybe he wanted to do the same. Maybe he wanted me, too. Was he wrestling with the same emotions as me? Desperate for more, but afraid of messing up a good thing? Afraid it would be a mistake?

Please, Jameson. Do it. Step forward and meet me halfway. Then kiss me. Kiss me and tell me to stay.

But he rubbed the back of his neck and stuffed his hands in his pockets. "I can get all this into the shop."

"Oh, right," I said, trying not to let the disappointment show on my face. "Are you sure you don't want help?"

"Nah," he said. "Hope you had a nice time, though."

"I did. Thanks for saving me from the squirrel."

He laughed, shaking his head. "Anytime."

We stared at each other for a moment, and there it was again. That glimmer in his eyes. But just as soon as I thought I'd seen it, it was gone.

"I should let you get back to work then," I said. "Bye, Jameson."

"Bye, Leah Mae."

He smiled—that adorable shy smile I loved so much—and watched me go.

Chapter Seventeen
Leah Mae

"Daddy," I said as I got out of my car. "Look at you."

He smiled at me from his rocking chair on the front porch. "Hi there, sunshine."

"You look so much better today," I said.

His skin was a healthy color, his lips no longer waxy and bluish. He rocked back and forth, resting his hands on his belly.

"I feel all right," he said. "And it's a beautiful day for porch-sittin'."

"That it is," I said and joined him, taking a seat on the bench next to his rocking chair.

He leaned a little so he could eye my left hand. "No ring back on that finger?"

"You can stop checking," I said. "It's been almost a month. There's no risk of me getting back together with Kelvin. Trust me."

He chuckled. "I know, I just like teasing you. Did you ever get him to ship your things to you?"

I sighed. I'd been trying to get Kelvin to send me my stuff—not that I owned a lot. I'd always traveled so much,

I'd never accumulated many things of my own. Most of the things in our apartment had been Kelvin's. But I still wanted my belongings back.

"I resorted to going around him and talking to his assistant," I said. "I think she'll get it done even if he wants to keep dragging his feet."

"Mark my words, sweetheart, he's trying to get you to come back to him," he said. "Holding your stuff hostage."

"Maybe," I said. "But it won't work."

"That's my girl," he said with a smile. "So tell me, what's going on between you and Jameson Bodine?"

"What do you mean?" I asked. "We're just friends."

"Is that so?" he asked.

I glanced down at my hands in my lap. Nothing had really changed between me and Jameson since I'd broken up with Kelvin. We both knew I was single. We still spent time together, just like we had before. But if anything, Jameson seemed *less* interested in me, not more. He certainly never acted like he wanted more than friendship.

It was better than nothing—I loved having Jameson in my life—but also hard. Spending time with him was great, but this unrequited crush I had made my heart ache.

"Yeah, Dad, that's so," I said.

I'd spent the last few weeks working on projects around my dad's house with Betsy. We'd gotten the yard into better shape and fixed a few things inside. Scarlett had come over and replaced the sagging boards on the porch and the steps. Then I'd repainted the whole thing. It looked great.

When I wasn't with my dad—either keeping him company or helping him around the house—I was with Jameson, or the girls. Scarlett, Cassidy, and even June had welcomed me into their circle. We'd been out for drinks or coffee a bunch of times. Scarlett seemed to be trying to take me under her wing and ease me back into single life—and life in Bootleg.

My phone rang, and I checked to see who was calling. "I'm sorry, I need to take this. It's Evelyn Peters, my lawyer."

"That sounds ominous," he said.

"I hope not. I'll be right back."

I'd called Evelyn after breaking up with Kelvin to get her assistance in dealing with my contract. She'd offered to reach out to her contacts in the industry to help me find new representation, so I hoped she'd have good news. I got up and walked out to my car to take the call.

"Hi, Evelyn," I said when I answered.

"Leah," she said. "How's America's least favorite reality TV star?"

I groaned. "I was fine until you reminded me."

She laughed. "I guess if you believe that any press is good press, you're in great shape."

"Do you believe that?" I asked.

"No."

I always appreciated Evelyn's blunt honesty. "Me neither."

"I have good news and bad news," she said. "The good news is, Crown Talent Agency is interested in representing you."

"Wow, that is good news," I said. "What's the bad news?"

"You need to come out here," she said. "Tomorrow, so you can meet with them Friday morning."

"Are you serious?"

"As a heart attack," she said. "Crown Talent is big league, Leah. You won't get another shot with them."

"Yeah, I know. I just wasn't expecting to have to come out there on such short notice."

"You busy out there in Radiator Springs?" she asked.

"Bootleg Springs," I said with a laugh. "And it's not that. This is just… unexpected."

"Leah, you broke up with your agent, hence fired your agency, which has left you unrepresented," she said. "You're hated in the media, although the show is doing phenomenally thanks to the drama. How much of that is real, by the way? Off the record."

"It's all fake," I said. "I didn't sleep with Brock Winston. And I know how to catch a freaking fish."

"I figured. But you never know. I've seen a lot of crap over the years."

"I'm sure you have," I said. "I'm getting tired of not being able to say anything about it, though. I can't tell you how many times I've almost posted the truth all over social media."

"God, Leah, don't do that," she said. "Trust me, you do not want to go up against Verity Studios in a breach of contract suit. They'll bury you alive."

"My reputation is shot," I said. "The country basically hates me."

"Is your pride worth your life savings? That's what we're talking about here. They'll ruin you. Keep your mouth shut and your fingers off those keys. Once you're signed with Crown, they'll get PR going on damage control. In the long run, you'll probably be okay."

I knew she was right, but I still didn't like it. "Yeah, I understand."

"Good. I took the liberty of booking you a flight out tomorrow," she said. "It's early, and out of Washington Dulles. You might want to drive out tonight and stay in a hotel."

"You didn't have to do that," I said.

"Technically, my assistant did it. But I figured I'd make it easier for you, considering you're going it alone at the moment."

Maybe I shouldn't have bristled at that, but I didn't like the idea that she thought I was helpless without Kelvin. "I do appreciate your help, but just because I don't have an agent doesn't mean I can't make a flight reservation."

"Okay, Leah Larkin has her big girl panties on," she said, and I relaxed at the note of humor in her voice. "Noted, and good for you. On a personal note, how are you?"

"I'm okay, I think. Honestly, I haven't watched the show since the supposed blow job incident. And I've been trying to ignore all the talk online."

"Don't read any of it," she said. "It'll go away eventually, and in the meantime, you'll just torture yourself."

"I know," I said. "And I realize breaking up with Kelvin leaves me in a bind, but I was just done."

"Honey, you don't have to justify yourself to me," she said. "I never liked Kelvin. I'm glad you're not marrying that cheap son of a bitch."

I laughed. Blunt honesty. "Thanks, I think?"

"I just wish my son would take a page from your book and get his head out of his ass," she said. Her son was my age, and she was forever lamenting his bad relationship choices. "I swear, Leah, I don't care that he's gay, but he has worse taste in men than you. It's too bad he's not straight. The two of you would be great together."

I laughed again. "Too bad. But thanks."

"My assistant will email your flight details," she said.

"Okay. Thanks, Evelyn."

"You're welcome."

I hung up and let out a long breath. Back to L.A. I'd known that was coming. Evelyn was right, I did need new representation, and Crown Talent Agency was one of the best. I was shocked they were willing to meet with me, although Evelyn had a lot of contacts. She'd obviously pulled some strings.

A last-minute trip to L.A. wasn't ideal, but it wasn't the end of the world. I'd meet with the agency, make sure any legal loose ends with my contract with Kelvin were handled, and then...

And then, what? Come back to Bootleg?

It would depend on my work schedule, if there was any work to be had. Landing another agency wouldn't guarantee they could get me any gigs—modeling, acting or otherwise. Everything was up in the air. I didn't have a permanent place to live, or a long-term plan. I'd have to figure out everything, and I didn't know how Bootleg Springs fit into any of it.

I didn't know how Jameson fit into any of it.

Jameson. The thought of leaving him made me slightly ill. I wouldn't be able to swing by his shop to see how his piece was coming. Meet him for sandwiches and take them down to the lake. Go out scrap hunting or help him pull apart that old car he'd found.

I could still keep in touch, and I certainly would. I wasn't going to let our friendship fade away like I had when we were younger. But I hated the idea of not being able to see him all the time.

I brought up his number and sent him a text.

Me: I have to go back to L.A. Flight leaves in the morning. I'm going to Washington tonight and getting a hotel.

There was a long pause before he replied.

Jameson: Sorry to hear that. Will you be gone long?
Me: Not sure. Depends on a lot of things.

Another long pause.

Jameson: Do you need a ride?
Me: Thanks, but I have to return this rental car anyway.
Jameson: OK, just thought I'd offer.

I chewed on my lower lip, wondering what else I should say.

Me: I'll text you when I get there.
Jameson: Please do.
Me: Thanks for everything. I had fun.
Jameson: Me too. We'll talk soon.
Me: OK

There were a million other things I wanted to say, but I didn't. I put my phone down and got out of the car to go tell my dad the news. I needed to find a hotel room. Go back to the cabin and pack. Let Scarlett know I was leaving. And I had a long day of travel tomorrow.

Chapter Eighteen
Jameson

And just like that, she was gone.

The morning after Leah Mae told me she was leaving, I woke up early to a summer rain storm. It was fitting. The sky was covered with gray clouds and water pattered against the roof. Ran in rivulets down the windows. The weather matched my mood.

Jonah dragged me through a workout before breakfast. I was quiet, and he didn't ask questions. Jonah was good like that. Seemed to be able to tell when I didn't feel like talking. That done, I went out to my workshop. I figured I'd get a good start on the work I wanted to do on my piece today.

I'd barely gotten started when my phone rang. It was Deanna.

"Hey, Dee," I said.

"Good morning," she said. "How's the piece coming?"

I walked a slow circle around my sculpture, glad she couldn't see me wince. Parts of it were coming along fine, but there was something missing, and I was struggling to figure out what.

"It's lookin' good."

"Will you send me some pictures?" she asked.

"Nope."

She groaned. "Jameson, it's not that I don't believe you that you're making good progress, but…"

"But you don't believe me."

"Don't take this the wrong way, but I make a living dealing with artists," she said. "I've been doing this for twenty years, and I've learned the hard way not to take the artist's word for it when it comes to meeting deadlines."

"All right, I'll send a picture." I held out the phone and tapped the screen to open the camera. Found an angle that made it look more finished, took a quick picture, and texted it to Dee. "Get that?"

"Hang on."

I was hit by a sudden rush of nerves. I hated showing my pieces to people before they were finished. In some ways, I hated showing my work at all. Not that I wanted to hide it away and keep it to myself. But showing what I'd created always left me feeling so intensely vulnerable. I was never sure how to cope with the rawness.

"Wow, this is different from what I was expecting," she said. "But it's beautiful."

I rubbed the back of my neck and shifted on my feet. "Yeah, I reckon it's coming along."

"Whatever you have going on out there that inspired this, keep it up," she said. "This is unlike anything you've done before, but Jameson, it's going to be incredible. I can see it already."

"Thanks, Dee. Appreciate that."

"Okay, I'll let you get back to work," she said. "And don't forget about the unveiling in Charlotte."

"Yeah, I know."

"Don't sound so excited," she said with a laugh. "And get back to work."

"Yes, ma'am."

I ended the call and put my phone in my back pocket. Kept eying the sculpture.

It wasn't what I'd planned to make for this client. When I'd started this commission, I'd had something more abstract in mind. A statement piece that would be decorative and beautiful, but less organic. More modern, like the building it would front.

But after watching Leah Mae on that show a few times, I hadn't been able to get the image out of my head—Leah Mae, locked in a cage. An angel behind bars, her light dimmed. Didn't seem to matter how hard I tried to concentrate on something else, that was all I saw. A beautiful angel with her hands gripping the bars, her wings faltering.

But something was missing, and I didn't know what. It was driving me a bit crazy. I knew it needed more—wouldn't look finished otherwise—but I didn't know what the missing element was.

Dee's reassurance helped a little, but I was still anxious about it. It was so personal. I always put myself into my work, but this was different—raw and real.

It had been terrifying to show it to Leah Mae. I'd been so afraid she'd be able to tell what it was—that it was her. She'd walked around the unfinished piece and I could have sworn I saw recognition in her eyes. Maybe even understanding. It was like she could feel it the way I did. Like she had a sense of what I was creating, and she could see herself in the piece.

But there I went thinking about Leah Mae again. I did my best to put her out of my head and got to work.

By mid-afternoon, it was time for a break. I also needed some things from the hardware store, so I changed into clean clothes and drove into town.

Without the distraction of my work, the first thing to come to mind was Leah Mae. I'd been beating myself up over her since I'd gotten her text yesterday. There were times in life when you had to take a chance. When you had to grab a situation—or in this case, a girl—and take the risk. And I hadn't. I'd let it slip through my fingers, and now my chance was gone.

It didn't matter that she hadn't been single for long. Or that I had no reason to believe she'd stay in Bootleg much longer. I shouldn't have let those things stop me. There were uncertainties, but I'd let them get the better of me. I could have kicked myself for it.

How many times could I have stopped what I was doing and kissed her? We'd spent enough time together over the last month or so, I'd had dozens of opportunities. So many moments when our eyes had met and we'd both gone quiet.

I had no idea what she'd been thinking. Hell, she could have been hoping I *wouldn't* kiss her. Maybe she'd already decided we were better off as friends, and me kissing her would have been a huge mistake.

I still wished I had taken that risk.

My hands were tight on the steering wheel as I drove into town. The more I thought about it, the more frustrated I was with myself. My dad's voice echoed loud in my head. Telling me I was too sensitive. That I needed to toughen up. Maybe he'd been right about that.

I got into town, heading for the Rusty Tool. I was about to pull into the parking lot, when something caught my eye further up the road. It couldn't be her—I must've been seeing things—but I kept going nonetheless.

Wavy blond hair hanging beneath a sun hat. Denim jacket over a loose blue dress. Long, graceful legs. Delicate hands holding a bag. She turned toward me and oh my god, it was her.

My tires screeched across the pavement as I stopped in the middle of the street, not a care in the world for whether someone might drive up behind me. They could go around. With my truck still running, I opened the door and jumped out.

Leah Mae's eyes widened as I walked toward her. She opened her mouth like she was about to say something, but I was a man on a mission, and this time, I was not going to fail.

Without a word, I slipped one hand around her waist and cupped her cheek with the other. And I just fucking kissed her.

Her lips were as soft and sweet as I'd always imagined.

Pliant and yielding against mine. At first my kiss was hard, my mouth decisive and forceful against hers—my hand holding her tight against me. I sold out. Laid all my cards on the table.

She gasped and stiffened but within a heartbeat, she relaxed, her body softening against me. I moved my lips, capturing more of hers. Our heads tilted and the desperation in my kiss melted into a mix of sweetness and passion. Of gentle softness and heart-racing intensity.

There was something happening around us—voices, feet shuffling. But I didn't pay them any mind. Now that I'd started kissing her, there was no way I was going to stop. I didn't care who saw or how much the town talked. This was my moment—our moment. I'd waited so long for this.

Chapter Nineteen

Leah Mae

Jameson Bodine was kissing me.

No, not just kissing me. Melting me. Making my knees weak and my legs tremble. I couldn't think. Could barely breathe. And just when I thought it couldn't get any better—that this moment had come to the brink of perfection—he parted my lips with his tongue and took the kiss deeper.

The caress of his velvety tongue felt like magic, and sparks danced across my skin. I had no idea what was happening around me. It was as if nothing had existed before this—before Jameson's mind-numbing kiss.

I wound my arms around his shoulders and pressed myself against him. Kissed him back with everything I had.

Gradually, he took the kiss from deep to shallow. The slow dance of our tongues became light kisses against soft lips. His fingers caressed my cheek and his strong arm held me tight.

Our mouths separated, but we stayed close, our noses brushing together.

"I thought you were gone," he said, his voice quiet.

"I came back."

He surged in, kissing me again, and my hat fell off behind me.

"Leah Mae, I don't know what happened or why you're back," he said, caressing my cheek again. "But I have something very important that I need to talk to you about."

"What the hell, Bodine?" a voice called from the street. "Move your damn truck."

Jameson cracked a smile and called over his shoulder, "Hold on a second." He turned back to me and ran his thumb across my lips, his touch making me tremble. "Will you come with me?"

I tried to say *yes*, but my voice wouldn't come, so I just nodded.

He clasped my hand in his and led me to his truck. It was parked in the middle of the street, still running, the driver's side door wide open. Vaguely, I was aware of people on the street watching us. But it was hard to think. Jameson had just kissed the hell out of me and my head was spinning.

We got in his truck and he drove the short distance to the beach. It had been raining off and on all day, and clouds still hung low in the sky. The lake looked deserted.

Jameson parked and turned off the engine. He shifted so he was facing me. "God, Leah Mae, I have something to say, but all I want to do right now is kiss you again."

I practically launched myself at him, and he pulled me onto his lap. Our mouths tangled, wet and insistent. He ran his hands through my hair while his tongue swept past my lips.

With my legs straddling his lap, my dress had hiked up, but—ever the gentleman—Jameson kept his hands in my hair. Kissed me deep and slow. He felt eager, but unhurried. Like every kiss was meant to be enjoyed. Savored.

Rain pattered against the window, a soft serenade. His hands caressed my back and I shifted in his lap. My body was on fire for him, a longing taking hold deep inside. My nipples brushed against his chest, tingling against the thin fabric of my bra. I wanted his hands all over me—his hot skin against mine.

I wanted him to forget his gentlemanly manners and rip my clothes off, right here.

He touched my face again, gently, and pulled back so he could look me in the eyes.

"Oh, darlin'," he said, his voice breathy and low. "I have wanted to kiss you for so damn long."

"Me too," I breathed.

His mouth hooked in a grin. I loved it when he smiled.

"I thought you'd be long gone by now," he said.

"I know," I said. "I was supposed to be on a plane."

"What happened?"

"I woke up this morning and I asked myself what I was doing—why I wanted this. I've been so focused on where I'm going next, I forgot to ask why I wanted to go there in the first place. I've been chasing the dream of a child who didn't know better—who didn't know what that dream really looked like. And it's crazy, because I don't have a backup plan. I don't know what I'm going to do with my life."

It was true. I'd never felt so adrift. But for the first time in a long time, I felt free.

"Do you mean you're giving it all up?" he asked. "No more modeling, or acting?"

"Would you think I was crazy if I said yes?"

"Why would I think that?"

"I guess… I know what others would say." I meant Kelvin, but I didn't want to say his name. Not here, in this moment. "They'd say I've worked too hard to quit now. That this show was just a stepping stone to something bigger and I'd be throwing it all away on a whim."

Jameson looked deep into my eyes. "Is it a whim?"

I shook my head. "No. I don't think I can be the person I want to be if I have to play their game. I've had to compromise too much of myself already. If I went to L.A. today—if I kept traveling down that same road—I'm not sure who I'd be at the end of it. I don't know what road I'm going to take now. I just know that one isn't right."

"I'm so proud of you," he said, his brilliant blue eyes still holding mine.

"Thank you." I nibbled on my bottom lip.

"Listen," he said, brushing my hair back from my face. "I realize things are up in the air, and you're not sure where you're going next. But there's something important I need to ask you."

"Okay."

"Leah Mae, I'm wonderin' if you'll be my girl."

My heart melted inside my chest, pooling into a little puddle of mush. "Your girl?"

"I know, it sounds silly," he said. "We're not kids anymore. But imagine we're sixteen again. You're here for the summer, stayin' with your daddy. We're down by the water and you're wearin' that pink and yellow swimsuit. Your hair's all wet 'cause we've been swimming since lunchtime, and the sun-kissed freckles all over that sweet little nose of yours."

"I remember those days."

He nodded. "I should have done this then, but I didn't. So I'm doin' it now. What do you say, darlin'? Stay. Stay and be my girl."

I leaned my forehead against his. "I will gladly be your girl, Jameson Bodine."

Our lips came together again, so warm and soft. His kisses felt like magic.

"I was coming to see you," I said when we pulled away. I didn't want him to think I'd have let him believe I'd left for L.A. "I wanted to surprise you, and I stopped in town to pick up something sweet to bring with me. And then you pulled up, and well… here we are."

"Here we are."

Smiling, I nodded and kissed him again. Kissing was good. I wanted more of that. A lot more. I could tell Jameson did too.

We made out in the front seat of his truck like we were teenagers again. Like it really was that summer when we were sixteen, and none of the last twelve years had happened. We weren't adults dragging the burdens of baggage and heartbreak.

With the stresses of families and careers and hard choices. We were just two kids who were a little bit crazy for each other, kissing in the front seat of a pickup truck on a rainy summer afternoon.

I wished it never had to end.

His mouth tangled up with mine felt better than anything I could remember. I'd certainly been kissed before, but never like this. This was warm summer sunshine and sweet tea all wrapped up in a pleasantly scruffy jaw, soft lips, and very capable strong hands. He touched and caressed me. Kissed away all the questions and uncertainties.

And for that brief moment, everything was perfect.

Chapter Twenty

Leah Mae

I tilted the picture I'd bought for the kitchen, making sure it hung straight. It was made of wooden planks and said *Home Sweet Home* in rustic white letters. I'd seen it in the window of Daisy Home Furnishings and it had tugged at my heart so hard, I'd gone in and bought it.

It had been a long time since any place I lived felt like home. In fact, it had been about twelve years, and that house was not a five-minute drive from my little cabin on the lake, here in Bootleg Springs. The house I'd lived in before my parents split up was the last place that had really felt like home to me. My dad had sold that house years ago and bought the little one he lived in now. It was easier for him to maintain, and living there alone, he didn't need more room.

My mom's house in Florida had been home of a sort. But in its own way, it had felt temporary. Like I'd been biding my time between summers when I could return here to stay with my dad.

Once I started modeling, I'd mostly lived in hotels, or

cheap apartments with roommates I barely knew. I'd moved in with Kelvin, but it had always felt like his place, not ours. Certainly not mine.

I glanced over at the stack of boxes that had arrived at my dad's place yesterday. Kelvin's assistant had helped me out, having them shipped here. I hadn't been sure where I would be, so she'd shipped them to Dad's, and I'd brought them here. They were still boxed up from our last move. Kelvin hadn't opened any of them.

This cabin wasn't exactly mine, but I'd arranged to lease it from Scarlett long-term, rather than as vacation rental. She'd been thrilled to hear I wanted to stay in Bootleg for a while. I wasn't sure what she knew about me and Jameson, exactly, but she'd been all smiles when she'd come by yesterday with the paperwork.

I was in a strange place in my life, not knowing what the future held for me. I'd spent so many years chasing a dream. But that dream had been tarnished beyond repair. I didn't have doubts that I was doing the right thing. I just needed to figure out what I was supposed to do next.

The prospect of starting over—of finding a new path for my life—was both exciting and scary. I had enough savings to live on for a while, but it wouldn't last forever. And I wanted to make sure my dad would be okay. I had a lot to think about.

But I was grateful that I could afford to take a little break and just be. Live here, in a place that was far removed from all the craziness of the outside world. Where I could ignore the gossip, and people didn't see me as a disgraced reality TV star.

Where I was Jameson Bodine's girl.

My heart fluttered, and my stomach did a little flip, just thinking about him. It had only been a few days since he'd kissed me on the street—and in his truck, and at my door. When he'd asked me to be his girl, I'd nearly died. It was the sweetest thing anyone had ever said to me.

And being Jameson's girl? Yes, please. I'd take all that and more, thank you very much.

I'd fallen a little bit in love with Jameson Bodine when I was a girl. When he'd been my best friend—the quiet boy who loved to draw and build things. Who took apart his toys and glued them back together to make something new. Who quietly observed the world around him, noticing things no one else did.

I was falling a little more in love with him now. With the man who saw beauty in the broken and discarded. Whose quiet stubbornness had built a career out of his passion. Jameson had grown up to be a man who was loyal and kind. Who loved his family and protected the people he loved.

The idea that Jameson—this man with such a soft heart and strong spirit—could possibly love me was enough to make me giddy.

To the outside world, my life probably looked like a mess. People blasted me on every social media platform I'd ever heard of—and probably all the ones I hadn't. Stills from the show had been turned into memes—none of them flattering—and the gossip all pointed to me as the bad guy in the *Roughing It* cabin.

For now, I ignored it all. I took everything but Instagram off my phone, and I only used that to post pictures of things like the giant slice of chocolate cake I'd indulged in last night. Or the flannel shirt I'd turned into a dress that looked perfect with my cowboy boots.

The online gossip and comments only made me feel terrible and small. So I pretended none of it existed. I knew I'd have to deal with it all at some point. I still had contractual obligations to the studio to finish out the season of *Roughing It*. But until then, I'd live for a while in Bootleg bliss.

My phone rang, and I wrinkled my nose at the very unwanted intrusion from the outside world. It was Kelvin. He'd texted and called several times since I'd broken off our engagement. Mostly he harped on the fact that I didn't have representation, or tried to talk me into doing another reality show.

"Hello?"

"Leah," he said, "I'm so glad you answered."

"What do you want?"

"We need to talk," he said. "I'm going crazy out here."

"I've already told you, I'm not staying with your agency, and I'm not doing that show."

"Right, fine," he said. "That's not what we need to talk about. We need to talk about us."

I rolled my eyes. *Now* he wanted to talk about us? "I think I've been pretty clear about that, too."

"Leah, I miss you," he said. "Nothing is the same without you here."

I took a deep breath and leaned against the counter. "I don't know what to say about that. I'm sorry if this isn't what you want, but I already told you it's over."

"But why, babe?" he asked. "We were great together."

"Were we, really?" I asked. "I think we were more convenient together than great."

"That's not true."

"Kelvin, you didn't love me," I said. "Maybe you loved things about me, or you loved my career. But you hated my hometown, you talked down to people I care about, and you had no interest in getting to know my family."

"Babe, you should come home so we can talk about this in person."

"That's not my home," I said. "And stop calling me babe."

"Leah—"

"I have to go," I said, and ended the call.

A few seconds later, my phone rang—Kelvin again. I declined the call just as Jameson knocked on my front door. I turned off my phone and left it on the counter. Kelvin could leave as many messages as he wanted. He was not ruining my day with Jameson.

"Hey, darlin'," Jameson said when I opened the door. Without hesitation, he stepped in and slipped his hands around my waist. Pulled me close and kissed me.

"Hi," I said, wrapping my arms around his neck.

"I think I need to do that again, just to be sure it's real." He gently brushed my hair back from my face and rubbed his nose against mine before leaning in to kiss me.

"What are we doing today?" I asked.

"Going to the rusty reef," he said.

"What's that?"

He grinned. "You'll see. Are you wearing your swimsuit?"

"Sure am." I was wearing my pink and blue bikini under a loose-fitting shirt I'd modified to hang off one shoulder, with a pair of cut-off jeans and pink sandals.

Jameson's eyes swept up and down, taking me in. The hungry look in his eyes made my tummy tingle.

"I reckon we should go," he said.

"Do I need anything else?"

"Just your pretty self," he said. "And maybe a towel. I took care of the rest."

I grabbed a beach towel and went out to Jameson's truck. We drove along the lake, away from town, and he pulled over to park on the side of the road. There were a number of other cars and trucks parked nearby. He took a cooler bag out of the back, and I got our towels, then followed him down an old dirt road.

We emerged on a wide beach. The land sloped upward on our left, flattening as it came toward the water. To the right was an expanse of sand bordered along the far side by trees and rocks that went almost to the edge of the lake. It made for a secluded section of lakefront.

People had blankets and towels spread out on the sand and a small fire sent a tendril of smoke into the air. Scarlett and Cassidy were laid out on a blanket, sunning themselves in bikinis. June sat beneath the shade of a wide umbrella, thumbing through a magazine.

Devlin and Bowie sat on a log next to the fire, poking at it with sticks. A few others sat nearby, with lunch or drinks. Heads bobbed in the water out from the shore, and the sound of their voices carried faintly over the water.

Jameson veered to the right and set our stuff down.

"There's more room over there," he said, nodding in the opposite direction. "But we don't want to be in the way."

"In the way of what?" I asked. There didn't seem to be anything over there.

The noise of a motor made me turn, and I watched as Gibson came tearing down the dirt road on a four-wheeler. He skidded to a stop just short of the water's edge. For half a second, I wondered what he was doing, until a shout came from higher up the slope. A rope was tied to the four-wheeler, and it led to a zip line. Someone—it looked like Jonah—was holding onto the handle and sliding toward the water at terrifying speed.

He flew out over the lake, let go, and fell in the water with a splash.

"That was a good one," Jameson said.

The girls clapped, then held up their fingers—rating his jump, apparently. Cassidy and Scarlett gave him a seven, June held up a distracted-looking eight.

"Did Gibson just pull Jonah on a zip line with that four-wheeler?" I asked.

"Sure did."

"That looks dangerous."

Jameson shrugged. "I reckon it is a bit. You just have to make sure to let go in time so you don't hit the rusty reef."

"What's the rusty reef?"

Jonah swam along the shoreline, then climbed onto something and stood tall, the water sparkling in the sun around him. It looked like he was standing on the water.

"That there is the rusty reef," Jameson said, nodding toward Jonah. "We used to tow the zip line with a truck, until Nash drove his old Ford into the lake and couldn't get it out. That's when we switched to a four-wheeler. Jonah's standing on the truck now."

"There's a truck out there?"

"Yeah," he said. "We moved the zip line a bit so we're less likely to crash into the truck—Buck learned that the hard way, but we appreciated him figuring out the physics for us."

"Oh my god, was he okay?"

Jameson waved his hand. "Broke a leg, is all. He healed up just fine."

I felt bad for laughing, but Jameson was so nonchalant about it.

"Are you going to do the zip line?" I asked.

"Course," he said. "It's a hell of a lot of fun."

"Hey Jame, I'm up," Gibson called. "You driving?"

"Yeah, I got you," Jameson said, then looked at me. "What do you think?"

I looked over at the zip line. It started up the slope and went out over the water. "I think I'll just watch."

One corner of Jameson's mouth hooked in a subtle grin. "You won't be sayin' that later."

I blinked, gaping at him. I wasn't sure if we were still talking about the zip line.

"Make yourself comfortable, darlin'." He winked and pulled off his shirt, letting it drop to the sand, then stepped out of his shoes. "I need to go take Gibs for a ride. It'll be your turn in a while."

He backed away a few steps, still facing me, in nothing but a pair of shorts, his fantastic torso on full display. I couldn't stop staring. He was lean and muscular without being bulky, and he had a tattoo across his chest and left shoulder that I'd never seen before.

I'd spent the last dozen years around models—male and female—and none of them had anything on Jameson Bodine. His appeal wasn't in being photogenic, although I was sure he was. It was in his slightly messy hair, his stubbly jaw, and his body that looked like it was built to be used, not just to look pretty. In his rough hands and the scars on his forearms. In that boyish smile and the little trail of dark hair that disappeared beneath the waist of his shorts.

He winked again before jogging over to the four-wheeler. I swallowed hard and had to resist the urge to fan myself. But god, he was sexy.

"He's really not bad, is he?" Cassidy asked. She was propped up on her elbows, looking over at Jameson from beneath her sunglasses.

"He's a Bodine; of course he's good-lookin'," Scarlett said without looking over.

"I mean no disrespect, Leah Mae," Cassidy said. "I'm just saying, objectively speaking, he's a fine-looking man."

I noticed Bowie scowling over by the fire, glancing back and forth between Jameson and Cassidy.

"My brothers are a right pain in the ass," Scarlett said. "Each and every one of 'em. But they're a good sort."

"Mm-hmm," Cassidy said.

I spread out my towel next to them and stripped down to my bikini. The warm sun felt good on my skin.

"Don't forget sunscreen," June said, tossing me a bottle of spray-on SPF-30. "Ultraviolet rays from the sun cause premature aging and skin cancer."

"Thanks, June." I sprayed on some sunscreen and rubbed it in. My skin was fair; I definitely needed it.

The four-wheeler started up again. Jameson drove it back down the dirt road while Gibson climbed the hill. They both disappeared from sight, and the sound of the four-wheeler faded. A moment later, Jameson drove down the road—fast—kicking up a cloud of dust in his wake. Gibson raced down the zip line at breakneck speed, then let go and plunged into the water.

The people on the beach cheered. He earned sixes from Cassidy and June, and a seven from Scarlett. Jameson smiled at me from across the beach, and damn it he was adorable. In all the time we'd been friends, I'd never seen him smile as much as he had in the last few days.

I was smiling a lot, too.

"Girl, you are plum sprung on that man," Scarlett said, grinning at me.

I adjusted my sunglasses and felt my cheeks flush. "Sorry. But… yeah, I am."

"Don't you apologize," Scarlett said. "I don't think I've ever seen my brother this happy. Whatever you're doing to him, you keep doin' it, and maybe don't ever stop."

I laughed, because I wasn't doing much of anything to Jameson. Not like that, at least. We'd kissed. Made out in his truck for hours. And it had been breathtaking. There was no doubt I wanted more, but I wasn't sure how *he* felt about it. Jameson was a bit old-fashioned. Maybe he'd want to wait before we took things further.

I hoped he didn't want to wait too long.

Gibson swam back in, and he and Jameson switched places. Jameson climbed the hill, towing the zip line handle with him, while Gibson drove the four-wheeler down the dirt road. My stomach fluttered with anticipation, and a little fear. A minute later, Gibson came roaring back on the four-wheeler, with Jameson riding the zip line just behind.

Jameson's muscles flexed, and he hollered as he rode the line down. Right when he let go, he leaned backward, tucking his legs, and did a back flip before plunging into the water.

I clapped and cheered, as did most everyone else on the beach, then held up both my hands for a perfect ten. Cassidy and Scarlett gave him tens as well, and June held up nine.

"Tough critic," Cassidy said to her sister.

June shrugged. "He could have straightened before hitting the water for less of a splash."

Cassidy laughed. "It's not the Olympics, Juney."

"I have my criteria, you have yours," June said.

Jameson swam to shore and got out of the water. I couldn't take my eyes off him as he walked toward me, dripping wet. He slid his hands through his hair, and the water ran in rivulets down his body, tracing the lines of his muscular frame.

He grinned and held out a hand. "Come on, darlin'. Your turn."

I took his hands in mine and he helped me to my feet. He looked down at me, biting his bottom lip. I'd always felt a little uncomfortable in my own skin. Growing up, I'd been the tallest girl in class. My limbs were long, and it had taken a lot of ballet and model walking lessons to learn any sort of grace. But the way Jameson was looking at me made me feel beautiful. Comfortable.

It made me feel other things, too, but I was very aware of the crowded beach. A crowd that included all his siblings.

He twined our fingers together and led me toward the slope, grabbing the zip line handle on the way.

"Tell you what," he said as we walked to the top. "I'll drive. All you do is hang on and let go when you're over the water."

"Promise I won't hit the rusty reef and die?"

He laughed and handed me the zip line handle. It was above our heads now, but I could still reach. "I'd never risk hurting you. It's a rush, and worth doing at least once. Besides, where else can you ride a zip line being towed by a motorized vehicle?"

"Good point." I nibbled on my bottom lip, my limbs tingling with anticipation.

He tapped my nose and planted a quick kiss on my lips. "I've got you. Just hang on until the rope starts to move, then lift your feet. I'll tell you when to let go, then I'll meet you in the water."

I took a deep breath and nodded. "Okay."

"That's my girl."

He ran down the slope and I heard the four-wheeler roar to life. A minute later, there was a quick tug on the rope and it started to move.

I gripped the handle tight and picked up my feet. Before I could take another breath, the rope went taut and I was flying down the zip line, the wind whipping my hair back. I went so fast, it felt like flying. The ground fell away beneath me as the beach sloped down, and I screamed—both in fear and exhilaration.

The water sparkled below me, and I heard Jameson yell, "Now!" And I let go.

Mostly by instinct, I straightened my legs, pointed my toes, and held my arms tight against my sides. I sliced through the warm water, taking a quick breath before my head went under.

I kicked up until my face broke the surface, coming up laughing. I raised my arms, like a gymnast who'd just stuck her landing, and the girls all held up both their hands, giving me three perfect tens.

Jameson swam out to meet me. He pulled me close and I wrapped my arms around his neck. My body pressed against his—nothing between us except my little pink and blue bikini.

We kissed like crazy in that bathwater-warm lake. Kissed like no one was watching, until Gibson yelled at us to get out of the way so someone else could have a turn.

Jameson just laughed and told his brother to shut his face.

After we swam back to shore, we laid out on our beach towels to dry off. My hair was tangled, the bit of makeup I'd been wearing had washed off, and the sun was probably giving me the smattering of freckles I'd always hated across my nose and cheeks.

But no one was going to complain that my photos would need retouching because of my freckles. Or care that there was sand in my messy hair. There was just Jameson, lying next to me, his blue eyes taking me in like I was the best thing he'd ever seen.

We ate lunch and drank a few beers and lay in the sun. Got back in the water when we needed to cool off. There was more zip lining, and the guys wound up playing a game of king of the mountain on the rusty reef that had the rest of us laughing until our stomachs hurt.

By the time the sun started to go down, I was warm, tired, and about the happiest I'd ever been in my entire life.

Chapter Twenty-One

Jameson

Leah Mae smiled at me from the passenger's seat of my truck. It was a tired, lazy smile—drenched in sunshine and lake water. Her shirt draped off her shoulder, showing the thin strap of her bikini, and her insanely long legs were crossed at the ankles. I couldn't stop looking at her, taking in her sun-kissed skin, her full lips. I wanted to nibble on that soft spot where her neck and shoulder met. Feel her nipples harden against my palms.

We'd spent the day half-naked and wet, and I'd enjoyed every minute. My biggest struggle had been hiding my constant hard-on when my sister was looking.

Not that Scarlett hid anything from her brothers. We had to deal with her making out with Devlin in front of us. The guy was damn lucky we liked him. Of course, that didn't stop us from chucking him off the rusty reef a few times for good measure. King of the mountain wasn't just a game. It was a reminder.

I parked in front of Leah Mae's cabin and got out to walk her to the door. We paused on the porch.

"I had so much fun today," she said, those beautiful green eyes sparkling at me.

"So did I."

Although I wasn't always good at making the first move, there was so much pent-up energy inside me, I couldn't help myself. I slipped a hand around her waist and drew her tight against me—didn't bother to shift so she wouldn't feel my erection. I let it press up against her, solid and wanting.

A breathy moan escaped her lips as I kissed her. She turned the doorknob and opened it, dragging me inside with her. If that wasn't an invitation, I didn't know what was.

I kicked the door shut and pushed her up against it, my mouth capturing hers. Her hands slid up my chest, around my neck, and into my hair. I kissed her differently this time—like this was just an appetizer. Like neither of us meant for tonight to stop at kissing. I sucked on her lower lip and licked into her mouth—wet and a little sloppy. But I'd been wanting this all damn day.

Kissing down her neck, I found the hollow at the base of her throat. I lapped my tongue against her sweet skin while she tilted her head to the side and moaned. My hand slid beneath her shirt, seeking more skin, more contact.

There was a time for fucking up against a door, but our first time wasn't it. I wanted to do this right. I backed us up, my mouth still lavishing wet kisses on her neck, until we half-stumbled into the bedroom.

I pulled up her shirt, slipping it over her head. The strings of her bikini tied at the nape of her neck, so I tugged on the ends to let the bow unravel. Silky pink and blue fabric fell away, revealing her firm, round tits.

My hands trembled a little, the realization that I was getting Leah Mae Larkin naked washing over me. Reaching around her back, I pulled the other bikini string and let it drop to the floor.

My cock ached to be inside her, but there would never be another first time. I held myself in check and focused on her. On worshiping her lithe body. I brushed my thumb across her nipple and traced a gentle circle, devouring her breathy gasps. Kissed my way down her neck, past her collarbone. Cupping her breast, I lapped my tongue against her hard peak. She tilted her head back, her hair falling around her shoulders, and a soft shudder ran through her body.

I pushed her onto the bed, even though I was still dressed, and I hadn't taken her bikini bottoms off. There was already so much to explore. I lay on my side next to her and palmed one breast while I slowly licked the other. She shuddered again as I took her nipple in my mouth and sucked—gently at first, then harder. Squeezing one of her tits, I sucked on the other, feeling her body respond to the rhythm. She moved her hips, shifting her body closer to rub against me.

Sliding my hand lower, I kissed her mouth again while I hooked my thumb beneath her bikini bottoms. She helped slip them off, then pulled my shirt up. I broke our kiss just long enough to get my shirt over my head. Her hands caressed my chest, and I trailed my fingers down past her belly button to the apex of her thighs.

"Yes?" I asked, my hand hesitating.

She tilted her legs open, inviting my touch, and whispered, "Yes."

I slid my fingers between her legs, nearly trembling at the feel of her silky soft skin. Looking down the length of her languid body, I wanted to pinch myself. Was I really here, with Leah Mae? With her naked body laid out for me, her lips whispering the *yes* I'd been dying to hear?

If this was a dream, I didn't want it to end.

"Mm, so wet," I said, tracing along her slit and dipping my fingertips inside her.

"I've been wet for you all day," she said.

Just that hint of dirty talk from her sent a rush of heat through my veins. I explored her gently, taking in every shiver and gasp. Rhythmic pressure on her clit had her hips moving, soft moans escaping her lips.

Making her feel good was pleasantly addictive. I drew it

out, caressing her, feeling for what she liked. Giving her more. I slid two fingers inside the soft, wet folds of her pussy, and she grabbed onto me, arching her back.

"Oh my god, Jameson."

I curled my fingers to stimulate the tender spot just inside while I clamped my mouth on her nipple. She bucked against my hand, breathing hard, gasping out her pleasure.

"How are you… oh god…"

"What do you want, baby?"

"I want you inside me," she breathed. "Please, Jameson. I want you to fuck me."

I growled, letting my teeth graze the hollow at the base of her throat, my cock throbbing. "Say it again."

"I want you to fuck me," she said, her voice a whimper.

Her pussy was hot and tight around my fingers. God almighty, that was going to feel good wrapped around my dick. I slid my fingers out and brought them to my mouth. Sucked her taste off them with a low groan.

I fumbled for the condom in my wallet, then took off my shorts, kicking them onto the floor. Leah Mae's hand traced down my abs, her fingers lingering in the trail of hair below my belly button. She met my eyes, bit her bottom lip, and wrapped her hand around my cock.

Her touch froze me. Until that moment, I'd been in complete control, slowly building the intensity. Making her tremble and moan, and enjoying every second. Now, I was putty in her hands, my brain completely short-circuiting. Sucking Leah Mae's tits and sliding my fingers in her pussy hadn't broken me, but her hand on my dick sure had.

I was done for.

She nudged me so I was on my back, the unopened condom still dangling from my fingers. Pumped her hand up and down my swollen cock a few times. Slow, deliberate strokes that had me paralyzed.

Swiping her thumb across the beads of moisture leaking out, she rubbed the sensitive tip. I watched, fascinated. Her hand stroking my cock looked as good as it felt. The pressure building in my groin was nearly painful, but it was an exquisite ache.

She leaned closer, her tits brushing against my chest, and brought her mouth to mine. I tangled my hands in her hair and kissed her deeply while she squeezed my cock.

"Jesus, Leah Mae," I said when she pulled away. "I need to be inside you."

Plucking the condom from where it had fallen onto the sheets, Leah Mae ripped it open and unrolled it onto my thick erection. I was hard as steel for her, dying to be inside that wet pussy. To feel her body melding with mine.

I started to roll her to her back, but she stopped me with a hand on my chest. She climbed on top of me, straddling my legs, her wet entrance just below the base of my dick. I rubbed her thighs, taking her in.

"You are so damn beautiful," I said.

She nibbled her lip and smiled, lifting up while I held my cock at the base, positioning it at her entrance. Our eyes locked and she slowly slid down, my dick moving easily through her wetness. It felt so good, I could barely breathe.

"Come here." I pulled her down so I could kiss her. Wrapped my hand around the back of her head and lost myself in the feel of her. She was overwhelming, permeating all my defenses. Her skin, soft and supple. Her tongue, warm and desperate. And that pussy. God, that hot pussy clenching around me. It was all I could do to keep from coming in her after the first stroke.

I'd never felt anything like this.

She rolled her hips to slide up and down my cock, moaning into my mouth. We weren't graceful or delicate. We were messy and raw, sucking and biting and kissing. I held her hips and thrust myself deeper, grunting low, and her tangled hair spilled around me.

I needed to fuck her harder. She'd awoken a deep, carnal need. A drive I couldn't contain. I rolled us over and braced myself on top of her. Thrust in hard, sheathing my cock to the hilt.

"Jameson." Her voice was breathy and full of desire.

"God, Leah Mae, you feel so good."

I pumped my hips, driving into her. She clung to me—dug her fingers into my back. Our bodies moved together, faster. Harder. Her nipples dragged against my chest and her breath was hot on my neck. I wanted to devour her—lick and suck every inch. Make her come so hard she'd never forget this moment. I knew I wouldn't.

Her pussy clenched and I could feel her heat build. Pink crept across her cheeks, down her neck, flushing her perfect tits. I was captivated by the way she felt, the way she smelled. The way her skin tasted. The pressure in my groin grew—heat and tension and bliss all rushing to break free from my throbbing cock. Waiting to unleash inside her.

She wrapped her legs around my waist and bucked her hips harder against me, letting out breathy moans with each of my thrusts. Even though it was our first time, I already knew her body. I could feel her getting close, on the brink of climax.

"You ready, baby?" I wasn't finishing without her.

"Yes," she said. "Don't stop, Jameson. Don't stop."

God, I loved hearing her say my name. I loved every bit of this. It was unlike anything I'd ever experienced before. The want, the desire. It was so much more than physical. Emotion unfurled inside my chest, an openness that made my head spin. I wanted to be real with her. To let her see me—feel me.

I grabbed her ass with one hand and slammed into her harder. My dick throbbed, my balls drawing up tight. I was riding the edge, ready to burst.

One more thrust and I felt her come apart. Her eyes rolled back, her mouth dropped open, and her pussy clenched so tight I lost my fucking mind.

The orgasm rolled through my body, a mind-numbing blast that made my back stiffen and all the tension in my groin release. Hot waves of pleasure left me reeling. I thrust my hips, coming in her so hard I couldn't see. All I could do was feel.

It left me gasping, my body slick with sweat. Slowly,

I opened my eyes and blinked at her. It was hard to think. I looked down at her brilliant green eyes and flushed cheeks and couldn't do anything but grin.

Her tongue slid across her lips, so I leaned in to kiss them softly while my brain started to function again. I kissed her nose, then got up to deal with the condom before getting back into bed with her.

I gathered her in my arms, her soft body curled against mine, her head resting on my chest. Kissed her forehead and stroked her shoulder with my thumb. We lay there for a while, silent. I wasn't sure how she felt, but I was too overcome to speak. She'd cracked me wide open, and I didn't think I'd ever recover.

Didn't think I wanted to.

"Are you okay?" she whispered, breaking the silence.

I looked down at her and tipped her chin up. Met her eyes. "I'm so much more than okay. You?"

Her lips turned up in a smile. "Yeah, me too."

It hit me then. I was falling in love with this girl. I'd always loved her in a way. But this was bigger than a little boy who loved his friend. Bigger than a man who had a crush on a girl from afar. This was so huge, it filled my chest. I wasn't sure my body could contain it all—all these feelings I was having. I wasn't quite sure what to do with myself.

So I held her. Closed my eyes and felt the warmth of her body against mine. Drifted in the sweetness of release. Smelled her hair and kissed her forehead.

I didn't worry about what would happen down the road. We'd figure that out when it came. For now, Leah Mae was mine, and I wasn't sure I ever wanted to let her go. A scary thought, that. But I held it and let it take root, because I knew it was real. It was true. And I wasn't a man to shy away from the truth, even if it scared me.

Chapter Twenty-Two

Leah Mae

I woke up in the morning wrapped in Jameson's arms. The bed smelled like him. Like us. His body was warm behind me, his chest moving gently against my back. I closed my eyes and breathed it all in.

Jameson, here with me. Our bodies close. His arm draped around my waist. His scent all over me.

Light peeked in through the curtain. I wasn't sure what time it was, but I didn't care. There was nowhere else I wanted to be.

Last night had been… it had been everything. Soft and sweet. Hard and rough. Jameson had somehow known every inch of my body. How to touch me, caress me, kiss me. When to hold back and when to unleash. It had been intense and dizzying.

The ache between my legs was satisfying and pleasant. I nestled in closer to Jameson, feeling his arm tighten around me. The sex had been fantastic—no one had ever fucked me the way he had. But it was more than that. I felt so close to him. Like something deeper had passed between us last night.

He shifted behind me and I felt his lips on the back of my shoulder. My eyes fluttered closed as he planted soft kisses along my skin. Nibbled my shoulder with his teeth.

"Mornin', beautiful," he said, his voice husky and rough.

"Morning." I arched my back a little and pressed my ass against his erection.

He groaned, a deep rumble in his chest. "God, Leah Mae, you have no idea what you do to me."

Grabbing my hip, he pressed his cock against me and sucked on the skin at the base of my neck. I arched into him, my body coming alive.

"If it's even half of what you do to me, I'm in trouble," I said.

"I reckon we both are."

I shifted so I was on my back, and Jameson propped himself up, partially over me. Our mouths came together in a wet, lazy kiss. Hands caressed warm skin beneath the sheets. His kisses were leisurely. Decadent. No hurry. Just our lips and tongues making soft love as we both came awake.

Morning sex was great, but it was even better after taking care of basic necessities. We kissed for a long while, then both got up to use the bathroom. After I came out, I got back in bed and waited, wondering if I should get dressed. Going back to bed with Jameson sounded a lot better, but I wasn't sure what he wanted.

The shower turned on and my heart sank. Was he going to shower and go?

He poked his head through the door and his shy smile made me melt all over again. "I reckon we should wash all that lake water off. Want to join me?"

"I'd love to."

I got up and went into the bathroom. The shower wasn't large, but that didn't matter. We got in and stood close together under the hot spray. He wrapped his arms around me, and I closed my eyes, enjoying the feel of him against me.

He turned me around and washed my hair. It was tangled after our day at the lake, but he gently ran his fingers through my tresses and massaged my scalp. His touch was arousing and relaxing all at once.

When my hair was rinsed, he moved it over my shoulder and sucked the water off my neck. I arched my back and rubbed against his hard erection while he growled and nipped at my skin.

Reaching around, he cupped my breast with one hand while his other slid down my stomach. His fingers found my clit and he caressed it gently. Warmth and pressure pooled between my legs. I leaned back into him, practically purring.

He played with my nipple, gently pulling, while his fingers worked some kind of magic on my clit.

"That feels so good," I said.

"I love hearin' you say that." He kissed down my neck. "And I love makin' you feel good."

I moved my hips, rubbing my ass up and down his solid length. He groaned and slid his hands all over my wet skin. My need for him grew, the sweet ache between my legs demanding more.

"My dirty girl," he growled into my ear. "We need to get you clean."

He lathered body wash all over me, and the addition of soap made our bodies slick. We rubbed against each other, teasing and tempting. I took his cock in my hand and stroked him hard while he played with my pussy.

"Baby, I need to fuck you," he said. "Now."

He spun me around, pushing me up against the tile. Lifting my leg, he propped it up on the little bench.

"Should we get out for a condom?" he asked.

"I'm on the pill."

He bit his lower lip. Grabbed his cock and stroked it a few times, his eyes locked with mine.

"If you're sure you're okay with this," he said, positioning his cock at my entrance.

"Yes, I'm sure."

With the water cascading over us, soap suds swirling at our

feet, Jameson thrust his cock inside me. I draped my arms over his shoulders and kept my leg up on the bench.

Looking down between us, I watched his cock slide in and out. My nipples were hard, and his abs flexed with each thrust. It was mesmerizing to watch him fuck me like this. To see his glistening erection plunge deep into my pussy, then move out again.

He held me with one hand and moved the other to massage my clit. His quick strokes had me panting, the exquisite pressure intensifying.

"Jameson," I said, nearly breathless. "Don't stop that."

Between the thrusting of his cock stretching me open, and the dance of his fingers across my clit, I was done for. I came in a rush of heat and pleasure, the climax rippling through me. I closed my eyes and moaned with the rhythm of his thrusts, riding the wave of intensity.

He slowed down so I could catch my breath. I reached between us and grabbed his hard cock as he pulled partway out.

"Oh darlin'," he said. "I'm about ready to come."

"I want to see it."

The corner of his mouth turned up and he plunged into my pussy a few times. His eyes rolled back a little and he grunted.

"Fuck, you feel so good."

His cock pulsed once, and he pulled out. I grabbed him and stroked, hard and fast, jerking my hand up and down his thick length. He braced himself with one hand on the tile behind me, his face close to my ear, and groaned, his body going rigid as the first rope of come burst out from the tip. Then another. Another. His cock throbbed in my hand as he came all over my stomach.

I loved the sight of his come all over me. I felt dirty in all the best ways. I'd never been so uninhibited with a man. It felt amazing.

He caught his breath and I eased my leg down off the beach. Taking my face in his hands, he kissed me—leisurely and sweet.

We cleaned each other off with more soap and gentle caresses. The water was cooling, so we got out and wrapped up in big fluffy towels. I sat on the edge of the bed while he used another towel to softly dry my hair.

Then we slipped back in bed, our clean bodies tangling beneath the crisp sheets. I nuzzled against him, warm and satisfied. He kissed my forehead and held me in his strong arms.

"Can I admit something that I'm a little bit afraid to say?" he asked, his voice soft.

"Of course."

He held me tighter, like he needed the reassurance of our bodies pressed close. I waited, breathless.

"I'm in love with you," he said. "I've never been in love before, but I'm certain of it. I'm crazy about you, Leah Mae. And it's kinda scarin' me right now."

I squeezed him, burying my face in his chest. Tears stung my eyes—tears of happiness and joy.

"Jameson, I'm in love with you, too," I said. "I'm so in love with you, I'm not sure what to do with myself."

"You are?"

I giggled softly and looked up at him. "Yes, I am. But why does it scare you?"

"I reckon I don't know a lot about love," he said. "I'm a bit worried I'll mess it up somehow."

I trailed my fingertips over his lips. Down his neck to his chest. "Don't be afraid. I'll take care of your heart if you take care of mine."

"Darlin', I'll take care of it like it's my most prized possession."

"Then it's yours," I said.

He tipped my chin up and kissed me. "I love you to the stars and back, Leah Mae."

"I love you too, Jameson. To the stars and back."

Chapter Twenty-Three

Leah Mae

My dad wasn't on the porch when I got to his house. His health had been steadily improving and he was no longer on oxygen full-time. I'd come over the other day to find him walking around with no tubes—no little cart with a tank of oxygen—and nearly burst into tears. His lungs were still delicate and prone to infection, so we had to be careful. And he tired quickly. But he was getting stronger every day, and the doctor had said he could go back to work soon.

I let myself in and almost dropped the bag of groceries I was carrying. Stopping in my tracks, I clamped my mouth shut and stared. I couldn't think to do anything else. There was my daddy, standing in the kitchen, kissing Betsy Stirling.

My eyes must have been wide as saucers. I was paralyzed, torn between clearing my throat to alert them to my presence, and trying to sneak out the door before they realized I was there.

Before I could decide what to do, they stopped—truth be told, it had been a very sweet kiss—and Betsy jumped, putting both her hands over her heart.

"Dear lord, you scared me," Betsy said, her face flushing red.

"I'm sorry," I said. "I didn't mean to interrupt."

My dad grinned. It was a little boyish, reminding me of Jameson. "Sweetheart, it's me who needs to apologize. Didn't mean for you to see that."

"Well…" I straightened and adjusted the grocery bag. "Can I ask if this is… a thing? Or did that just happen right then?"

They looked at each other and I already knew the answer.

"I suppose, I hope it's a thing," Dad said, his eyes on Betsy. "I haven't been well enough to court you properly, but I certainly intend to."

Betsy smiled. "I'd like that very much."

"If that's all right with you," Dad said, turning to me.

"Oh Daddy," I said. My heart wanted to burst. "Of course it is. This is just… it's just lovely."

"Are you sure you don't mind?" Betsy asked. "I was telling Clay we really ought to talk to you before we let things go any further."

"Mind? No, this is…" I struggled for words, looking between the two of them while my eyes stung with happy tears. "This is so sweet. I'm so happy for both of you."

I set the groceries down on the floor—who could worry about canned goods at a time like this?—and rushed forward to grab them both in a hug. It felt so good to see my dad smile, it was all I could do to keep from sobbing.

After I'd hugged them a few times and wiped away the tears that trailed down my cheeks, we all went out to the porch. Betsy brought out sweet tea, and instead of taking his rocking chair, my dad sat on the bench so he could sit next to her. I sat in the rocking chair, tipping it back and forth slowly as I sipped my tea.

"I don't mean to be nosy, but how did this happen?" I asked.

Dad took Betsy's hand and twined their fingers together. "Well, Betsy's been spending a lot of time here, helping me out and whatnot. We often got to talking, especially when I was too sick to get out of bed."

"We have a lot in common," Betsy said. "And enjoy each other's company quite a lot."

"And recently, I decided I wasn't going to keep lettin' life pass me by," Dad said.

Betsy blushed again. "He kissed my hand first, and asked if he could trouble me for a real kiss."

I put my hand on my chest and sighed. "Oh, Daddy, you are a romantic."

Dad laughed. "I reckon. I'm just happy she didn't smack me."

Betsy nudged him with her arm. "I'd been wonderin' if you were ever going to get around to it."

"I'm relieved you're all right with this," Dad said. "Been a bit worried about how you'd take it. Guess I got myself all tied up over nothing."

"You sure did," I said. "I'm so happy for you both. Really."

"Do you have plans to see Jameson tonight?" Dad asked.

"I do, as a matter of fact," I said. I'd seen Jameson every day for the past couple of weeks—ever since our day at the lake and the magical night that had followed. We'd had picnics and dinner dates. He'd taken me out on his four-wheeler again to recover more scrap metal from the old car. Last night we'd driven outside town and lain in the bed of his truck to look at the stars. We'd talked and kissed for hours. Then he'd made love to me out there in the open air. My core tingled a little just thinking about it.

"You planning on staying in Bootleg long-term, then?" Betsy asked. "Seeing as how you're getting cozy with Jameson Bodine and all."

I nibbled my lip and shrugged. "I'm not sure. I do have to think about making a living."

"You'll find a way," Dad said. "I always knew you'd make your way back to Bootleg. I'd sure love to see you settle down here."

"Thanks, Daddy," I said.

I'd been a little nervous to tell my dad I was dating Jameson. Turned out, there was no need, considering Jameson had beaten me to it. The day after he'd kissed me for the first time, he'd come to visit my dad for a little man-to-man chat. He hadn't asked my dad's *permission* to date me—and my dad hadn't expected that of him. Dad was old-fashioned, but not quite that old-fashioned. But Jameson had told me it was important to him to let my dad know we were dating, and that his intentions toward me were honorable.

It had certainly been the right move if Jameson had been hoping to win points with my dad. He admitted he liked to do things old-school. So even though I was a grown woman, he'd appreciated Jameson's gesture and later told me, more than once, he hoped I'd *settle down* with Jameson Bodine. It was a far cry from his reaction to Kelvin.

I stayed a bit longer to chat with Dad and Betsy. They were so cute together, it gave me all kinds of warm squishy feelings. Betsy had brought over supplies to cook dinner for the two of them, so I said my goodbyes and left.

It was early yet, and Jameson wasn't picking me up for several hours, so I decided to stop for some coffee and a pastry. Yee Haw Yarn and Coffee had the best blueberry muffins, so I found a parking spot and went inside. It was busy, but there were still a few open tables. I ordered at the counter and took my coffee and muffin to a table near the back.

The table next to me had a group of ladies with knitting needles clicking away. They talked quietly over their coffee as they knitted. A group of younger women dressed in tank tops and shorts over swim suits—probably tourists—came in a few minutes later and sat behind me.

I flipped through my Instagram feed while I sipped my coffee. The cell signal was good in here, which wasn't the case everywhere around town. I followed a number of fashion bloggers and designers, and it was always fun to see their posts and creations. I had a lot of unread comments on my posts, but I left them be. Most of them were probably about the show, and nothing I wanted to read. I might have been missing the odd supportive post, but it wasn't worth it to see all the negative ones.

My phone buzzed, the little text icon popping up at the top of my screen. I swiped to see who it was from. Kelvin. I didn't even read it. He'd started texting me again a day or two ago. The first one had just said, *you need to call me*. I'd replied, *no thanks*. He'd responded with *it's important*, but I'd ignored it. Yesterday he'd texted again to say I needed to call him, but I had decided to stop replying. If he kept it up, I was going to figure out how to block his number. The guy needed to move on.

The conversation the girls behind me were having caught my attention. I didn't mean to eavesdrop, but one of them had said something about *Roughing It*.

"I can't get enough of that show," she said. "I don't even know why. Like, it's ridiculous, right? But it's so addictive."

"Oh my god, I know," the other girl said. "It's like a car wreck. You know you should turn it off, but you can't look away."

"Exactly," she said. "I can't even with Leah Larkin. Like, who does she think she is? It was obvious from the first episode that she was going to be all over Brock Winston."

I swallowed hard and bit my lip. They obviously hadn't seen me sitting here. My hair was braided, and I was wearing one of Jameson's Bootleg Cock Spurs baseball caps, so I wouldn't be as recognizable in public.

"I know, right?" the other girl asked. "And what was Brock thinking? Leah Larkin isn't even that pretty. She's all bony and weird looking. That gap in her teeth? Oh my god, they're called braces, sweetie."

"Oh, I know."

"I guess I can't blame her about Brock, though," the other girl said. "He is hot."

"Yeah, but he's married," she said. "That's low."

"Some girls don't care."

"I'd care," the first girl said. "Anyone who stoops to stealing another woman's husband is a special kind of whore."

I pulled the ball cap down and squeezed my eyes shut to stop the sudden rush of tears. I was not going to cry sitting here in Yee Haw Yarn and Coffee. Not over this. These girls didn't know me.

"You know she's supposedly here, right?" the second girl asked.

"Here?" she asked. "Like, here, in this town? What is she doing here?"

"Running around with some guy," she said. "James or Jamie or something like that. I don't know, I saw it this morning. He's probably married, too."

"Oh my god, I have to see this," the first girl said. "Can you imagine if we saw her in person?"

There was a pause—I figured they were looking things up on their phones—and I should have left. But I held my breath, waiting. James or Jamie… did that mean the media knew about Jameson?

The first girl gasped. "You're right. Look at this. Oh my god, he's hotter than Brock. I guess when Brock went crawling back to Maisie, Leah went and found herself a rebound. Who is this guy?"

"According to this, he's just some random guy," she said. "Jameson Bodine? How did she even meet him? It's so weird."

"I hope he knows what he's getting into," the other girl said. "I wonder if they even know about the show out here. Oh my god, maybe he has no idea who she is. Wouldn't that be crazy? He's just some poor, innocent country boy, thinking he lucked out with a hot girl. What's he going to think when he finds out the truth?"

"I don't know, but according to this, his dad is being investigated for the murder of a sixteen-year-old girl," she said.

"Holy shit."

Oh, no. My chest felt like it had caved in on itself and a swirl of nausea rolled through my belly. I grabbed my phone and searched my name, clicking on the first result. It was an article in a gossip column. I skimmed it quickly and my fears were confirmed. It mentioned me, Bootleg Springs, and Jameson Bodine.

But it didn't stop there. It said that Jameson was a local artist, but then went into the Callie Kendall case and his father's possible connection to her disappearance. I felt sicker by the second.

With Leah Larkin's failed attempt to steal Brock Winston away from his wife, Maisie Miller, she has apparently taken refuge in the backwoods of West Virginia, in a little town called Bootleg Springs. And she's not alone. Confirmed photographs show Leah Larkin with local Bootleg Springs artist Jameson Bodine. But if Leah was hoping to keep her fling with the hot country boy out of the press, she should have chosen someone with a lower profile. Jameson Bodine's father, the late Jonah Bodine, is being investigated as a person of interest in the disappearance of Callie Kendall, a sixteen-year-old girl. Kendall, the daughter of Judge and Mrs. Kendall, went missing from Bootleg Springs twelve years ago, and her disappearance has gone unsolved. Recently uncovered evidence points the finger at the Bodine family, and resulted in the reopening of the case.

I closed the article, my heart in my throat. I wanted to believe it was just this one gossip column, but if this site was reporting it, that meant it was everywhere. They didn't bother with little stories. They always went for the big stuff.

Leaving my muffin untouched and my coffee still half-full, I rushed out. I needed to talk to Jameson.

Chapter Twenty-Four

Jameson

My face broke into a wide smile when Leah Mae came rushing into my workshop. I pulled off my leather gloves and pushed my safety goggles up to rest on top of my head.

"Hey, darlin'," I said, but my smile quickly faded. Something was wrong.

She came in wearing one of my plaid shirts she'd asked for. But it no longer looked like mine. She'd belted it at the waist and added something that sparkled around the buttons. Her hair hung in a long braid over one shoulder and she had my Cock Spurs hat on. She looked so damn adorable, I wanted to eat her up.

But the stricken expression on her face had me scooping her into my arms as fast as I could get to her. "Baby, what's wrong?"

She breathed in a slow breath and pulled the hat off. Looked me in the eyes. "Jameson, I'm so sorry."

"Sorry for what?" I didn't like the way her voice sounded. "What's goin' on?"

"Someone found out I'm here, in Bootleg," she said. "The gossip columns know, and now they're printing stories about it."

"Well, that was bound to happen," I said. "It's not like you've been in hiding."

"No, but someone took pictures of us," she said. "They found out who you are, and they're talking about you, too."

I blinked at her a few times. "What do you mean?"

"I mean the gossip columns," she said. "They're saying I came out here to hide and hooked up with some local guy. And there's stuff about you, and your art."

"All right," I said, trying to process what she was saying. I didn't like the idea of being talked about in the media, but I'd known it was possible. Hoped we could avoid it, but with all the attention on her show, it wasn't too surprising. "That's not the end of the world, now is it? Were you afraid I'd be mad?"

She nibbled her lip and fiddled with the end of her braid. "They're reporting things about your dad, and Callie Kendall."

That made my back stiffen, so I took a deep breath. "Well, I guess that's just something we'll have to deal with."

"I'm so sorry," she said. "I've been having so much fun with you, I sort of forgot the rest of the world exists. I should have been more careful."

I gathered her into my arms again and kissed her forehead. "This isn't your fault. What were we going to do, wear disguises every time we went outside? We'll just lay low for a while. Stay in more than we go out."

She rested her hands on my chest. "I didn't want to subject you to this."

"I know." I leaned down and kissed her. "First of all, you're worth it. And second, I think we can find things to do that keep us out of the way of any stray cameras."

She finally smiled. "I think so too."

I kissed her again, tasting her cherry lip balm—which had recently become my favorite flavor. "Tell you what. I'll see your bad news and raise you some good. Jonah is gone, and I don't expect he'll be home until late tonight. That means we have the place to ourselves."

"I'm a little bit crazy about you, Jameson Bodine," she said. "I hope you know that."

"The feeling's mutual, darlin'."

————

I'd assured Leah Mae that me turning up in the press with her wouldn't be a big deal. But after a while, I wasn't so sure I'd been right about that. Turned out, it *was* kind of a big deal.

They had indeed published photos of me and Leah Mae. I reckoned some nosy tourist had recognized her and snapped some pictures. Somehow they'd figured out who I was, and next thing we knew, the Leah Larkin story had a whole new level of scandal.

Not only had she supposedly tried to break up a marriage, now she was running around with the son of a man being investigated for killing a teenage girl.

Didn't matter that it was technically a missing persons investigation, considering Callie's body had never turned up. And it also didn't matter that a dead man couldn't be charged with murder. The gossip columns weren't much different than the studio behind *Roughing It*—not interested in showing the facts or the truth. Very interested in sensationalism and ratings. Or in this case, clicks and advertising dollars.

Dragging my family's name through the mud, just like they were dragging Leah Mae's, made for a juicy story. And apparently they were going to take full advantage, no matter who they hurt in the process.

I insisted Leah Mae come stay with me for a while. I didn't want her alone at that cabin. She still went to see her dad most days, and it wasn't like I'd stop her. But I worried about who was lurking around town, hoping to get some pictures. And this way, we could hide out somewhere safe and wait for it to all blow over without adding fuel to the fire.

People still found us, though. I went with her to get some

of her things at the cabin, and there was someone parked just up the road, waiting. Snapped some pictures of us before we could get inside. Neither of us could go into town without being followed. Leah Mae said the best thing to do was ignore them, but it wasn't easy.

I knew things were about to get worse when I got a text from Scarlett, calling for a family meeting at Bowie's.

Jonah and I drove out to Bowie's place early the next morning. Bowie was in the kitchen cooking up breakfast, but the lack of waffles told me everything I needed to know. This was about me. I sank down into a chair and waited for Scarlett and Gibson to arrive.

The wait wasn't long. Scarlett and Gibs came in a few minutes later. By the look Gibson gave me, I could tell he was mad. He always looked angry—to people who didn't know him, at least—but there was a difference between the everyday-Gibson scowl, and an angry-Gibson scowl. I was getting a ragey vibe from him the moment he walked in the door.

Bowie, Jonah, and Scarlett all dished up some breakfast. I didn't bother to get up, and Gibson sat down across from me, leveling me with a glare.

Shit.

"All right, I think y'all know why we're here," Bowie said.

"Yep," Gibson said, not taking his eyes off me.

"The stories circulating around are gettin' out of hand," Bowie said. "Started off with just stuff about Leah Mae and Jameson. I'm sure you didn't like that too much, but it seemed harmless. But then they started in on the Callie Kendall case and the possible connection with Dad."

"And now the whole goddamn country is talkin' about the Bodine family secret," Gibson said. "Like it was ever a fuckin' secret."

Bowie tipped his head, like he was acknowledging what Gibson had said, but he would have found a more diplomatic way to say it. "Right. I don't know what's happening with the investigation."

"It's not like the cops are going to give us a call and let us know if they find anything," Jonah said.

"Exactly. But now all these stories are bringing attention to the case," Bowie said. "I think we need a public statement. At least that way the press will have the truth."

"Devlin and I can work on that with Jayme," Scarlett said.

"Thanks, Scar."

"This is bullshit," Gibson grumbled.

"Simmer down, Gibs," Scarlett said.

"No, *you* simmer down," Gibson said. "The whole thing was going away until knucklehead over there had to go and start dating some reality TV tramp."

I stood and lunged at Gibson. Got an inch from his face before Bowie and Jonah's strong grips on my arms held me back.

"You watch your fucking mouth," I said.

Gibson's eye twitched. "This is on you, Jameson. There are pictures of you two all over the place. You were dumb enough to let it happen."

I strained against Jonah and Bowie, but the two of them together were strong enough to keep me away from Gibson. Barely.

"I swear, if you say one more word about her, I'll break your fucking nose, you hear me?" I growled.

"Outside, then," Gibson said, standing.

"Boys," Scarlett snapped. "Enough. Y'all aren't helping anything by going at each other's throats."

"It's his fault," Gibson said.

"Oh my god," Scarlett said, rolling her eyes. "Next you're gonna say *he started it*. Don't make me act like your mama or I will box your ears and stick you in the damn corner."

Gibson scowled and sat. Jonah and Bowie released their grips on me and I straightened my shirt.

"You think I like this?" I asked. "This is the stuff of my nightmares. It was bad enough when it was just the town talking about whether Dad murdered Callie. Now it's all over the damn country? In case you haven't noticed, people lookin' at me is not my favorite thing. And I have far more of it than I'm comfortable with at the moment. So you can all just back the hell off."

"I'm sorry, Jame. I know this has been rough," Scarlett said.

I nodded, and almost went after Gibson again when he glowered at me, but my phone buzzed in my pocket.

Leah Mae: Kelvin is in town. I agreed to meet him at Moonshine.

My anger at my brother had nothing on the wave of rage that poured through me, sizzling through my veins like liquid steel. Grinding my teeth, my back and arms clenching, I typed out a quick reply.

Me: Be there in five.

"What's wrong?" Scarlett asked.

"Leah Mae's asshole ex showed up," I said. "She's meetin' him at Moonshine."

"Oh, hell no," Jonah said and we all glanced at him. "Bootleg justice, right?"

"You are definitely a Bodine," Bowie said, patting him on the back. "Let's go."

We poured out of Bowie's front door, piling into cars. Scarlett declared she was *not* missing this, so she got into Jonah's car with me and Bowie. Gibson brought up the rear in his Charger. He was by himself, but he did come. I was still mad over what he'd said about Leah Mae, but I appreciated that he wasn't going to leave this one to us.

We were still brothers, after all. This was how we did things.

Leah Mae was already inside Moonshine when we pulled up, sitting in a booth across from that asshole. I had to admit, the look on his face when the entire Bodine family walked in that restaurant was worth the price of admission and more.

Chapter Twenty-Five

Leah Mae

Kelvin stood when I walked into Moonshine. Instead of his usual business casual attire, he was dressed in a black hoodie and track pants. Of course, they were Lululemon. The guy managed to be pretentious even when he was dressed down.

I nodded at Clarabell, then took a seat across from Kelvin. She eyed him with open skepticism—maybe even a touch of hostility—as she came over to our table.

"Mornin'," she said. "Coffee?"

Kelvin ignored her and sat back down.

I met her eyes. "Sorry. I guess not. Maybe give us a few minutes?"

"Sure thing, honey," she said, and took her coffee carafe back to the kitchen.

"What are you doing here?" I asked.

"You stopped answering my calls," he said. "You won't text me back. What was I supposed to do?"

"How about move on?"

"Leah, I don't know what game you think you're playing

out here, but slumming with some backwoods West Virginia hillbilly is low."

My eyes widened so much I thought they might pop out of their sockets. "Excuse me? You did not just call Jameson a hillbilly."

"Well, it's the truth," he said. "The man's father murdered some girl."

I rolled my eyes. "Oh my god. Is that why you came out here? You saw the story about me and Jameson, and you just couldn't let it go?"

"You're throwing away everything we worked for," he said. "I know you still don't have an agent. Who's working for you? Who's making sure your next gig is lined up? What the hell are you going to do with yourself out here? Open up a moonshine slushy stand?"

I paused for a second, because a moonshine slushy stand would do very well in Bootleg, especially during the summer months.

"Jesus, Leah," he said. "You're thinking about that, aren't you?"

Before I could reply, the color drained from Kelvin's face, leaving him stark white—maybe even a little green. His eyes were on the door and I knew immediately what—or more importantly, who—he must be looking at.

Not two seconds later, our booth was surrounded by Bodines.

Gibson leaned against the table across the aisle. It wasn't empty, but the couple sitting there just glanced at him and went back to their breakfast. Jonah and Bowie took a slightly more subtle approach and sat at an empty table—facing us. Scarlett joined them, an amused smile on her face.

Jameson crossed his arms and casually leaned against the back of Kelvin's side of the booth.

"Really?" Kelvin asked, his voice thick with disdain.

Jameson didn't answer.

"Are these assholes for real?" Kelvin asked.

I glanced around at each of them, my gaze stopping on Jameson. He picked at his fingernails like he was bored.

Clarabell came out with a stack of menus and held them out, offering to anyone who needed one.

"We won't be needin' those, sweetheart," Gibson said.

I sighed. I didn't need Jameson to fight this battle for me—and I really didn't need the rest of his family doing it, either. I was about to say something to Jameson, but Kelvin started in again.

"You think you know her?" Kelvin asked, twisting to look up at Jameson. "You don't get to come in here and speak for her."

"No one's speakin' for Leah Mae," Jameson said. "She's perfectly capable of doing that all on her own. We're just here to make sure you behave yourself is all."

I bit my bottom lip to keep from smiling. They weren't here to rescue me, or fight my battle because they didn't think I could. They were just here to make sure I was okay. And their presence helped. With Jameson and his family backing me up, I felt like I could take on the world. Or, my ex-fiancé-agent, at least.

"This town is insane," Kelvin muttered under his breath and scooted farther from Jameson.

"No, I'd say what's insane is you flying all the way to West Virginia because you saw gossip about me with another man," I said. "You're the one who kept insisting my so-called relationship with Brock Winston was a good thing. And let's not forget, you were willing to put me on dating show with not one bachelor, but six."

Jameson raised his eyebrows. Gibson cracked his knuckles.

Kelvin glanced around, like he didn't want to talk with so many people around. I didn't blame him, but I certainly wasn't going to ask them to leave. I folded my hands in front of me and pressed my lips together, waiting.

He lowered his voice, but of course everyone could still hear him. "Those were strategic decisions for the benefit of your career."

"My career went down the toilet because of you," I said. "But you know what? I'm glad. I'm glad everything happened the way it did. Because if things had been different, I might not have realized what a lowlife bottom feeder you really are."

"Leah, I made you," he said. "You'd be nothing without me."

Gibson growled—he actually growled—but Jameson held up a hand and then nodded to me, as if to say it was my move.

"You made me?" I asked. "I made you, asshole. Your agency was nothing before you signed me. I was the one who broke you into high fashion, and you've been riding my coattails ever since. Without me, you'd be nothing, and we both know it."

Someone whistled; I wasn't sure who, but it might have been Scarlett.

"That's bullshit," Kelvin said. "We worked together for everything we had. You can't just walk away from that."

"Actually, I can, and I did."

A vein in Kelvin's forehead looked like it might burst. "This is what you want? To go back to being a country bumpkin and be this redneck's whore?"

"Now you're finished, son," Jameson said. "You shouldn't have called her a whore."

He grabbed Kelvin's shirt and hauled him out of the booth like a rag doll before Kelvin had a chance to react. Gibson took one side while Jameson held him on the other and a second later, Bowie and Jonah were ahead of them, holding the door open.

I got up and grabbed my handbag while they dragged Kelvin outside. Scarlett paused next to my table.

"They aren't going to actually hurt him, are they?" I was frustrated and annoyed at Kelvin for having the gall to show up here, but I didn't want anyone to get hurt.

"Nah," Scarlett said. "He just needs to be taught a lesson. My brothers are good at this sort of thing. Best to just let it happen."

Scarlett and I followed them outside. Kelvin struggled, but Jameson and Gibson held his upper body while Jonah and

Bowie each took a leg. Together, the four Bodine men handled him like he weighed nothing.

I glanced around, expecting to see people with their cell phones out, taking pictures or video. But it was early enough, no one was around. I breathed out a sigh of relief at that.

"What the hell are you doing?" Kelvin asked, his voice bordering on panic.

The Bodines didn't answer—just hauled him around the side of the building while Kelvin struggled in vain.

A car pulled up, *Bootleg Springs Sheriff* in large letters across the side. The Bodines all paused as the window slowly lowered.

"Mornin', boys," Sheriff Tucker said.

"Sheriff," Jameson said.

"Oh, thank god," Kelvin said. "Sheriff, make these psychos put me down."

Sheriff Tucker just raised his eyebrows.

"Public assholery," Jameson said. "Clarabell and Scarlett can vouch."

"Dumpster?" Sheriff Tucker asked.

"Yep," Jameson said.

Sheriff Tucker tipped his hat. "Carry on, then."

"What?" Kelvin screeched. "Are you serious?"

"Well, there is a town ordinance against public assholery," Sheriff Tucker said. "Just mind his head, Bodines."

"Will do, Sheriff."

The Bodines started moving again, hauling him through the parking lot. Sheriff Tucker drove on.

"What kind of backwoods shithole is this?" Kelvin asked, still trying to struggle out of their grip.

I stopped and tried to keep myself from laughing. They were heading toward the huge dumpster. "Are they really going to put him in there?"

Scarlett stood next to me, her arms crossed. "Of course. It's the appropriate response to public assholery. Like Sheriff said, it's a town ordinance, and he was clearly in violation."

"On three," Jameson said.

They swung Kelvin on one and two, and when they got to three, they hurled him over the edge of the dumpster. There was a wet thud and Kelvin started in on a string of curses that could have made a sailor blush.

Jameson brushed his hands together and walked toward me.

"Oh my god!" Kelvin's muffled voice came from inside the dumpster. "What is that... oh god, it's wet. And sticky. Get me the fuck out of here!"

"Are you just going to leave him in there?" I asked.

Jameson shrugged. "Garbage pickup is tomorrow, so it's mostly full. He shouldn't have any trouble gettin' out. And if he does, Hamish'll give him a hand."

"Who's Hamish?" I asked.

"Garbage man."

"Do you fuckers know how much these pants cost?" Kelvin shouted, struggling to get over the side of the dumpster.

Scarlett left with Jonah and Bowie, and Gibson stalked off. He glared at Jameson as he walked by, but neither of them said anything.

Jameson tucked my hair behind my ear. "I didn't mean to overstep. But no one speaks to you that way when I'm around."

"It's okay," I said.

He put his arm around me and we walked back around the corner. It sounded like Kelvin was getting out, but I wasn't worried about him anymore. And I was pretty sure I'd heard the last of him, thanks to some good old-fashioned Bootleg justice.

"Thanks for backing me up, but letting me say what I needed to say."

"Course, darlin'," Jameson said. "I don't know about you, but I could use some waffles. Can I buy you breakfast?"

"Waffles sound great to me."

Chapter Twenty-Six

Leah Mae

My skin still tingled from the facial I'd gotten earlier today, and my muscles felt loose. Scarlett had invited me to come to the spa with her, along with Cassidy and June Tucker. We'd been scrubbed, steamed, and rubbed until our faces glowed and we were relaxed as could be. I was convinced Lula, the spa owner, had magical hands. I felt amazing.

I lounged on the floor in Scarlett's living room, my back resting on the couch. She'd put out an assortment of snacks on the little coffee table and made drinks for everyone. We were all dressed in comfy clothes or pajamas, making it feel a bit like a slumber party.

If I had too many of these drinks she was mixing, it might turn into one.

"Thanks again for inviting me," I said. "Today was much needed."

"Glad you could make it," Scarlett said. She tossed a few more pillows on the floor and balanced her drink in one hand as she sat. "Seemed like you could use a little pampering, with everything that's been goin' on."

I nodded. She was certainly right about that. I'd made the mistake of reading more of what the gossip columns were saying, and it wasn't good. I was a home-wrecker, a vixen, a seductress, and an attention whore. Jameson was a hick with a tragic past and the shadow of his father looming over him—although the stories always emphasized that he was hot. Someone had taken pictures of him at the lake—shirtless of course. Images of Jameson Bodine in nothing but board shorts, running his hands through his wet hair, had gone viral.

"Yeah, the last few weeks have been ridiculous," I said.

"Did your ex quit buggin' you after the little incident at Moonshine?" Scarlett asked.

"Incident with the ex?" Cassidy asked. She sat up a little straighter and tilted her head. "I heard something went down."

I laughed. "My ex showed up in town after he saw the story about me and Jameson. I agreed to meet him at Moonshine, mostly so I could get rid of him."

"And of course you know who showed up," Scarlett said.

"Let me guess," Cassidy said. "A big wall of Bodine men."

"Scarlett was with them," I said.

"Hey, there was no way I was missin' that," Scarlett said. "And I have to give it to my brothers. They were on their best behavior."

"Best behavior? They tossed Kelvin into a dumpster," I said.

"Nothin' he didn't deserve." Scarlett glanced at Cassidy. "Public assholery."

"Typically in West Virginia, disorderly conduct carries a fine of up to four hundred dollars," June said. "Or a night in jail."

"Well, in Bootleg, we just toss your ass into a dumpster and call it a day," Scarlett said.

Cassidy and Scarlett both raised their glasses and clinked them together.

"So what did the asshole ex do after being served up a cup of Bootleg justice?" Cassidy asked.

"He left town," I said. "And I haven't heard from him since."

June tapped her chin thoughtfully. "It appears to have been an effective measure."

"I'd say so," Scarlett said. "We know how to do things right, 'round here."

I grabbed a handful of potato chips and popped one in my mouth. "I still can't believe he flew all the way out here."

"Sounds like you dinged his pride," Cassidy said. "Men are like toddlers. They don't appreciate what they have until someone else wants it. Then they throw a tantrum."

"I think the good ones get it," Scarlett said. "They appreciate what they have, when what they have is good."

Cassidy groaned. "Scarlett, I love you, but I don't need to hear any more about the amazing Devlin McAllister. You found the perfect man. We know."

"Aw, Cass, you'll find a man who's perfect for you, too," Scarlett said.

"I don't think he exists," Cassidy said.

"Approximately ninety percent of Americans get married before the age of fifty," June said. "The numbers are still in your favor."

"That's not exactly a comfort, June Bug," Cassidy said.

June just shrugged and picked up her phone.

"Are you still striking out, Cassidy?" I asked.

She groaned. "I swear, I think I'm going for some kind of record. Most terrible dates before the age of thirty or something. I didn't think it could get worse than the guy who picked me up on his riding lawnmower."

"It got worse than a guy picking you up on a riding lawnmower?" I asked.

Cassidy shook her head slowly. "You have no idea."

"Spill it, Tucker," Scarlett said, pointing a chocolate-covered pretzel at her. "We need to know."

"All right, so I met a guy from Perrinville," Cassidy said. "We talked a few times before we decided to go on an actual date. And, honestly, he told me up front that he had a particular... interest. I just didn't take him seriously."

"Uh oh." I wasn't sure where Cassidy was going with this story, but I'd met a lot of people in the fashion industry who were into some kinky stuff.

"The thing is, he was very funny," she said. "He had me in stitches every time we talked. So when he told me he liked wearing women's underwear, I thought it was another joke."

Scarlett coughed, almost spitting out her drink. "He likes what now?"

"Women's underwear, but that's not even the worst of it." Cassidy sighed. "I met him for dinner, and that was pretty nice. He had me laughing through most of the meal. Afterward, he walked me out to my car and leaned in, like he was fixin' to kiss me goodnight. I kinda put my hands on his chest and I felt somethin' there."

The three of us stared at Cassidy, enthralled. Even June.

"I felt around a bit, and he noticed. When he asked if everything was all right, I said, 'well, it feels like you have something strange under your shirt.'"

"Oh god," Scarlett said.

"Yep," Cassidy said. "It wasn't just women's panties. He was wearin' a bra."

We all burst out laughing. Scarlett fell over, her head in Cassidy's lap. June snort-laughed so hard she dropped her phone. I covered my mouth, trying to contain myself, but it was no use. Fortunately, Cassidy laughed as hard as the rest of us.

I clutched my stomach and wiped a few tears from the corners of my eyes. "I'm sorry, Cassidy. I shouldn't be laughing at you."

"It's okay," she said, still trying to catch her breath. "It's so ridiculous, of course it's funny."

"I have so many questions," I said. "Why was he wearing a bra? Did he have man boobs?"

Scarlett started laughing all over again.

"No," Cassidy said. "He was tall and thin—couldn't have filled out an A-cup."

"Was it stuffed?" Scarlett asked.

Cassidy laughed again. "I don't think so. Although I didn't keep feeling around to find out. Kinda jumped back when I realized what he was wearing."

"What happened then?" I asked.

"Well, he seemed a bit surprised by my shock, since he'd been up front and told me beforehand that he was into that sort of thing," Cassidy said. "I explained that I'd thought he was joking. Then I blurted out, *why?* And he said it made him feel complete and he couldn't imagine his life without his special undergarments."

"Oh my god," I said. "Did he use the phrase *special undergarments?*"

"That he did," she said.

"Does this mean you won't be seeing him again?" June asked.

"Yeah, Juney," Cassidy said. "I won't be datin' a guy who wears a bra. I don't like to be too judgmental about what other people like, but that was a bit much for me."

"At least he was honest," Scarlett said. "That has to count for something."

"I suppose it does," Cassidy said. "But honesty or no, bra-wearing is a hard limit for me in a man."

"I don't blame you," I said.

"That is an odd quirk," Scarlett said. "Well, maybe you just need to find someone a bit more conventional."

"I don't know," Cassidy said. "I'm wondering how long before I just get a bunch of cats and call it good."

"Stop," Scarlett said, playfully smacking her leg.

"Yes!" June yelled, and we all startled.

"You okay?" Cassidy asked.

"I am excellent," June said. She had her phone out again and she was busy typing with her thumbs, her eyes on the screen. "I just acquired Thompson."

"Who?" Scarlett asked.

June furrowed her brow, like she was confused at the question. "George Thompson, also known as GT, starting receiver for Philadelphia. Buck was foolish enough to release him from his fantasy football team, and I was able to take advantage of his miscalculation."

"Y'all playing for money again this year?" Cassidy asked.

"We are, although the gambling aspect is not why it appeals to me," June said.

Cassidy glanced at me. "If you hadn't noticed, Juney is a sports nut. Football is her favorite."

"Baseball is a close second," June said. "But I find the number of variables in football to be particularly stimulating."

"You sure it's not the big strong men smashing into each other that you find stimulating?" Scarlett asked.

June got that confused look on her face again. "No."

"She likes numbers," Cassidy said. "Has fun with all the statistics."

"People like to believe there's a high level of intuition involved in putting together a winning fantasy team," June said. "But it's all there in the numbers. Thompson's total yardage has gone down, but his reception-to-touchdown ratio is in the top five in the league. He's clearly the superior choice."

"That's great," Cassidy said. "I bet Dad will be jealous."

"He will be envious of my newly updated roster," June said, nodding.

Cassidy laughed and patted her sister's shoulder.

"How is it I wasn't following your Instagram, Leah Mae?" Scarlett asked. She swiped her phone screen with her thumb. "Look at that cake. You get that from Opal?"

"Millie Waggle, actually," I said.

Scarlett groaned. "What I wouldn't give for a plate of her brownies."

"Her cake was amazing," I said. "It was so sweet of her to bake it for me. But I haven't been looking at my Instagram all that much. Too many comments I don't want to see."

"I don't know, this doesn't look all that bad," Scarlett said. "Mostly people are talkin' about your clothes."

"Really?"

"Well, not on the cake picture," Scarlett said. "I'm just skimmin' these comments, but that's mostly what I see. People asking about your clothes and where you got them. This one here says, *who cares if she sucked Brock's dick, look at her jeans.*"

We all burst out laughing again.

"You're kidding," I said.

Scarlett handed her phone over to me.

I thumbed through some of the comments on my photos. I did see a few references to my supposed scandal on *Roughing It*, but Scarlett was right. There were a lot of comments about what I was wearing. I was very pleased to see all the likes and comments on the photo of my cowboy boots. People loved them.

Take that, Kelvin.

"You ever thought about doing something with this?" Scarlett asked.

"With what?"

"With your sense of style," she said. "I basically want to steal all your clothes every time I see you."

"Same here," Cassidy said, raising her hand.

"Thanks," I said, and took another sip of my drink. "I've always liked to have fun with what I wear. It's kind of like art to me. Art you wear around with you all day. Want to hear something weird?"

"Sure," Scarlett said.

"It all started with Callie Kendall," I said. "Her mismatched button. Remember how we all copied her that summer, and changed the top buttons on all our cardigans? Just the idea that I could change my clothes to make them unique kind of blew me away. I started modifying more of my clothes, then. At first it was just buttons, but it wasn't long before I was ripping seams and resewing things. Making new silhouettes, or adding accessories."

"Is that why you're always so cute?" Cassidy asked. "Because I kinda figured it was just something models innately knew how to do that the rest of us don't."

"I guess," I said. "Remaking my clothes and styling new outfits is… well, it's what I do for fun. It's relaxing."

"So when are you coming over to remake my wardrobe?" Scarlett asked.

I laughed. "Anytime."

"I'm gonna hold you to that," she said. "Tell you what, that's payment for dragging my poor quiet brother into the media with you."

She smiled and winked at me, and I knew she was kidding. But I still felt bad.

"I feel awful for what they've put him through," I said.

"Yeah," Scarlett said. "This kind of thing is hard on Jameson. When the rest of the town found out about Callie's sweater turning up at Dad's place, he pretty much disappeared. I think he came into town for groceries once, but that was about it. It was almost impossible to get him to come out of hiding."

"Wow, I didn't realize," I said.

"He's never liked it when attention is on him," she said. "If he could find a way to be invisible, I think he'd do it. He tends to withdraw, even from people he loves."

I remembered how scared Jameson used to get when we'd have to go up in front of the class when we were kids in school together. I could still see him, putting his head down on his desk, like he hoped the teacher would forget he was there. As soon as she'd call on him, he'd get this stricken look on his face—broke my heart, even then.

We'd had a system back then. If he got called up in front of the class, I'd give him a special signal—tug my ear twice and wink. It was such a silly thing, but each and every time I'd done it for him, the terrified look in his eyes had melted away, and he'd given me that sweet little boy grin.

But I knew all too well how much Jameson hated the very sort of attention he was being subjected to right now. I'd been worrying about it since the first article with his name in it had come out. Although he'd assured me it was okay, I wondered if he was just telling me what I wanted to hear.

Eventually, the media attention would die down. But I was pretty certain it was going to get worse before it got better. I still had to fly out to L.A. for the end-of-season media event and party. That would have me back in front of cameras, and would probably breathe one last gasp of life into the Leah Larkin gossip mill.

Once that was over, the stories and attention would wane. Some new scandal would pop up to take its place. I no longer wanted to pursue a career in the entertainment industry, so it wouldn't be long before my name faded from the public's memory.

In the meantime, I wondered if Jameson would decide I was no longer worth all this hassle. If he'd withdraw from me, too.

Scarlett's phone blared the chorus of a country song, and she picked it up to answer the call.

"Hey, sexy," she said. "How's poker night?"

She was quiet for a moment and I could hear Devlin's muffled voice.

"They're what?" she asked, her voice a half-screech, half-laugh. "You're kidding, right? You're not kidding? They are? Oh my god. Okay, we'll be right over."

"What happened?" I asked.

"Apparently the menfolk are little out of hand at poker night," she said. "I think we should go over there and help sort it out."

That didn't sound good. "Sort it out?"

She shook her head. "I can't even explain. We'll just have to go over there and see what's what."

Chapter Twenty-Seven

Jameson

With Leah Mae at the spa with my sister, I spent the afternoon in my shop. My deadline was looming, and I still didn't know how to finish the piece.

Dee had told me in the beginning that the client loved my style, and he'd prefer to let me use my creativity, rather than him dictating what he wanted. I had the front elevation of the building—a drawing that showed what the façade was going to look like—and the location he'd reserved for my sculpture. But aside from that, I didn't have any direction.

I'd been excited by that in the beginning. It meant I could take any direction I wanted. And at first, I'd planned to create something that echoed the lines of the building. But what I'd actually sculpted was completely different than anything I'd done before.

I walked around her in a slow circle. She was ten feet tall and no doubt one of the heaviest things I'd ever made. It was going to take an engine hoist and probably some creative engineering to get her on the truck that would haul her to Charlotte. But we'd manage.

Usually my work looked like what it was—something made of scrap metal. That had its own beauty, and I was proud of my other pieces. But this didn't look like she'd been made of scrap—hardly looked like metal at all. I'd taken so much care with each section, making everything flow together smoothly.

She sat in a cage shaped like an old-fashioned birdcage, her knees against her chest, her hands gripping the bars. Large wings drooped from her back, the tips brushing the ground outside the bars. Her head tipped forward, her face angled down.

An angel in a cage.

But she still wasn't finished. And it was killing me that I didn't know why.

I was running low on time, but I couldn't deliver a piece that wasn't done—wasn't perfect. As she stood, I was proud of her. There was no doubt in my mind it was the best work I'd ever done. But I had to figure out what else she needed. I'd never had this problem before, and it was driving me crazy.

My phone rang, making me jump. Luckily I didn't have something hot in my hands. Didn't want to admit how many little burn scars were the result of being startled when I was lost in thought out here.

It was Deanna.

"Hey, Dee."

"Jameson," she said. "Please tell me you're almost finished."

"I'm almost finished."

"Are you lying?" she asked.

I cleared my throat. I wasn't strictly lying. *Almost* was a relative term, and I was sure once I figured out what she needed, it wouldn't take too long to finish. I hoped. "No. I'm looking at it now, and there's not much left to do before it'll be ready."

She let out a noisy breath. "Oh thank god. Okay, they're beefing up security at the opening, what with you being a sudden gossip-celebrity."

I groaned. "Don't remind me."

"Kind of hard to avoid," she said. "The girl's pretty, though. You sure you know what you're doing with her?"

A flicker of anger made me clench my fist, but Dee simply didn't know the truth. "Yeah, I've known Leah Mae since we were kids."

"Huh," she said. "Regardless, your client is of course aware of the circumstances, and everyone there will be prepared."

I still hated that I had to go, but there was no use grumbling about it. "All right, good to know. Thanks, Dee."

"Sure," she said. "You bringing her with you?"

"I'd like to."

"Okay," she said. "If she was just some sweet country girl from Bootleg Springs, it wouldn't matter too much. But since she's Leah Larkin, it does."

I sighed. "She *is* just a sweet girl from Bootleg."

"Right. Well, I'll have the shipping company get in touch. I have you on their schedule, but they'll need to coordinate with you for pick-up."

"Sounds good. Thanks."

"No problem," she said. "Talk soon."

"Bye, Dee."

I hung up the phone and put it in my back pocket. At least she wasn't trying to set me up with her niece anymore.

Tonight was poker night with my brothers, so after covering the sculpture, I went inside to shower and change.

―――――

Poker night rotated locations, and players, but the basics were always the same. Food, beer, cards, and betting. We didn't usually mess around with big money, especially when Scarlett was playing—that girl always cleaned up. Five or ten to buy in was standard, and the most I'd ever won was a hundred bucks. It was more about having a good time than winning a bunch of money off each other.

Truth be told, I kept my winnings and just kept rotating them in each new game. Sometimes I was up, sometimes I was down, but so far, I always had a bit of poker cash. Reckoned if I ran out, that was my cue to quit going to poker night.

Devlin was hosting tonight, and he had us out at Build-a-Shine. It had once been an old speakeasy, and now you could craft your own moonshine from their impressive selection of flavors. They also had a back room you could reserve for things like poker or birthday parties.

Jonah and I drove into town together and found our way to Build-a-Shine's back room. A round table surrounded by chairs was in the center, and there was food off to one side. My mouth watered. Dev had found someone—I knew it wasn't him, he was a worse cook than my sister—to serve up a taco bar. There were tortillas, meat, cheese, beans, guacamole, and all the fixin's you could ever want. That spread was worth losing some money for.

Devlin was at the table with a beer and a plate, as was Bowie. Nash occupied another chair. I said my hellos, grabbed myself a plate, and loaded it up with tacos. Grabbed a beer from a bucket of ice and found a seat.

Gibson sauntered in and I slumped a bit. I'd been hoping Gibs might decide to sit this one out. He and I still hadn't patched things up after our almost-fight at Bowie's. Granted, he'd backed me up when it came to Leah Mae, but that didn't mean what was going on between us was over.

Not that I expected an apology. Bodines didn't generally apologize, and Gibson had taken that trait to a new level of stubbornness. But I'd be glad when we could both look at each other without angry glares. I had enough on my mind without dealing with my grumpy-ass brother.

As if he wanted to make sure I knew he was still angry, he paused next to the table, held the back of a chair, and glared at me. I glared right back, meeting his eyes. Gibs was older, and bigger, but I was not going to let him intimidate me. I'd go toe to toe with him any day of the week. If he was gonna be like Dad and think I was weak, he was dead wrong.

"Grab some food and let's get started," Devlin said.

Apparently a taco bar was a bigger draw than trying to stare down his younger brother, because Gibs tore his eyes away and loaded up a plate. When everyone had taken a seat, we all tossed in our cash, got our chips, and Dev started dealing.

I kept my eyes on my cards and sipped my beer. Bowie and Jonah got into a heated, but good-natured, discussion about football. Gibson stayed mostly quiet, but that was typical. We played a few hands, ate some food, and drank our beers. I relaxed a bit. Seemed like tonight was going to go just fine.

My phone buzzed, so I checked. Leah Mae had texted me a photo of her and Scarlett with something smeared all over their faces, and they looked to be laughing. It said, looking sexy at our spa visit earlier.

Me: There's my beautiful girl.

"Quit texting during the game," Gibson said.

I eyed him. He was looking to start a fight, and I wasn't sure if I was going to indulge him or not. Probably best to ignore him. But just to show that I wasn't letting him get to me, I sent her another text.

Me: Have fun tonight.

"God, Jameson, quit being an ass," Gibson said.

"I'm pretty sure I'm not the ass here." I put my phone down. "You have that title squared away nicely."

The tension in the room thickened, eyes darting around over fanned-out cards. Looking between me and Gibson.

"At least I'm not draggin' everyone else through my shit," Gibson said.

"Why the fuck are you making this about you?" I asked. "You're not the one being followed around town. Who has to duck when he goes anywhere because every person with a cell phone has a damn camera. Why the hell are you letting this piss you off so much?"

"Because you didn't give a shit about what this would do to our family," Gibson said. "You were just thinkin' with your dick."

206

"Fuck you, Gibson."

Gibson tossed his cards on the table. "No, fuck you."

"Guys, come on," Bowie said. "Let's just play."

My first instinct was to throw my cards on the table and walk out. Go home. My brother could go fuck himself. I didn't have to take his shit. But I was getting damn tired of Gibson's angry streak being aimed at me. Growing up, I hadn't ever been Gibson's target. He'd usually been the one sticking up for me, both at home and at school. I didn't like being the recipient of his assholery.

"You need to back the hell off, Gibs," I said. "Mind your damn business."

"This is my business." He took a slice of olive off his plate and popped it in his mouth.

That smug bastard. I grabbed a chunk of tomato and flicked it at him. "No, it ain't."

The juicy tomato stuck to his shirt and slid slowly down his chest, leaving a wet trail and a few seeds behind. His jaw worked, his teeth grinding.

Maybe I shouldn't have, but I did. I dug at him a little more. "You got something on your shirt, Gibs."

Bowie snickered, and it was all over.

Gibson tossed an entire taco at me. The contents— mostly meat and cheese—spilled into my lap. Bowie shouted something, but Gibson had already thrown food in his direction.

"You ass," Bowie said, and tossed some avocado at Gibson.

I grabbed what was left of Gibson's taco and threw it at him—hard.

Gibs tried to retaliate at Bowie, but the taco I threw distracted him and he hit Jonah instead. Jonah tossed something back, Devlin scooted away from the table, Nash ducked, and seconds later, all hell broke loose.

Gibson stood and threw more food from his plate. He wasn't even aiming anymore. Someone hit him with a scoop of sour cream. I tossed chunks of marinated steak across the table, then threw a lime wedge at him. He grabbed a bowl of salsa and I dove for cover.

Salsa sprayed across the table and onto the floor behind me. Bowie crouched next to me and nodded. Together, we tipped the table upright to make a barricade to hide behind. We grabbed whatever was near—chips, olives, avocado, lime wedges, tomato, tortillas—and tossed them over the edge of the table.

"Shit," Gibson growled.

"I'm hit!" Nash shouted.

Bowie and I were running out of ammo, and Gibson was closest to the food table. The steady stream of taco fixin's flying over our heads indicated he'd gotten to it.

"Jonah, reload," I said.

Jonah had taken cover behind a chair. He nodded and crawled closer to the food. Bowie and I hurled the last of what we could reach at Gibson while Jonah reached up and pulled a few bowls off the table.

"Just toss it," I said.

Gibson noticed Jonah and his lips curled in a sneer. He scooped a handful of pico de gallo and tried to throw it, but most of it just splattered all over the floor. Jonah slid a bowl of sliced onions our direction, then the chopped lettuce. Bowie and I made good use of them, pelting Gibson with vegetables as fast as we could throw.

There was a lull in the action, and for a minute, I thought maybe Gibson had relented. Bowie and I waited, our backs against the bottom of the table, handfuls of cheese and lettuce at the ready. Jonah had moved further from Gibson—couldn't blame him—and I had no idea where Devlin had gotten to. Nash seemed to have bailed on the scene at the start.

Bowie nodded, and we inched our way up so we could look over the top edge of the table. I caught the evil in Gibson's eyes just before mine were hit with a fistful of guacamole.

"Goddammit, Gibson!" I ducked behind the table and wiped the guac off my face. "Quit being such an ass!"

"You're an ass," he said, and more guacamole went flying over my head.

Scarlett's voice came from somewhere to my left. "I'd say you're all asses at this point."

I couldn't see her from my hiding spot, but the heat in her voice made me cringe. I was certain she had her hands on her hips. Probably shaking her head in disbelief.

"Oh my god." That'd be Cassidy.

I rolled my eyes. No doubt June was with her. Great, an audience.

"Y'all get up," Scarlett said. "Come on, now."

Bowie and I glanced at each other, understanding passing between us.

"Nope," I said. "Not until he does."

"Fuck that," Gibson said. "I ain't getting up first."

Scarlett let out an exasperated sigh. "Then get up at the same time. Put down the guacamole, Gibs. What's wrong with you? I swear, y'all are grown men. Quit acting like children."

"Jameson?" Leah Mae asked.

"Stay back, darlin'," I said. "Gibson, if you throw anything at her, I will kick your ass."

"I ain't throwing shit at the girls," Gibson said, although it sounded like a reluctant concession.

"Okay, fine," I said. "I call a truce. We all drop our weapons and stand on three. Agreed?"

My truce offering was met with a chorus of *aye*s. Including Gibs.

"Count us up, Scar."

"One," she said. "Two... three."

Bowie and I nodded to each other, dropped the food in our hands and stood, looking warily over at Gibson. He held his empty hands up slightly, and we did the same.

"Y'all clean up this mess," Scarlett said. She went over to the cooler and started pulling out beers—handed them to the girls. They dragged chairs to the side of the room and sat, like they were standing guard over the clean-up. Probably not a bad idea, that.

Gibson grumbled, but got to work. Bowie and I righted

the table and we picked all the shit up off the floor. Money, chips, cards, and a ton of food. Took a solid forty-five minutes before the room was in decent shape again.

Sonny Fullson, Build-a-Shine's owner, came in and appraised the room. His dark hair was shaggy and his black apron had the store's name in white. "What the hell happened back here? Someone cheatin' at cards?"

"Nah," Bowie said, stepping up, as he usually did, to be the diplomat. "Sorry about all this, Sonny. We got a little carried away. We'll all chip in extra for clean up."

I half-expected Sonny to throw us all out and ban us from coming back. Instead, he put his hands on his hips and shook his head.

"Tell you what," Sonny said. "Y'all make sure the Cock Spurs win next time you play the Perrinville Bootleggers. Those filthy buggers had no right using *Bootleggers* as their mascot. You win, we're even. If not, we'll work something out."

"Sounds fair." Bowie shook his hand.

Sonny went back out to the front. I'd avoided Gibson during clean-up, and he left first, sparing me the need to say anything to him. Leah Mae gave me a sympathetic smile when I grabbed my jacket and headed toward the door. I didn't know what money was mine, and I didn't much care. I just wanted to get out of there and be done with it.

Thankfully, Scarlett didn't try to interrogate me. Just patted me on the arm before I left. I followed Leah Mae out and we got in my truck. Drove silently back to my place.

Under different circumstances, I'd have been laughing over it all. A bunch of grown men throwing food at each other. Certainly wasn't the first food fight that had broken out between the Bodine brothers. But I had a sick feeling in the pit of my stomach. The weight of everything was heavy on my shoulders. The gossip. My dad. Callie Kendall. My sculpture. Fighting with Gibs just made everything worse.

And Leah Mae. She was my refuge, yet there were still unanswered questions between us. Was she going to stay in

Bootleg Springs? Was she making plans to go? I knew she wasn't moving back to L.A., but where was she going next? Was this just a stopover while she figured things out? Was I just a distraction? I wasn't sure.

All I knew was that I didn't want to talk about it tonight. We got back to my place and I cleaned up. We curled up on the couch together to watch TV. Later, I took out some of my pent-up aggression on her, in ways she liked quite a lot. Fell asleep with her in my arms, exhausted and drifting in the scent of her…

…with a hint of guacamole.

Chapter Twenty-Eight

Jameson

Avoiding Gibson was easy, with Leah Mae staying with me and plenty of reasons to not go out. Truth be told, I avoided all my siblings. Even Jonah. He was around, as roommates generally are, but he had a lot of clients in town now, so that kept him busy. Leah Mae visited her dad, and I spent time in my workshop.

Then, about a week after the taco fight, she dropped a bomb on me.

"I have to go to L.A. next week," she said, her voice casual, like that wasn't big news.

We were sitting out on the back porch while the sun went down, sipping some apple pie moonshine. I had on a thick flannel over my t-shirt to keep off the chilly September air, and she was wrapped in a light gray sweater, her cowboy boots dangling over the side of the wooden deck chair.

"I'm sorry, what was that?" I asked.

"The show's final episode airs next week, so we're all supposed to go to this big end-of-season party," she said.

"Is the media going to be there?"

She nodded. "They will be at the beginning. They'll want to take pictures and do interviews. Then they'll have a private party afterward."

"How long have you known about this?"

"A while," she said. "I wasn't sure if I was going to go, but I should. It's in my contract. Plus, it would feel like admitting defeat if I didn't."

"Makes sense. Is this a social type thing? Like where people bring dates?"

"Yeah."

"Good," I said. "Then I'm comin'."

She swung her legs around so she was sitting upright in her chair. "Jameson, I can't ask you to do that. It's going to be crazy. All these cameras and people shoving microphones in your face—you'd be miserable."

"Darlin', last I checked, my balls are still in place," I said. "A man does what needs to be done, even if it's outside his comfort zone. I'd never let you face that shitshow by yourself. Of course I'm going with you."

"That would make it a lot easier."

I shifted forward in my seat and leaned closer so I could tuck her hair behind her ear. "That's exactly why I'm going."

She smiled and pressed her lips to mine. I kissed her back, softly. I wasn't surprised she'd assumed I wouldn't be willing to go with her. Took a man to stand up and do what was necessary. Last guy she'd been with hadn't been much of one. She wasn't used to someone standing by her side when things got tough.

"You didn't need to keep this to yourself," I said, touching her face with the backs of my fingers. "Next time, let me know. I love you, Leah Mae. I'll walk through hell and shake hands with the devil himself if you need me to."

Not that I was thrilled with the prospect—of the devil, or this party. A studio event in Los Angeles sounded about as far outside my realm of experience as you could get. And the media being there? Hell, it was liable to be a disaster. But I still wasn't going to let her face that disaster by herself.

But I wasn't too proud to get a little advice on the matter. So the next day when Scarlett asked me to swing by and help her with a few things at Dad's old place, I thought I might mention it. See if she had anything to say. Trouble was, conversations where things like *feelings* were going to be front and center were about as easy for me to face as a crowd of people wanting to hear me speak.

Scarlett was ripping up the linoleum in the kitchen when I arrived. I'd brought work gloves, so I put them on and without a word, got down to helping her.

We worked for a while, with Scarlett doing most of the talking. She'd recently had brunch with Devlin's parents, and it had gone well. Seemed she'd been her usual sassy self, rolling over them like a tornado in a trailer park.

She stood and brushed her gloved hands together. Her hair was in a ponytail and she wore a dusty t-shirt, jeans with holes in the knees, and a pair of brown work boots.

"Not bad for an afternoon's work. Thanks, Jame."

"Anytime," I said. "Sounds like things with Dev are goin' all right."

"Yeah," she said with a smile, her eyes sparkling. "They sure are."

"Good."

I rubbed my neck and glanced away, not sure how to bring up the trip to L.A. Seemed like a simple thing—nothing I should get nervous about. But it wasn't travel tips I was looking for. And I had no idea how to start a conversation about my relationship. Or how I was feeling about it all.

"Everything all right?" she asked.

"Sure."

She laughed. "Jameson Bodine, you act like I'm not your sister who can read you like… well, like a book or a magazine or just about anything. What's wrong?"

"It's not that something is wrong," I said.

"Okay, what then?"

I shrugged. "Well, Leah Mae has to go to a studio party in L.A. next week."

"That doesn't sound like much fun."

"No, not especially," I said. "I'm going with her."

She grinned at me. "Course you are. You worried about what to wear or something?"

I paused and blinked at her a few times. "Well shit, Scar, I hadn't thought to worry about that, but now that you mention it…"

"Leah Mae will help you with that," she said. "Or Devlin knows all about dressin' up. You can ask him."

"Thanks."

She took off her gloves and tossed them on the dusty counter. "So are you going to keep making me pry this out of you? Because I have a lot more work to do today."

I put my hands on my hips and looked down. "It's just that… I'm not sure how this is going to go. I'll face the cameras or whatever I have to do. That's fine. But this is her world I'm steppin' into. A man's supposed to lead in a dance, not follow."

"Good thing it's not really a dance," she said.

"It's a metaphor."

She laughed. "I know, and I hear what you're saying. Look, I can't speak to being the man in this scenario. But I can tell you I've been in your shoes. I had to go to that charity barbecue with Dev and it was like being on an alien planet—one where the natives were hostile toward visitors."

"I'd imagine that wasn't easy," I said.

"Actually, it was pretty great," she said. "I understood Devlin a lot better after seeing that side of things for myself. It helped me see where he'd come from. I think it did a lot for our relationship."

"So, you mean, getting out of your element and into his was a good thing."

"Absolutely," she said. "It'll be good for you and Leah Mae, too. Think of it as a chance to show her off to the world. She'll be perched on your arm, lookin' all sexy in a fancy dress. You'll be there to make sure she can hold her head high and look all those assholes in the eye."

"That's exactly why I'm going."

"Then what are you so worried about?" she asked. "You've got this."

I shrugged. "Yeah, I reckon."

"God, Jameson, I don't think you realize just how adorable you actually are," she said. "All those Hollywood people are going to eat you up with a spoon."

I wasn't sure about all that. But supporting Leah Mae—backing her up so she could face a tough situation—that I knew I could do. And maybe Scarlett was right. Maybe it would be good for us, like it had been good for them. I certainly hoped so. As strong as my feelings were for Leah Mae, there were still a lot of unknowns. And I wasn't sure how much more pressure the two of us could take.

Chapter Twenty-Nine

Leah Mae

There was something about a man with manners.

Jameson Bodine left a trail of melted panties from the mountains of West Virginia all the way to sunny California. From the ticketing agents, to the waitress in the airport restaurant, to the flight attendants on our cross-country flight, to the hotel staff in L.A. He said *pardon me,* and *please,* and *thank you ma'am* in that adorable Appalachian drawl. Tipped his hat. Gave them his boyish grin. Didn't want to trouble anyone for anything, but sure was grateful for it all, even when they were just doing their jobs.

I caught at least half a dozen women watching him with dreamy eyes. The flight attendants fawned over him. The waitress at the airport looked like she would have slipped him her number if I hadn't been there.

The farther we got from Bootleg Springs, the more pronounced the Jameson effect became. The woman who checked us in at the hotel fanned herself—actually fanned herself—as soon as he started talking.

Maybe some women would be jealous of their boyfriend getting so much attention from other women. Not me. I loved it. It wasn't that I needed other women noticing him to realize what I had. It was just so adorable. He clearly had no idea the effect he had on women. I was sure that to him, he was just being polite. He didn't seem to notice their reactions at all.

And yes, I did indulge in a little satisfaction over knowing he was mine. Besides, I could hardly blame them. I found him irresistible, too. I was just the lucky girl who got to keep him.

"The hotel's nice, at least." He put our bags down and surveyed the room, his hands on his hips, a battered ball cap on his head. "I reckon we'll be comfortable."

Our room wasn't fancy, but it did have a big king-sized bed with a fluffy white comforter. I kicked off my shoes and hung up my garment bag with my dress for tomorrow night.

It was strange being back in L.A. From the moment we'd walked off the plane, I'd felt odd. I'd been hiding away from the outside world while I was in Bootleg Springs, and here I was, smack in the middle of it again. I felt like a different person from the woman who'd been living here with Kelvin Graham. Leah Larkin had been convinced she wanted to be famous. She'd clung to a little girl's dream long past the time she should have moved on.

Going home to Bootleg Springs had opened my eyes. It had reminded me of who I was—who I'd been before agents and managers and fashion clients had told me who to be. And that girl—Leah Mae—knew there was a better life for her out there somewhere. And it wasn't chasing fame in Hollywood.

I had no qualms about walking away from this place—this life. Leaving L.A. for good and finding a new dream. The problem was, I still didn't know where I was going. Back to Bootleg Springs? To do what? I couldn't very well just live in Scarlett's cabin, date Jameson, and do nothing else. I'd run out of money, for one. I'd earned a good living as a model, but my lifestyle with Kelvin had been expensive. I certainly hadn't earned enough to retire at twenty-eight. And I had my dad to think about. He was getting better, but I wanted to be able to help him financially if he did get sick again.

It wasn't just the money. I needed something—a vocation or a career. I needed to be productive. Have purpose to my life outside of the man I was dating.

I was still adrift, floating in a sea of indecision and uncertainty. I'd taken aptitude tests and career path quizzes. I had interests, and ideas, but I still felt like I didn't know what to do with the rest of my life. And how that life could be lived in Bootleg Springs.

I loved Bootleg. It was home in a way no other place in the world would ever be. But jobs in a small town were scarce. It had been easy to get lost in Jameson, and in Bootleg's magic. Where time seemed to move slowly, and the cares of the outside world weren't so important. I'd indulged in that for too long now, and soon I'd need to make some hard choices.

Jameson stretched out on the bed, and I hung his suit next to my dress. We'd gone into Perrinville to buy it a few days ago. Bootleg Springs didn't exactly have a store with formal menswear. I almost hadn't recognized him when he'd come out of the dressing room. It was the one good thing about this studio event. I was definitely looking forward to seeing him all dressed up. Jameson Bodine cleaned up good.

Glancing over at him, I smiled. His ball cap had shifted partway down his forehead, almost covering his eyes, and he'd fallen asleep. I wasn't surprised. It had been a long day.

I climbed onto the bed next to him and got comfortable. I wasn't sure how to properly express how much it meant to me that he was here. A part of me didn't want to face tomorrow. I wanted to stay hidden—cozy up with Jameson in his bedroom and pretend the outside world didn't exist. That I'd never done that stupid reality show, and no one believed I'd seduced Brock Winston and convinced him to cheat on his wife.

But like I'd told Jameson, that would be admitting defeat. I needed to show my face. Smile for the cameras. Get through this one last obligation, and I could finally be free.

Jameson's chest rose and fell slowly. He looked so cute, lying there in his faded blue *Support Local Farms* t-shirt and worn jeans. He was about as out of place in L.A. as anyone could be. And it made me love him all the more.

I shifted closer, and he reached out to wrap an arm around me—drew me against his chest. His body was relaxed and warm. I curled myself around him, nuzzling my face into his neck. The stubble on his jaw was pleasantly rough against my cheek and he smelled so good. I breathed him in as he traced gentle circles on my arm.

My lips found the sensitive skin at his throat. The vibration of his low groan tickled, lighting little sparks that raced down my spine.

His muscles flexed, and he pulled me on top of him. I took his hat off and tossed it on the floor. Those brilliant blue eyes took me in, devouring me with just a look. I loved seeing my desire for him reflected at me. It heightened my senses, awakening my body.

Letting my legs slide down each side of his hips, I pressed myself into his growing erection. He took my mouth in a deep kiss, groaning as I rubbed against him. Our bodies moved together, slowly—grinding and rubbing. Intensifying our need for each other.

I broke the kiss and crawled down his body. When I got to his waist, I pushed his shirt up, revealing the hard ridges of his abs. He groaned again as I ran my tongue along his skin.

His belt buckle clinked as I unfastened it. I opened the top button of his jeans and lowered the zipper. He dragged his teeth over his lower lip, watching me.

"Darlin', I like where this is going."

I licked my lips and smiled, then pulled his underwear down. His cock was thick and hard. I ran my tongue up his length, reveling in his sharp intake of breath. Grabbing him around the base, I licked him, paying special attention to the sensitive ridge around the tip. His eyes rolled back, and he groaned again.

There was nothing like hearing him moan because of me. I took his cock into my mouth and moved slowly, teasing him. Gradually, I moved faster, plunging down, taking in as much as I could. I worked the shaft with my hand, letting the tip slide in and out of my mouth.

He moved his hips and stroked my hair. I picked up the pace, squeezing the shaft while I drew his hard length in and out. His cock thickened, stiffening with his impending release. I tasted his flavor on my tongue.

The feeling of his growing climax was intensely arousing. Pressure built between my legs, warm and insistent. My heart raced, and my cheeks flushed as I kept drawing his cock in and out of my wet mouth. Harder. Faster.

"Baby, I'm almost there," he said.

His rough voice sent a thrill down my spine. He was breathless, losing control. His muscles flexed beneath me, his hips thrusting himself deeper. I moaned, feeling his cock begin to pulse.

The first spurts of come hit the back of my throat and he groaned, a low sound that reverberated through me, setting me on fire. I took him all in, every last bit, reveling in the way it felt to give him this pleasure. I loved it. He was lost, his body stiff, jerking into me as the orgasm overtook him.

When he finished, I slid his cock out of my mouth and quickly swallowed. He was breathing hard, his eyes glassy.

"Good lord, baby," he said between breaths. "That was unbelievable."

"I'm glad you liked it."

I adjusted his underwear and crawled back up his body. He rolled me onto my back and kissed me deeply, his tongue sweeping through my mouth with lazy strokes. My body trembled with a rush of anticipation as he slid one hand up my thigh, beneath my skirt. He nudged my legs open and stroked my clit with gentle fingers.

"These panties are awfully wet," he said between kisses. "I reckon I ought to do something about that."

He slipped his fingers beneath my panties and teased my clit, making me shiver and moan. His touch was soft, leaving me desperate for more.

Without warning, he pushed his fingers deep inside me. My back arched, and I groaned. I bucked my hips against his hand, seeking more—more friction, more pressure. He pumped his fingers in and out a few times while he nibbled on my bottom lip.

"I want a taste of you," he said, drawing his fingers out. He brought them to his mouth and sucked my wetness off, closing his eyes and groaning. "God, you taste good. I need more."

With rough hands, he yanked my panties off and pushed my skirt up. Positioning himself between my open legs, he licked up each side of my slit.

"Jesus, Jameson," I said, my voice halting. The feel of his tongue on my sensitive skin was electric.

"Relax, darlin'," he said. "I'm just getting started."

His tongue moved with slow strokes and the sensation was overwhelming. I closed my eyes and sighed his name. He lapped against my clit, sending jolts of pleasure rushing through my core. God, he was good at this. His wet tongue slid and swirled until I was panting, hardly able to catch my breath.

The tension between my legs built, a deep surge of heat and pressure. Jameson sucked on my clit, and I moaned, running my fingers through his thick hair. He licked and sucked and stroked until I was ready to burst.

He slid two fingers inside me, and I cried out in ecstasy, my body shuddering. He growled into my pussy as he worked my clit relentlessly with his mouth. His fingers curled, and I thought I might die. I gasped, clutching at the sheets, the intense sensation crashing over me. He had me at the peak of climax, on the brink of coming apart.

But he wasn't finished with me. He held me in that place, where the pleasure is at its height and the intensity is overpowering. I writhed and whimpered, digging my heels into the mattress. My pussy was hot and throbbing around his fingers, my body desperate for release.

His tongue strokes became rhythmic—warm, wet pressure against my clit—and I came undone. Wave after wave rolled through me as I came, the sensation taking over. I grabbed the sheets and gasped for breath, losing myself in the hot rush of my orgasm.

Jameson gently kissed between my legs and the insides of my thighs while I lay panting on the bed.

"I don't know what you just did to me."

He kissed me again, just above my opening, the soft pressure of his lips soothing in the aftermath of such an intense orgasm.

"I just like makin' you feel good," he said, then kissed me again.

He moved higher up the bed and we finally stripped off our clothes. Although I was sated, I needed to feel his skin against mine. He wrapped his arms around me and held me close. I relaxed against him, reveling in the warmth of his body, the feel of his rough jaw against my cheek.

"I love you," I whispered.

He drew back to look me in the eyes and touched my face. "I love you, too."

Our mouths came together, soft and sweet. His lips caressed mine, our tongues sliding together. I felt like I could have spent a lifetime kissing Jameson and it would never be enough.

His cock hardened, and he pressed it against me. I felt good—my pussy warm and wet from his tongue—but I wanted more. I wanted him inside me—filling me. Stretching me open and connecting my body to his.

He seemed to have the same idea. He pushed me onto my back again and settled between my legs. My need grew as he kissed me deeply and pressed his cock against me without going inside. I rocked my hips against him, rubbing my clit along his hard length. He groaned into my mouth, then sucked on my lower lip.

"I need you inside me," I said, the urgency for him growing.

I ran my hands down his back and pressed against his ass,

hoping to nudge his cock inside me. He grinned and kissed me again, like he was enjoying this game.

"You want this?"

I took his lower lip between my teeth and tugged gently. "Yes."

He groaned again but instead of thrusting inside, he moved off me. Grabbing my hips, he flipped me over and pulled my ass into the air. I propped myself up on my forearms and looked back at him over my shoulder.

He grabbed my ass and slid his thumbs up and down my slit a few times. "God, you're fucking sexy. I love the way you look on your knees for me."

Taking his cock in one hand, he rubbed the tip against my opening. Jerked his hand up and down his thick length a few times. I rocked my hips back, seeking more.

"I want you inside me," I said. "Please."

"Baby, I'm gonna fuck you until you can't see straight." He positioned himself at my entrance, grabbed my hips in a tight grip, and thrust inside.

I cried out as his thickness filled me and arched my back to take him in deeper. He held my hips and plunged in and out, drawing my ass into his groin with every stroke. I loved it when he unleashed on me like this. When he showed me this side of himself—primal and raw. Strong and commanding. To the outside world, Jameson Bodine seemed like a quiet and sensitive soul, but in the bedroom, he was fierce. And I loved every second of it.

He pounded into me with hard thrusts, his grip on my hips tight. Hot tension built again, deep in my core, as waves of pleasure rolled through me. I lost myself in the feel of him fucking me, forgetting everything. The studio, the gossip, the uncertainty of my life. It all melted away.

I looked back at him again, watching his abs flex. The tattoo across his left pec and shoulder glistened with a light sheen of sweat, and his brow furrowed. He grunted low in his throat with each thrust.

Our eyes met, and he stopped, his cock buried deep inside me. His chest rose and fell and his grip on my hips was tight. Slowly, he blinked and licked his lips.

He pulled out and turned me onto my back again. Crawled up between my legs and slid his cock inside. Touching my face with gentle hands, he kissed me slowly while his hips began their rhythmic motion.

"I love you," he whispered into my mouth, kissing me again. Deep, wet kisses, like he wanted to devour me.

I held him and kissed him back, moving with his slow thrusts. "I love you, too."

Like a dance timed perfectly to music, our bodies moved in sync. My nipples dragged across his skin as he thrust his cock in and out of my pussy. He kissed down my neck and licked the hollow at the base of my throat. Grazed my skin with his teeth. I held on tight, rolled my hips, and drew him in as deep as he could go.

He moved faster—harder—and I could tell he was close. His cock pulsed inside me, and I whimpered with the need to come again. Sensation pooled between my legs, like every nerve ending led there. Then he shifted, a subtle movement of his hips, and took me to a whole new level of ecstasy. My eyes rolled back, the pressure so intense I could scarcely breathe.

"Fuck, Leah Mae," he said, low in my ear. "Baby, I'm gonna come."

"Come in me. Oh god, Jameson, come in me now."

His body stiffened, his cock pulsed, and the first waves of his orgasm sent me over the edge.

My climax swept through me, sparks and tingles and hot swells of lust. I closed my eyes, held Jameson tight, and let it overtake me. Reveled in the release—in the feel of him emptying himself into me. In the heat of his skin, his body joined with mine.

When the last tremors faded, we lay together, arms and legs tangled. We were hot, sweaty, and exhausted. And utterly satisfied.

Chapter Thirty

Jameson

This was, hands down, the strangest thing I'd ever done in my life. I was dressed in an expensive suit, about to walk my girl through a jungle of reporters at a studio party in L.A. It was a far cry from anything this kid from West Virginia had ever experienced before.

Leah Mae looked stunning. Her long gold dress shimmered when she moved, and her heels made her almost as tall as me. Bright red lips begged me to kiss them and with her hair up, the smooth skin of her neck taunted me. I wanted to lick her all over.

I hoped I was a good counterpart. My suit was nice—fit well. She'd told me a dozen or more times how good I looked. It wasn't the most comfortable getup, but I appreciated it for what it was. Felt like I fit in—on the outside, at least.

As soon as we arrived at the hotel, a man in a slick suit appeared out of nowhere and snatched Leah Mae from her perch on my arm, pulling her aside. Adrenaline pumped through my veins and I was ready to beat this guy's ass. I was back at her side in an instant, but she didn't seem upset. In fact, she was leaning in close so she could listen.

"Okay, sugar, here's what you're doing tonight," he said. "Be sweet as apple pie. Lean on those country roots a little bit. We want you likable, but not too friendly. Don't answer direct questions about Brock. Keep them guessing. Imply whatever you want with your nonverbal cues, but don't deny or admit to anything."

She nodded.

"We have Brock and Maisie arriving shortly," he continued. "They're putting up a united front. Smile at Brock, but feel free to glare at Maisie when he's not looking."

Leah Mae just nodded again. I glanced at her. Was this for real?

The guy seemed to notice me for the first time. "As for you, just… don't talk. Be the strong silent type."

"Pardon me?" I asked.

He cringed. "Yeah, no talking."

"Just who in the hell are you?"

"This is Rich Baumgartner," Leah Mae said. "He's one of the producers."

"You've done beautifully, sugar," Rich said. "We couldn't have asked for anything better. Perfection, babe. Keep it up."

He gave her a quick peck on the cheek and disappeared back into the crowd.

"Was that guy serious?" I asked.

"That's just how he is," Leah Mae said. "He doesn't mean anything."

"He told me to keep my mouth shut."

"Don't let him get to you." She tucked her hand in the crook of my arm and squeezed. "Besides, you don't want to talk to the press anyway."

Before I could reply, she nudged us toward the waiting sea of reporters. From the corner of my eye, I could see her smile. It looked as fake as Misty Lynn Prosser's boobs. Made my back tense, and I reached up to stretch my shirt collar a bit. I'd known I'd feel like a fish out of water, but it wasn't just the unfamiliarity making me uncomfortable. This whole place reeked of insincerity, and I didn't like seeing Leah Mae playing into it so easily.

We started down the long walkway toward a photo backdrop with the studio logo. As soon as the first set of eyes hit Leah Mae, reporters swarmed like bees around a hive.

The first one to reach us, a woman with platinum blond hair and more makeup than I'd ever seen on one person, held up a small microphone.

"Leah, you look beautiful tonight," she said.

"Thank you," Leah Mae said, her red lips parting in a false smile.

"You've been quiet since *Roughing It* wrapped," the reporter said. "Is it true you went into hiding when you found out the show was exposing your affair with Brock Winston?"

"After filming, I decided to take some time off," she said. "I've been visiting family."

"Have you seen Brock since the show ended?" she asked. "Did you attempt to continue your relationship?"

"Like I said, I've been visiting family. Filming the show was a great experience. I enjoyed meeting the entire cast and we all had a great time, even though it was a challenge."

We moved on and another reporter stepped forward. Leah Mae kept her hand tucked in my arm and tilted her chin. Too late, I realized people were taking our picture. I tried not to fidget.

"Leah, you've been subjected to a significant backlash since the infamous back room episode aired," the next reporter said. She had more makeup than the first. "Do you feel the vitriol was deserved?"

"There have been a lot of comments and opinions shared about the show," she said. "I'm just glad people have been enjoying it. Mostly, I try to project the positivity that I'd like to see in the world."

"Is this Jameson Bodine?" the reporter asked, turning her gaze on me. "How did you meet Leah?"

I opened my mouth to reply, but Leah Mae cut in.

"We're old friends," she said.

"Jameson, what do you think about the accusations against your father?" the reporter asked. "Do you believe he murdered Callie Kendall?"

"Well, I—"

"The Bodine family has mourned the loss of Callie Kendall for the last twelve years," Leah Mae said, cutting me off again. "Just like the rest of Bootleg Springs."

And before I could say another word, we were moving on down the line again.

The rest was much of the same. Questions about Brock and Maisie. About her connection to Bootleg Springs. About me, or my father. In every case, Leah Mae gave the same non-answers. Her voice was hollow, and her words sounded practiced, like she was reading from a script. She smiled, turned her chin, posed for pictures.

I stayed quiet, merely tipping my head to the reporters. Felt a bit like an accessory and didn't much like it. But I figured she was just trying to get us through as quick as she could.

A stir went through the crowd, and heads turned toward the entrance. I recognized the couple who'd come in. Brock Winston and Maisie Miller.

Brock was shorter than they made him look on TV. Dark blond hair. A cocky half-smile. He was dressed like he didn't give a shit that this was a formal event. Sunglasses, a leather jacket, and black jeans.

His wife, Maisie, looked like a porcelain doll. Shiny dark hair, smooth skin, and blue eyes that almost seemed too big for her face. Her bright red dress didn't leave much to the imagination.

They walked in, all smiles, and were soon surrounded by reporters, much like we were. It was hard to tell what Brock was looking at, with his eyes hidden behind his sunglasses, but I had a feeling he was glancing over at us in between answering questions. Maisie seemed to be pretending we didn't exist.

By the time we got to the photo backdrop, my back was stiff, and my palms hurt from clenching my fists. I took a deep breath and tried to relax.

Leah Mae gave my arm a squeeze. "You're doing great."

We stood for a minute, and I had no idea which way to look. It seemed as if there were a hundred cameras. I concentrated on Leah Mae, like I was just a pedestal for her to stand on so she could look her best. Despite my brief brush with notoriety, she was the one people were here to see.

There were a few more people to talk to once the photos were done. I wasn't sure who they were—reporters or people from the studio, or perhaps a bit of both. Leah Mae kept right on smiling and talking like she'd been told by the producer. Didn't say much of substance or answer hard questions. And she certainly didn't deny that she'd had an affair with Brock.

Which led me to wondering... why not?

"The worst is over," she said as we walked down a short hallway. "There won't be any press for the rest of the night."

There were already dozens of people in the ballroom where the private party was being held. Tables were set with white linens and fancy dishes. The lights were low, and music hummed in the background—just loud enough to intrude on conversation, but not loud enough that we'd need to yell over it. I recognized several other cast members from *Roughing It*. A few stood together, talking near the bar. Rudy Barron, the basketball player, stood talking to another man, with a woman who looked to be his wife—or at least his date—at his side. Everyone was dressed in suits and formal dresses, and most had drinks in their hands.

A drink sounded like just the thing—a nice glass of whiskey to take the edge off—but someone stopped Leah Mae to chat almost as soon as we got into the room.

My mind wandered from her conversation. No one wanted to talk to me, anyway. More people came in. A few I recognized, but most I didn't. I reckoned they were more people who worked for the studio.

I adjusted my jacket. The air in the room felt thick, making it a bit hard to breathe. People wandered past, some greeting Leah Mae—calling her Leah, of course. Something about that grated at me, but she never corrected anyone. Of course, to these people, that's who she was, and she seemed to be determined to keep playing their game.

We worked our way deeper into the room, and I started to wonder how long this was going to last. I had no idea what was supposed to happen at a studio party. Would we just shift around the room, making small talk with different people? How long did she need to stay in order to feel like she'd done what she had to do? I wanted to ask her, but a couple of the other cast members were chatting her up about the show.

I glanced toward the entrance just in time to see Brock and Maisie walk in. She held onto his arm like she was afraid of letting go. He finally pulled those damn sunglasses off his face. Dark as it was in here, he probably couldn't see enough to walk with them on. He tucked them in the inside pocket of his leather jacket and led his wife into the room.

For the first time since they'd arrived, Brock acknowledged Leah Mae. He held up a hand and nodded to her. She smiled back, giving him a little wave. Maisie didn't exactly glare, but she didn't look all too friendly, either.

The people Leah Mae had been talking to—she'd introduced me, but I'd already forgotten their names—finally moved on and I pulled her closer to the edge of the room. I didn't know about her, but even though no one was talking to me, I needed a break.

"How are you doing?" she asked. "You hanging in there?"

"I reckon." I adjusted my jacket again and tugged at my tie. "It's a bit warm in here."

"You must be hot in that suit. I'm sorry, I know this has been miserable. We don't have to stay much longer. I just want to make sure I talk to Thomas Spencer, the show's other producer."

"All right," I said. "But why are you actin' so weird?"

"What?" she asked. "How am I acting weird?"

"You're not acting like yourself. The way you're talking to everyone, you don't seem like you."

"It's just part of the job," she said. "I don't want to rock the boat, and it's almost over anyway."

I wasn't quite satisfied with that answer, but I didn't want to argue with her here. I rubbed my hand up and down her arm, taking solace in the feel of her soft skin against my finger-tips. "Should I get us drinks?"

"That would be nice." She touched the side of my face and leaned in to kiss me lightly on the mouth. "Thank you for this."

"I've got your back, darlin'."

"You're amazing."

Her smile soothed my discomfort a bit. I kissed her cheek and headed toward the bar. I still wanted that whiskey.

The bartender was a young woman with a shiny bob and dark lipstick. I ordered our drinks and waited, glad to finally have something to do. I hated the way people were talking over and around me, like I wasn't there. Reminded me too much of growing up. I'd drifted around like a ghost, always trying to stay out of the way. Remain unseen. Being noticed usually meant being yelled at in my house, so I'd stayed invisible.

But being invisible had started to eat at me after a while. More than once, I'd wondered if I just wandered off and left home, how long it would take before anyone would notice. I couldn't count the number of times I'd looked at those posters with Callie's face, pretty sure if it had been me, they'd never have been made.

"Hi, there."

The woman's voice startled me from my thoughts. I looked over to see Maisie Miller standing at the bar next to me.

"Pardon me," I said. "Afraid I wasn't paying attention."

"Sorry about that." She held out her hand. "I'm Maisie."

"Jameson Bodine," I said, shaking her hand. "Pleasure to meet you."

Her smile widened. "You really are from West Virginia, aren't you?"

"Born and raised."

I glanced around, but didn't see Brock. I wondered if I was supposed to be talking to Maisie, or if all that mattered now that the show was done and the press wasn't around. Wasn't sure why she was talking to me, either. Reckoned she was just being friendly.

"Have you been to L.A. before?"

"I haven't," I said. "I've been a fair few places on the East Coast, but never out west."

"What do you think so far?"

"It's… different."

She laughed a little and nodded slowly. "I'm sure it is."

Something seemed to catch her eye and her smile faded. My eyes darted in the direction she was looking, and I saw Leah Mae and Brock standing together, talking.

My back clenched all over again. They were standing close, talking with a certain familiarity. Granted, they'd spent two months filming a show together, so a bit of friendliness didn't mean anything. But I didn't like the way he was looking at her, and truth be told, I liked the way she was smiling back at him even less.

Maisie didn't appear to be any happier about it than I was. Her lips pressed together in a thin line and a flicker of emotion passed across her features. I only caught a glimpse of it before she took a breath and smiled at me again. But now her smile looked forced.

The bartender put our drinks out, and she grabbed her martini. Took a sip.

"It was nice to meet you," she said. "Good luck."

"Nice to meet you, too," I said, but she was already walking away.

I picked up my whiskey, and Leah Mae's gin and tonic, and moved in her direction. She was still talking to Brock, but Maisie had found someone else in the crowd to speak to.

Just before I reached them, Brock stepped in and hugged Leah Mae. Her back was to me, so I couldn't see her face, but he smiled and said he'd see her later.

I stepped up next to her and leveled Brock with a hard stare. I wasn't the jealous type, but this was the guy she'd supposedly slept with. A guy who had a wife in this very room. He needed to move the fuck on.

Brock didn't acknowledge my existence any more than the rest of the people here. He just walked away, heading in the direction of his wife.

"You didn't have to glare at him," Leah Mae said, taking her drink from my hand.

"I wasn't glaring."

She smiled. "Yes, you were."

"He was being a little too friendly, is all."

Her brow knitted together, like she didn't understand. "We were just talking."

I let it drop and swallowed back half my whiskey. The burn of it felt familiar—the only thing I recognized in this place. I'd expected to be uncomfortable. Worked myself up to it and thought I'd been prepared. But there was a discomfort of a different sort that had taken root in my gut, and I wasn't sure what to do about it.

Maisie Miller caught my eye again, standing next to Brock in that bright red dress. She was looking up at him with the same look she'd had before, when we'd been standing at the bar. A look that said exactly what I was feeling, and I reckoned she was thinking the same as me, too.

What had happened between Leah Larkin and Brock Winston on that show?

I'd never asked. I'd seen the way they were settin' it up in the early episodes, but after that, I hadn't watched. Sort of felt like a betrayal to Leah Mae, even before we'd been seein' each other. So I'd avoided the show. I'd heard things second hand—from people around town, a few articles I'd bothered to read, and the little bit that Leah Mae had told me.

But we'd never really talked about it outright. And I'd been going on the assumption that nothing had happened, and Leah Mae's distress was because the entire thing had been faked.

But what if it hadn't been? What if something had happened between them, and she was upset and ashamed because they'd been caught?

I felt bad for thinking it, but at the same time, how would I know? Turned out, she was an excellent actress. She hadn't seemed like herself since the moment we'd arrived. I could see her doing it—playing a role. She was playing Leah Larkin, and it made me wonder who she'd been playing when she was filming the show. How deep had she gone?

It was deeply uncomfortable to feel like there was suddenly a whole lot I didn't know about Leah Mae Larkin. About what had really gone on behind the scenes when she was filming that show. What had she been willing to do for that career she'd wanted so badly?

She hadn't ever denied the affair. Not to me. Not to the media. Why not? What else did she have to lose, now that the show was over? She'd had reporters asking her questions out there. Why hadn't she told the truth?

It didn't make any sense. Unless there were parts of the truth she wanted to avoid telling.

I kept up my role for a little longer while Leah Mae took little sips of her drink, smiled that fake smile. Talked to some more people who looked right past me. Thankfully, she decided we could leave before they served dinner. The thought of eating a meal among these people turned my stomach sour. I reckoned there were decent folk around, but I was damn tired of feeling like a ghost, or a bodyguard. Someone who just took up a bit of space, but wasn't worth talking to.

We went back to the hotel and ordered room service. Leah Mae suggested a bath together, but I told her I was tired. Truth be told, I had a lot swirling through my mind. Wasn't sure what to do with all of it. I needed some space to think, so I turned in early.

Chapter Thirty-One

Jameson

I was almost out of time.

The shipping crew was going to be here in the morning. I walked around my piece, eying her for what felt like the millionth time. The forge was hot, my tools laid out, ready for me. My t-shirt was damp with sweat, and my leather apron hung from my neck. I had everything I needed.

I'd tried to convince myself she was done. That no one else would think she wasn't right. That didn't satisfy me. I'd smoothed her out. Adjusted the tiniest details. Made sure every last bit of her, from the feathers on her wings to the tiny eyelashes brushing against her cheeks, were perfect.

But she wasn't finished, and I knew it.

It didn't help that my mind was full of turmoil. Our trip to L.A. hadn't been the good-for-our-relationship experience Scarlett had assured me it would be. I'd come back feeling unsettled. Frustrated. I was having a hard time reconciling the Leah Mae I thought I knew with the girl I'd taken to that studio party.

The unanswered questions between us weighed on me. I needed to get the hell out of my own head and focus.

I closed my eyes and took a few deep breaths. Thought about why I'd made this sculpture in the first place. I'd been inspired by Leah Mae—by the vision of her in a cage, being made to perform.

The angel fit my vision perfectly. She was forlorn. Sad. Almost weeping. Looking at her aroused a deep sense of melancholy.

And maybe that was the problem. She was locked inside, her wings faltering. Her spirit diminished, without any hope of escape.

My eyes flew open, the realization hitting me in a rush. Hope. That was what she needed. She needed a way out.

I went over to a shelf and rifled through the contents of my bins. I had it, now. I could see it. It wasn't going to be easy to finish on time, but now I knew what she needed.

———

The shipping crew was going to mangle my sculpture and there wasn't a damn thing I could do about it.

They'd arrived late, and now that we were finally getting her on the truck, they seemed hell bent on fucking up months of hard work. As if her being made of metal meant she didn't need to be handled with care.

The engine hoist jerked and my back tightened. She was wrapped for shipping, but scratches were still a possibility. I could buff them out when I got to Charlotte, but the less of that, the better. There were parts of her where the texture was more vulnerable than others. If these assholes ruined my piece before they even got her on the truck, I was going to lose my damn mind.

"Careful, there," I said.

None of them answered me, just kept right on adjusting the straps with her dangling in the air. I held my breath as they got it moving again. Let it out when she was on the dolly they'd use to roll her in the truck.

Showing no care whatsoever, as far as I could tell, they worked on getting her up the ramp. One of them stood in the truck and pulled a strap they'd tied around her. The other two pushed from the behind. Between the three of them, they got her on—barely. I'd warned them she was heavy.

I'd been up most of the night finishing her, but I wasn't yet feeling the lack of sleep. I was still buzzed, on a creative high that I reckoned would keep me up a few more hours before I'd crash.

They started tying her down, and I pushed my way in.

"I'll get this." I took the strap from one of the movers.

He just shrugged and they all gave me space to work. I reckoned they thought I was being overly fussy about it all, but I didn't give a shit. I'd worked too hard on this piece to let them bounce her around down the highway all the way to Charlotte.

My phone rang as I got the last strap tied down to my satisfaction. It was Dee.

"Hey," I said, wiping my forehead with my sleeve.

"How's everything going over there?" she asked. "Did the movers get the piece?"

"We just finished loading her."

"Just now?" she asked. "They should have been on the way to Charlotte hours ago."

I jumped out of the back of the moving truck. "I'm aware of that, Dee. They were late, and it's taken some doing to get her in the truck."

Dee's huff sounded highly annoyed. Or maybe she was just as stressed about all this as I was. "Well, okay, are they on their way?"

"Soon enough. And Dee, I swear to god, if there is a single scratch on her—"

"Calm down," she said. "These guys are good. I use them all the time."

I wasn't nearly as confident as she seemed to be, and it bothered me that I wouldn't be in Charlotte to help unload when they arrived. Wasn't much I could do about it, though.

"Well, she's on the truck, so that's something," I said.

"Okay, good. I'll see you in Charlotte."

"I reckon you will." I hung up the phone and slid it in my back pocket.

The movers closed the back and piled into the truck. One of them stuck his head out the passenger's side window. "Looks like you have a flat tire."

The moving truck roared to life and they started down my long driveway. I cringed at how much it bumped up and down and hoped I'd secured my sculpture well enough.

I glanced at my truck. Front tire was indeed flat. "Well, shit."

I walked over to inspect it but couldn't find what had caused the puncture. I'd have to put on the spare and take it in. Probably need a new set of front tires. I stood up and kicked the tire. I didn't have time for this shit. It was a six-hour drive to Charlotte, and I had to leave first thing in the morning.

The crunch of gravel made me look up. Figured it would be Jonah, but it was Leah Mae.

She was still driving that silver rental car. Struck me as odd that she hadn't bothered to buy something. She must have been spending a fair bit of money on that rental—money that could have bought her something decent enough to drive, even for just a short while. Hell, I could have helped her find something if she'd have asked. But she hadn't. She was still living in that vacation home of Scarlett's, too—when she wasn't staying at my place, that is. But it wasn't like she had a home.

It all bothered me, maybe a fair bit more than it should. But I couldn't stop thinking about L.A., and Brock Winston, and how she'd acted at that party. There were a lot of unanswered questions between me and Leah Mae, and seeing her come up my driveway didn't make any of that better. Made it worse, in fact, because I knew I wasn't in any state to talk to her.

She parked and got out of the car, smiling at me. She was dressed in strapless top covered in silver sequins with a skirt that looked like a pink tutu. By itself, the outfit might have looked a bit ridiculous, but she'd paired it with her cowboy boots, and the ensemble looked damn adorable. Course, she always looked adorable if you asked me.

"Hey," she said with a big smile. Her makeup was done, and her hair too. Looked real pretty, but I wondered what was up.

"What's with the outfit?" I asked, pointing to her clothes. "You goin' somewhere?"

"I thought we could go out. I know we have to leave in the morning, so we won't stay late. But I figured you could use a distraction. And now that your sculpture is on its way to Charlotte, it's not like you have to work tonight."

I rubbed the back of my neck. "I'm not sure I much feel like going out tonight."

"Really?" she asked. "Gibson's band is playing the Lookout. It's always a good time."

Now I definitely wasn't going out. "I don't want to be shoved into a crowded bar with my brother. Sorry you went to the trouble to get all dressed up, but I'm stayin' in."

I glanced at the flat tire again and just shook my head. I'd have to deal with it in the morning, which would mean getting a late start.

"What happened to your truck?" she asked.

"Flat tire."

"I can see that," she said. "I thought maybe you'd tell me how it happened."

"I don't know how it happened. Look, I'm going to have to get an early start tomorrow to fix this before we leave."

"I know," she said, like she was trying to mollify me. "But you've been hiding out here ever since we got back from L.A. Don't you think it might be good to get out for a little bit? Take your mind off everything?"

"You're starting to sound like my sister."

"Maybe your sister is onto something."

I sighed. "Not tonight. If you want to come in, that's fine, but sittin' in a bar with my angry bastard of a brother is not happening tonight."

"How long is this feud going to last?" she asked.

"How in the hell am I supposed to know? Until Gibson finds someone else to be mad at?"

"Maybe you could talk to him," she said. "He seems like he's in a good mood when he's playing. Could be a good time to deal with it."

I shook my head. "Darlin', Gibson is never in a good mood, playing guitar or not. And don't worry about me and my brother. This sort of thing happens. Eventually we'll both forget what made us mad and we'll go back to the usual way we ignore each other—without the anger."

"That's… that's awful."

"It's not awful," I said. "It's just how things are between us."

I was a lot less confident about that than I sounded. I'd never fought with Gibson before. I'd seen him fight with Scarlett. Even Bowie a few times. And that pattern seemed to hold. Some time would go by and tempers recede. I didn't expect there were ever many apologies from anyone—except maybe Bowie. But he was good with this kind of thing, and the rest of us weren't. I didn't rightly know where Bowie had learned it. Maybe in college. Certainly hadn't been from growing up with Mom and Dad.

But I didn't know how this thing between me and Gibson was going to end, and it wasn't something I wanted to think about tonight. Not with everything else I had on my mind.

"Okay, no Gibson," she said. "But what's going on with you?"

"What do you mean?"

"You've been acting weird," she said. "Since L.A."

I rubbed the back of my neck. My head was starting to hurt. We'd been back for a week, and I'd been busy from dawn till dusk trying to get my piece ready to ship. The days I lost taking her to L.A. had taken their toll.

"I've just been busy."

"Yeah…"

"But what?" I asked, not bothering to hide the annoyance in my voice.

"I didn't say but."

"You trailed off like you were agreeing with me, but getting ready to tell me how you're not agreeing with me."

"It seems like it's more than that," she said. "Are you upset about something?"

"I don't think now is the time for this."

"When?" she asked. "Is that how you do things too? You ignore your girlfriend until you forget why you were mad and hope everything turns out okay?"

"I'm hardly ignoring you. I'm standing here now, talkin' to you, ain't I?"

"Yes, but you're clearly upset, and I don't understand why you won't talk to me about it."

Frustration burned in my veins, running through me like molten steel. Clenching my fists, I turned and started back to my house.

"Jameson, don't you walk away from me."

I whirled around, anger sitting like a hot coal in my gut, searing me from the inside. "You want to talk about why I'm upset? All right, let's talk. What the fuck happened between you and Brock Winston on that show?"

Her eyes widened, and she froze, almost like I'd slapped her. "What?"

"You've never told me what really happened between the two of you," I said. "And I never asked because I assumed if there was somethin' to tell, you would have been up front with it. But now I'm not so sure about that."

"You can't be serious."

Her cheeks flushed, and it pissed me off more. I loved the way she looked when her skin got that hint of pink. Damn it, I was angry, not turned on.

"I'm dead serious, sweetheart," I said. "Lay it out for me."

"Nothing happened."

"Nothing? Not a damn thing? You just went around makin' eyes at each other all season long, but nothing else happened all those times you two were alone?"

"Making eyes?" she asked. "I was supposed to flirt with everyone. I did. Shamelessly, and I'm not proud of that. The show edited the rest of it out to make it look like I was only flirting with Brock."

"What about all those times you were alone, away from the cameras?"

She put her hands on her hips and my eyes drifted down to the shape of her legs under that skirt. God, she looked good.

"Why don't you just say it? Ask," she said.

I blinked, tearing my eyes away from her sexy legs and back to her face. Damn it, why was I getting hard? This was ridiculous.

"Did you suck Brock's dick in that back room?"

Her nostrils flared, her jaw tightened, and I knew in an instant that I'd just fucked up. Badly.

"No, I did not," she said, her voice laced with anger. "I followed him into that back room because I knew he needed to talk. He was worried about Maisie, and the producers weren't letting us have any contact with the outside world. He'd been trying to get them to bend the rules for him, since she'd been injured. He'd told me earlier that they'd said no, and I felt bad for him. He needed someone to talk to. That was all."

"Were you tempted?"

"Was I tempted to blow Brock Winston?" she asked. "God, Jameson, why would that even matter? Even if I was, how could you hold that against me? We're talking about something that happened before we were dating. Do I have to answer for every blow job I've ever given?"

I almost said yes, but thankfully I stopped myself before it came out.

"He was married, and you were engaged," I said. "Although you were lying about that to everyone, so I don't know what that means. If you were tempted, that's an issue."

Every time I said *tempted*, my cock got harder. She was feeling it, too. I could tell. The two of us were fixin' for a good angry fuck. And maybe that was what we needed.

She stepped toward me, her tits straining against that little top. "Me being tempted by another man before we met is an issue?"

"It wasn't before we met. We met when we were five."

"Oh my god, you know what I mean," she said. "Do you know how crazy you sound right now?"

I threw my arms up in the air. "You make me fucking crazy. I don't know what the hell I'm doing with you."

She stopped, her posture changing. We were outside, but it was like something had sucked away all the air. She stared at me, her lips parted, and blinked a few times.

The last thing I'd said hung in the space between us. *I don't know what the hell I'm doing with you.* The truth of that hit me square in the chest. Took all the fight out of me. The lust, too.

What *was* I doing? Fanning the flame of anger so we could angry fuck and pretend that was making up? Sounded an awful lot like my parents. And they'd been miserable together more often than not.

I had no idea what I was doing with her.

Leah Mae had spent almost half her life away from here, living in a world about as far removed from Bootleg as you could get. And how much of that life had she really left behind? How much did she *want* to leave behind? She'd slipped right back in easily enough, soon as we were in front of all those Hollywood people. She'd done what they said, like she was happier with someone telling her what to do.

I'd hated it. Hated seeing her like that. I didn't understand it, and it made me realize, I had no idea what I was doing with her.

I probably wasn't cut out for a relationship with any woman, but with Leah Larkin? I was damn lost.

"I'm goin' alone tomorrow," I said, my voice quiet. "Go home, Leah."

Then I turned and left her standing there.

Chapter Thirty-Two

Leah Mae

I stared at Jameson's closed door longer than I should have. The sound of it banging shut seemed to hang in the still air, an echo with no real sound.

He'd told me to go home. And he'd called me *Leah*.

He never called me Leah. Always Leah Mae, from the first time we'd bumped into each other at the Pop In. Just now, he'd flung my shortened name at me like an insult. Like he didn't see me the same way anymore. I wasn't the girl who'd been his friend when we were kids. Maybe not even his girlfriend, anymore.

Had Jameson just broken up with me?

I was too angry to go after him. I got back in my car—my rental car, I reminded myself—and peeled out in the loose gravel. How could he ask me if I'd given Brock a blow job? He knew me better than that. I was insulted, and hurt, and those were definitely not tears stinging my eyes. I blinked them back, determined not to cry. I was angry, and angry people didn't cry.

When I got home, I sat in the car, not sure I wanted to

go in. I hadn't actually slept here in a while. Despite Jameson's long hours in his workshop this week—and how distant he'd been toward me—I'd still been sleeping at his place. Sleeping, and nothing else since L.A., which now I could see was a bigger red flag than I'd realized. I'd thought he was just worn out from working so hard, and maybe a little stressed about the unveiling.

Apparently it was a lot more than that.

The cabin was dark. Looked cold. And just like the car, it wasn't mine. Regardless of my arrangement with Scarlett, it was a vacation rental, not a place meant for someone to stay long-term. Nothing in my life was long-term.

But that wasn't new. When was the last time anything had been static in my life? I'd moved more times than I could count since high school. I'd hardly spent more than six months in any one place—often less. For years, Kelvin had been the only constant in my life. Looking back, I could see that's why I'd been with him. In a life where travel and change were the norm, having one person who was always there was a comfort. I'd mistaken that comfort for love.

Had I done that again with Jameson?

I went inside, the tears starting to spill, despite my best efforts to hold them in. I sniffed my way through undressing, tossing my clothes aside, and rooted around the dresser for something to sleep in. I didn't care that it was early. I just wanted this day to be over.

Although I'd been staying with Jameson, about half my stuff was still here. I was caught in between, existing in a place where I had no real home. No real roots. No real future anywhere. Everything was temporary.

I slipped on a tank top and shorts and fell into bed.

———

I was up early the next morning, wondering if I had a text from Jameson. No messages. I showered and dressed. Had some tea and breakfast. Still nothing.

The longer the morning dragged on, the angrier I got. Was

he really going to Charlotte without me? He wasn't even going to apologize?

Pacing around the cabin wasn't doing me any good. I was fuming, frustration simmering in my belly like water boiling in a tea kettle. If I'd have been a cartoon, I would have had steam coming out of my ears.

For lack of anything else to do, I drove over to my dad's. Jameson was probably on the road by now, and it was clear he'd meant it when he said he was going alone. I almost turned up the road to Jameson's instead, just to see if he'd gone. But I didn't. Went straight to my dad's house. If that was how Jameson wanted to be, he could go to Charlotte all by his damn self.

When I pulled up to my dad's house, I was relieved that Betsy's car wasn't out front. I was happy for Dad and Betsy, but I didn't feel like doing this—whatever this was going to be—in front of her.

The front door opened, and Dad stepped out onto the porch as I got out of the car. He must've heard me drive up. Tears stung my eyes again, but I swallowed them back.

"Hey, sunshine," he said as I walked up the porch steps. I could tell by his voice that he could see something was wrong. His demeanor had that soothing dad quality.

"Hi, Daddy."

He gave me a sympathetic smile. Held out his arms for me and wrapped me in a hug. He felt stronger than he had since I'd been here.

"Come on in, sweetheart."

Instead of me waiting on him, like I'd been doing when he was sick, he sat me down on the couch and went into the kitchen. Came out a few minutes later with two glasses of whiskey on ice.

"It's nine in the morning," I said, taking the glass from him. "I was expecting lemonade or sweet tea."

"I have a sneaking suspicion this isn't a lemonade or sweet tea kind of visit." He sat down in his recliner and rested his glass on the arm. "Wanna talk about it?"

I took a sip of my drink and shrugged. "I suppose. I think Jameson and I broke up last night."

"Hmm," Dad said, and I couldn't tell what he was thinking. "What happened?"

"Well… I went to his house to see if he wanted to go out," I said. "But he said no, and then we got in this big fight."

"About going out?"

"No. I guess it kind of started out that way, but we ended up fighting about… well, about his brother Gibson, and then the show." I didn't really want to get into the details of all that with my dad. I had a feeling he could figure it out, anyway.

"Gibson Bodine, huh," he said, the words coming slow, like he was turning that over in his mind. "He's had a tough time, that one."

"Has he?"

Dad shrugged off my question. "Yeah, but what about the show? Why were you fightin' about that?"

"I don't know, it was like he was just ranting at me," I said. "He asked me about things he should already know, and it hurt that he'd think that of me."

"So he kinda blew up at you?"

"Yes, exactly. And then he told me to go home. And he…" I paused, feeling tears trying to well up again. "He called me Leah. He never calls me that."

"Is this all surprising to you, sweetheart?"

I blinked at him. "What? Of course it's surprising. Why wouldn't it be?"

"Well… Jameson Bodine is a quiet sort. Keeps to himself."

"Yeah…" I didn't understand what he was getting at.

"And lately, he's had a lot of attention heaped on him," he said. "Not all of it putting him or his family in the best light."

"Yes, I know. I feel terrible about that."

"I'm not sayin' it's your fault," he said. "I just mean he's a man who's been under a lot of extra pressure recently."

"Right."

"So, him blowing up at you makes a lot of sense."

"I…" I paused, unsure of what to say to that. I had a feeling my dad was trying to make me feel better, but he was only confusing me. Wasn't he supposed to be on my side? Mad at Jameson for breaking up with his daughter? "Daddy, I have no idea what you're talking about."

He shifted in his seat. "Sweetheart, people tend to blow up at the ones they trust the most. A child will behave for everyone but his mama, because he knows his mama is going to love him even if he's bad. Grown men do it, too. It ain't right, necessarily, but it's human nature."

"So you think Jameson and I got in a fight because he trusts me?" I wasn't quite buying his logic.

"In a manner of speaking," he said. "We let go when we're with someone safe. With someone we think is going to love us anyway. I'm not sayin' he thought it through. If he had, I reckon he wouldn't have fought with you at all."

I took a sip of the whiskey. "The show made it look like I had an affair with a married man while we were filming. I didn't, and I don't think Jameson believes me. He asked me last night and I just… how could he think that about me?"

"You've told him you didn't?" he asked. "Before last night, I mean."

"I didn't think I had to. I thought he knew."

"You thought…" He sighed. "A man doesn't know what he doesn't know. And he sure as hell doesn't know what a woman is thinking. I fell into that trap with your mama."

"It's not that I expected Jameson to read my mind. But I thought he knew me better than that."

"There's always things to learn about someone," he said. "Good or bad. And making assumptions isn't a good idea, even with someone you know inside and out."

"Daddy, are you trying to tell me you think this is my fault?"

He smiled, a warm, gentle smile, his eyes crinkling at the corners. "No, sweetheart. And if I thought Jameson had mistreated you, I'd be of a different mind. So you tell me if I'm wrong, and that boy needs a whoopin'. I'll visit some Bootleg justice on him right quick."

"No, he didn't mistreat me."

"All I'm saying is that I understand him a bit," he said. "I've seen the two of you together, and I know how he looks at you. If he picked a fight with you last night, it's because he's hurtin' inside. Not because he doesn't love you."

"I think he left for Charlotte without me," I said. "He told me he was going alone, and I haven't heard from him this morning."

"Stubbornness is a virtue among us Bootleggers," he said. "Sweetheart, do you know why Betsy and I fell in love?"

Confused by the sudden change of topic, I stared at my dad for a few seconds. "Um… I guess because you spent a lot of time together and realized you cared for each other?"

"That's part of it," he said. "But there's more. Betsy saw me at my worst. Now, that's because I was sick, not because I was angry and blew up at her. But I knew there was something special about her when it hit me that she was seeing me at my worst, and she wasn't walking away from that. Because honey, when you find someone who can see the ugly parts of you—because lord knows we all have them—and love you anyway, that's a rare thing. So I suppose my question to you is this: Does seeing a bit of Jameson's ugly side make you want to walk away? If that's a deal breaker for you, that's quite all right. Nothing wrong with it. Maybe he's not the man for you, and fightin' with him last night made you see it clearly."

"No," I said, surprising myself with my vehemence. "No, that's not how I feel at all."

He nodded slowly and took another sip. "And perhaps Jameson saw a bit of your not-so-good side, too. I don't know, that's just a guess. Maybe he saw it last night. Or maybe he saw it before, and he's not sure what to do with it. It's disconcerting when it happens. But the real test is in what two people decide to do about it."

I settled deeper into the couch. Was my dad right? Had

Jameson blown up at me like that because he thought I was safe? Far from making me feel better, that thought made me feel worse. Anger was a heady emotion, easy to hold onto and still be certain you were in the right. Letting go of it meant hurt was creeping in to take its place. Hurt and sadness.

It had hurt when Jameson had asked me about Brock. But my dad might have had a small point. I'd never specifically told Jameson that I hadn't slept with Brock. We just hadn't talked about it. It had been easier not to—easier to ignore the outside world and live in our little bubble. It wasn't so easy now that our bubble had burst.

My heart sank as I realized something else. Not only had I never been clear with Jameson about Brock, I'd never denied it publicly, either. It had felt like I didn't have a choice. What had Evelyn said? My life savings wasn't worth my pride, and if the studio went after me, I'd lose everything.

But what was Jameson supposed to think? If I'd never been straight with him about Brock, and I kept quiet about it publicly, was it any wonder he'd question the truth?

Maybe he wasn't the only one who needed to do some apologizing.

I put my whiskey on the coffee table and stood. "Thanks, Daddy. I need to go."

"Course you do," he said. "Take care, sweetheart."

"I will."

Chapter Thirty-Three

Jameson

There were hours yet before the sun would come up, but I couldn't sleep. I'd slept the evening away after Leah Mae had gone, and woken up around midnight. Since then, I'd been tossing and turning, replaying everything in my mind.

What the hell had happened? I'd been angry, no doubt about that. But how had it turned into me storming off, leaving Leah Mae outside in the cold? Telling her I was going to Charlotte alone. And I'd called her *Leah*.

I'd meant to. Wasn't proud of that. Lying in my bed, staring at the ceiling at four o'clock in the morning, I could hear how cold it had sounded. It had been downright mean, and I knew it. Too late to take it back, now.

Since I wasn't sleeping anyway, I got up and went out to my workshop. Flicked on the lights. The place was a wreck. There was stuff everywhere—discarded bits of scrap, nails and screws, tools. It was typical for the aftermath of finishing a project. I tended to create a bunch of chaos while I worked. When I finished, I'd clean it up so I could start over again.

I couldn't leave for Charlotte until I got my tire fixed, so I went to work on setting my workshop to rights. Put stuff away, returning bits of metal to their bins. Found new places for the smaller pieces that I could use later. Tools went back in their drawers or on hooks on the wall.

There was a stack of boxes over by the door that I hadn't dealt with yet. Stuff from my dad's place. I stood in front of it, my hands on my hips, eying it all with suspicion. More than likely, there was nothing in there but junk. Scarlett had said to save pictures, but everything else could be tossed out or given away.

I blew the dust off the top box and opened the flaps. There was an odd assortment of things. Faded papers, old bills, one of Scarlett's report cards. A discipline slip with Gibson's name on it. A half-empty roll of tape. Some brittle ribbon and an old sewing kit. I figured there wouldn't be much else of interest, but I dug around a bit more.

At the bottom, I found a large yellow envelope stuffed with old pictures. Scarlett would want these, for sure. I pulled out a few and thumbed through them. Mostly us as kids. There were a bunch of Gibs. I could tell it was him by his big, cheesy smile. Didn't see that expression on him often nowadays, but he'd always hammed it up for pictures. Got yelled at for it, too.

And then I found one of her.

My mama had been a pretty lady. Scarlett took after her. She'd had long auburn hair and freckles on her nose and cheeks. Big gray eyes. She was wearing a Sunday dress—all covered in pink flowers—and holding a baby. It was hard to tell who the baby was. One of us boys, to be sure, judging by the blue outfit. By her smile, I reckoned it was Bowie. He'd always been the easiest of us all. He'd probably made Mama smile all the time.

I blew out a long breath. I missed my mama. She'd been the only one in the house who'd really seen me. There hadn't been much she could do about Dad, but at least she'd noticed me some of the time. When I'd drawn her pictures, she'd put them up on the fridge. Granted, they'd always seemed to get knocked down and trampled. But at least she'd told me she liked them.

Although, truth was, she hadn't been the only one who'd seen me. I'd stayed out of Dad's way as much as possible—life had been easier that way. Bowie had always been busy with all his friends, and Scarlett was the baby. We'd had to raise her ourselves for the most part.

But Gibson had paid attention to me, in his own way. He'd made sure I had a lunch every day. Kept the bullies at school off my back. Showed me the best hiding places for when Dad was drinking and it was best to be scarce. Maybe that was why fighting with Gibs was bugging me so much. Gibson and I didn't fight. He kept a lookout for me and ignored me the rest of the time. Been that way since we were kids. I wondered if it would ever go back to that, or if I'd screwed it all up by dating Leah Mae.

I tucked the pictures back in the envelope and set it on a shelf. I didn't much want to keep going down memory lane. I'd give them to Scarlett and she could do what she wanted with them.

The next box was the same size. I picked it up to move it to a shelf, but it was oddly heavy. Out of curiosity, I opened it up.

Looked a lot like the other box—papers and so forth. There was another big envelope and I peeked inside. Instead of photographs, this one had newspaper clippings. A lot of them, in fact.

The newsprint felt brittle between my fingers, so I pulled them out carefully. There was an article about Gibson playing football senior year at Bootleg Springs High School. Bowie winning an award. An announcement about the Bootleg Springs Historical Society charity lunch with a big photo of Mama and a smiling six-year-old Scarlett.

There were full newspapers, too, folded in half. Three of them. I pulled them out and my heart felt like it was stuck in my throat. The front-page story on two of them was Callie Kendall.

The photo I'd come to know so well from her missing persons posters smiled back at me from the front page of the *Bootleg Springs Gazette*. It declared her missing and seemed to be reporting on the search. The second paper was more of the same, from about a week later. I reckoned a lot of Bootleggers had kept these papers. It had been a defining moment in the town.

The third newspaper had me especially confused. I didn't see anything about Callie on the cover. Spreading it out on my workbench, I paged through it, wondering why my parents had kept it. Then, on page five, I saw something that surprised me more than anything.

It was me.

Way at the bottom, there was a small photo of me standing in front of a sculpture I'd done. Wasn't metal, but I'd worked with a lot of materials as a kid. This one was clay, and I'd entered it in an art contest. Won first place.

The article was barely a caption. Just my name, and age—eleven—and a sentence or two about me winning. I didn't remember ever seeing this—didn't think I'd known my picture had been in the paper. But my parents had kept it?

Couldn't hardly be a mistake. There didn't seem to be anything else of interest in the entire issue. And the fact that it hadn't been cut out like the others made me wonder... had my dad hung onto this? Seemed like Mama would have cut out the little snippet about me, not kept the whole paper.

But that didn't make a whole lot of sense. My dad had never liked me doing any kind of art. Said it wasn't manly. I'd shown him things, but he'd always scowled. Had he kept this?

I folded up the paper and put it all back. That didn't explain why that box had been so heavy, so I moved a few things out of the way.

And just when I'd thought I'd been as surprised as I could possibly get, I saw what weighed so much.

I pulled out a hunk of metal that was roughly in the shape of a dog. At least, that's what I'd been going for when I'd made it. It was the very first metal sculpture I'd ever made. The thing that had made me fall in love with the medium.

I'd talked Clint Waverly, the local mechanic, into teaching me to weld after seeing a video at school about an artist who worked with metal. It had been fascinating to watch, what with the sparks flying and the heat and electricity coming together to forge pieces of hard steel together.

Once I'd gotten the hang of it, he'd let me come over and use his tools as long as he didn't need them. I'd found some rusty old wrenches in the garage—stuff my dad had probably forgotten was even out there—and used them to make this. Didn't look much like a dog, now that I looked at it through the eyes of an adult. But at the time, I'd been mighty proud of it.

I'd given it to my dad. And gotten yelled at for stealing his tools.

He'd asked me where I'd gotten the wrenches, so I'd told him. I could still see his face, getting red with rage. He'd said it was stealing, and no son of his was going to be a thief. He'd yelled that I'd ruined his perfectly good tools, grounded me for a month, and thrown the sculpture out the back door.

I held it in my hands and stared at the messy welds. They looked like frosting spilling out between the edges of a cake if you pressed down too hard.

But he'd kept it.

I didn't understand what that meant. He'd been so angry at me, I'd been a bit afraid he'd smack me for it. Dad had never laid a finger on us, but he'd yelled loud enough, it had felt like being hit. Had to me, at least.

Why had he kept this all these years? Had he known it was in here, or had my mama rescued it and put it away? Somehow, I didn't think so. Mama hadn't been home when I'd shown him. I didn't think she'd ever known about it. By the time I'd gone looking for the sculpture, it had been gone. I'd always figured Dad had thrown it away.

While I was upstairs, cowering in my bedroom, had he gone outside and picked it up? Dusted it off and tucked it away in his closet?

I'd never really understood my father, and I didn't understand him now. But suddenly, I saw things a little differently. Maybe he hadn't hated me like I'd thought. A terrible feeling, to think your daddy hates you. I'd thought it many times. The times he'd been nice, and even affectionate, had only confused me more. But maybe those times had been more true than I'd known.

Maybe my dad had been proud of me.

That was enough to get my chest worked up tight and my throat feelin' thick. I swallowed hard and put the sculpture away. Maybe I'd get it out again and put it somewhere in the shop—a nice reminder of how far I'd come. But for now, I couldn't bear to look at it any longer.

I finished tidying the workshop around the time the sun came up. I had a long drive ahead of me, so I got cleaned up, made some coffee, and packed my bags for my trip. Checked my phone, thinking maybe Leah Mae would have texted. Wondered if I should text her.

In the end, I didn't. I put the spare tire on my truck and drove into town to get it fixed. Then without allowing myself to think too much about her, I got on the highway and headed out of Bootleg. It was probably better this way. I'd just disappear. Fade into the background and let her move on. I was pretty good at that—had a lot of practice over the years. Lord knew I had no idea what to do to fix things between us, or if they could be fixed at all.

Or whether I was worth the trouble.

Chapter Thirty-Four

Jameson

The humid air made my shirt cling to my back. It was warm for October, but I reckoned that was just Charlotte for you. The fact that I couldn't seem to stop pacing didn't help much, either.

I was outside in a staging area near the central courtyard where we'd installed my piece this morning. She'd arrived safely from Bootleg Springs—not a scratch on her. They'd unloaded her fine, and I'd put on the finishing touches, securing her to the metal base where she'd live out her days.

I didn't think I'd ever been more proud of a piece of art than I was of my angel. She looked magnificent—perfectly proportioned. Soft, organic lines. She looked like she ought to be breathing.

My client, a man by the name of Everett Davis, had come to see her around the time I'd finished up her installation. At first, I hadn't been sure what to make of his reaction. He'd stood stock still, just looking at her. His mouth had parted, and after standing a while, he'd walked slow circles around her. When he'd finally spoken to me, he'd seemed to have trouble deciding what to say. All he'd managed was, *it's beautiful.*

I took that to mean he was pleased. Hoped so, at least.

"Jameson!" Deanna power-walked her way past security, wearing a flowing black shirt and wide-legged slacks. Her dark hair had streaks of silver, and it was pulled back in sleek ponytail. She took off her sunglasses. "Oh my god, Bodine. Mr. Davis is basically in love with you right now."

"How's that?" I asked.

"He loves the piece so much, you left him speechless."

"I reckon he didn't say much."

She laughed. "You have outdone yourself. Even after seeing pictures, she absolutely blew me away. I knew you were good, but this… Jameson, the piece is stunning."

I gave her a polite nod. Would have tipped my hat, had I been wearing one. "Thank you, Dee."

"I hope you're ready to get back to work," she said. "Hits to your website are up by a thousand percent. I'm not kidding. I've had inquiries from all over the country. You're about to be more in demand than you thought possible."

"Wow… that's great news."

"I hope you're excited under that humble exterior of yours," she said with a smile. "Your career is taking off."

"I'm just a little overwhelmed is all."

"God, you're adorable. Too bad you're taken. My niece is here."

I rubbed the back of my neck and glanced away. "Yeah… um, thanks, Dee."

"Where is she, by the way?" Dee asked. "No Leah Larkin after all?"

"Um, no."

"Is everything all right?"

I cleared my throat. "She couldn't make it. Is there water around here anywhere? I'm hotter than a sinner in church."

"Yeah, of course," she said. "I'll be right back."

"No, no, just point me in the right direction, and I'll fetch some myself. Don't need you going to any trouble."

She stared at me a moment, a strange look on her face. I was about to ask her what she was looking at, but she finally answered. "If you go in through the main lobby doors, there's a big table with bottled waters."

I nodded again. "Thanks."

The lobby was blissfully cool, the air conditioning in the brand-new building working like magic. I grabbed a water and took a few sips. We were starting soon, so I didn't linger. I grabbed another bottle in case Dee was thirsty and went back outside.

People meandered around the courtyard, checking out the new building, but my sculpture was covered. A platform stood next to it with a podium, microphone, and big speakers. A man was up there—seemed to be checking the wiring.

I headed back toward the staging area, but something—or rather someone—caught my eye. I had to do a double, then a triple-take. Was that Gibson?

He stood near the covered sculpture, his arms crossed, sunglasses on his face. I stopped and stared at him. Was I seeing things? He seemed to notice me and sauntered over. It was indeed my brother.

"What in the hell are you doing here?" I asked. Maybe not the nicest thing I could have said, but I wouldn't have been more surprised if my dead father had been standing there.

"You should have told us about this," Gibson said. "Why didn't you say anything?"

"Told you?" I asked. "Why?"

"Are you fucking kidding me?" he asked. "This is a big deal."

"What, my sculpture?"

Gibson shook his head, then swiped his glasses off. "Yes, your sculpture. Jesus, Jame. Are you serious? This is one of those *you've made it* moments. Don't you get that?"

"I reckon."

"You reckon," he said, shaking his head. "You know, most people aren't good enough to make a living the way you do. Or brave enough to take the risk to try."

I stared at him, dumbstruck. It was hands down the nicest thing Gibson had ever said to me. Maybe the nicest thing he'd ever said to anyone—that I knew about, at least.

"Thanks."

"If you'd said something, we all would have been here. I came down 'cause…" He trailed off and looked away, clearing his throat. "Because I wanted to make sure you weren't here alone."

I looked down at the ground, feeling a bit choked up. Those weren't tears stinging my eyes. Just a little breeze stirring up something in the air. "That was good of you."

"I, uh…" Gibson paused again. Seemed like he was having some trouble figuring out what to say. "I was here this morning and saw your sculpture before they covered it up. It's, um… it's real good."

"Thanks, Gibs."

He put his sunglasses back on. "Yeah. All right, don't think about all the people and shit. Just be proud of your work. You earned this."

I nodded and he punched me in the arm before walking away. And just like that, the Bodine brothers were good again.

Dee found me again while I was still a bit dumbstruck over seeing Gibson.

"Are you okay?" she asked. "They're almost ready to start."

"Yeah, fine. Water?"

She took the bottle. "Thanks. We'll wait over here."

I followed her to the platform where a few people, including Mr. Davis, had gathered. He shook my hand again and said how much he appreciated me being here. I just tried not to think about all the people congregating in front of the platform. One second, it looked like just a handful; the next it was getting downright crowded. Someone had obviously signaled that things were about to begin, and the crowd in front of me swelled.

My heart beat hard in my chest, but I took a few deep breaths to calm my nerves. I could do this.

We all stepped up onto the platform, and a man I didn't know started in on a long introduction, talking about Everett Davis. He had an impressive list of accomplishments leading up to opening the beautiful building behind me.

Mr. Davis took the microphone and said a few words, mostly thanking people. Talked about his vision, and his hopes for the future. He was a good speaker—held the crowd's attention quite well.

"Now for the moment I've been waiting for," he said. "When I discovered the artwork of the young man standing next to me, to say I was impressed would be a vast understatement. I understand architecture and design, but Jameson Bodine understands beauty. I was fortunate enough to commission a piece from him, and I have to say, it blew all my expectations out of the water. And they were high expectations."

He signaled for the sculpture to be uncovered. I watched, my heart hammering, palms sweating, as two men pulled the canvas sheet down.

A collective gasp rippled through the crowd, followed by a low murmur of sound as people reacted to her.

"It's my great pleasure to introduce you to the artist of this remarkable piece, Jameson Bodine."

The crowd applauded, and Mr. Davis gestured for me to take his place behind the podium.

I swallowed hard and blew out a quick breath. My stomach was queasy, but I squared my shoulders and stepped up to the microphone.

And then I saw her.

Leah Mae moved closer to the platform, slipping her way through the crowd of onlookers. Her hair was in a loose braid, hanging over one shoulder. She wore a pretty yellow dress with a chunky turquoise necklace and her favorite cowboy boots.

She smiled and winked, then tugged on her ear twice. Our signal. She'd done that for me back when we were kids, anytime the teacher made me get up in front of the class. I'd focused all my attention on her, forgetting anyone else was looking at me.

I grinned back at her, doing the same thing now.

"Hi," I said, and the speaker cracked. I turned to the side and cleared my throat. "I'm Jameson Bodine of Bootleg Springs, West Virginia. I have to admit, speaking in public is not my biggest strength. I tend to prefer to stay behind the scenes and let my work speak for me."

I paused and glanced over at my sculpture. I hadn't planned to say much, but I looked back at Leah Mae, and the words poured out.

"I'd planned to make something different. But after seeing something on TV, this image came into my head. It was a woman. Someone I used to know. And she'd always been happy and smiling with a light in her eyes like summer sun glinting off the still waters of a mountain lake. But this time, when I saw her, the light was gone. And I couldn't stop thinking about how she looked like an angel to me. But not an angel who was free to fly. Like a caged animal in an old-fashioned circus, being made to do tricks.

"So, I took a chance and followed my vision. I'd never created anything quite like her before, and truth be told, I wasn't sure I was capable. But I guess when a man is as inspired as I was, there's not much that can keep him from seeing it through. In any case, I'm glad y'all like it. It means the world to me."

Stepping back, I nodded, and the crowd erupted with applause. But I hardly noticed they were there. All I could see was Leah Mae. Her wide smile. Her eyes shining with tears.

Mr. Davis shook my hand again and stepped up to the microphone. I wasn't too sure what else was said. A few more words, a few more people to thank. Then we stood for photos, and after what seemed like an eternity in the fires of hell, I was finally free.

Leah Mae waited near the sculpture, her head upturned. She looked toward me as I approached her. I wasn't sure what I was supposed to do. Run up and scoop her into my arms? Kiss her? Walk slowly so I didn't scare her off?

"Hi," she said.

"I didn't think you'd be here."

She tucked her hair behind her ear and nibbled on her bottom lip. "I wasn't sure if you wanted me."

"Oh darlin'." I stepped closer. "I want you more than anything in this world."

I stopped thinking about what I was supposed to do—how to do this right—and grabbed her, pulling her against me. She melted in my arms, her body soft. I kissed her hair and breathed her in—held her tight.

"Baby, I'm sorry," I said, my voice quiet in her ear. "I'm so sorry."

"Me too." She pulled back so she could look me in the eyes. "I'm sorry for how I acted in L.A. And I need you to know, nothing happened with me and Brock. I promise."

"I know." I caressed her cheek. "I'm sorry I doubted you."

"It's okay," she said. "It wasn't fair of me to assume you'd know the truth when I didn't tell you."

"I still shouldn't have yelled at you."

She let her nose rub gently against mine. "I guess… sometimes we let go with the person we love the most because we know they're safe. We know they're going to love us anyway."

"I reckon you're right about that," I said. "I don't want to live that way, though."

"We won't," she said, her lips drawing closer to mine. "All we can do is our best. And when things are hard, we work it out."

"You make it sound awfully easy."

"Simple, but not easy," she said. "But you're a good man, Jameson Bodine. One of the best I've ever known."

"I love you like crazy, Leah Mae Larkin."

"Just tell me I'm still your girl."

I cupped her cheek and looked into her bright green eyes. "You're still my girl."

Our lips came together and I nearly shuddered with relief. Without a care for who was watching, I kissed my girl. Kissed her until we were both breathless and had to come up for air. Then I kissed her some more.

She giggled as I kissed her sweet lips a few more times. Finally, I stepped back, just enough so we weren't quite so obscene.

Leah Mae looked up at my sculpture. "Can I ask you a question?"

"Of course."

"I feel silly even asking, but… is that me?"

I smiled. She had known. That first time she'd visited my shop, I'd dismissed the look she'd had in her eyes—figured it hadn't meant anything. But I'd seen it, and deep down, I'd known. We'd both known this was her.

"She is."

She touched her fingers to her lips and her eyes glistened. "You added more since I last saw her."

I nodded. "Pulled an all-nighter to finish."

"But… whose hands are they?"

I'd crafted two hands reaching up, as if from below—hands intent on rescuing her. One gripped a bar, like he was hoisting himself up. The other held a key.

"I reckon they're mine."

A tear trailed down her cheek and I swiped it away with my thumb.

"You did set me free," she said. "You, and Bootleg Springs."

"Bootleg has a way of doing that," I said. "I guess it has the right sort of magic."

"It most certainly does. And so do you."

Chapter Thirty-Five
Leah Mae

The smells coming out of the kitchen in the Brunch Club made my tummy rumble. We were here for brunch and booze, as one does when they go to the Brunch Club, and I was starving.

Jameson sat next to me, his hand on my thigh. The way he kept sneaking his fingers beneath the hem of my skirt was making me tingle—in all the best ways. He leaned in and kissed my cheek—sweet, and appropriate for public display. What he kept trying to do beneath the table was anything but.

I loved it.

As soon as we'd returned from Charlotte, requests for Jameson's work had poured in. He was booked up solid for the next year, and had actually had to turn down several commissions, simply because he didn't have time. Being able to pick and choose what he wanted to work on was a dream come true for him. He was living his dream, and I was so proud.

Scarlett and Devlin sat across from us, engaged in their usual PDA. It didn't seem to bother Jameson, even though I knew he still felt protective of his sister. I figured he was too busy teasing me under the table, enjoying how it made me squirm.

Bowie, on the other hand, kept rolling his eyes and telling Scarlett and Dev to *knock it off, already.* That only made Scarlett giggle. Bowie even threatened them with detention, which made us all laugh.

The waitress brought our first pitcher of sangria and I helped pour. Gibson walked in and nodded, but didn't say much. Just pulled up a chair, turned it around, and straddled it backwards. Jameson tipped his chin to him and Gibson tipped his back. I was so relieved that the two of them were getting along again—even if *getting along* simply meant Gibson wasn't glaring at Jameson all the time.

I'd seen Gibson at the unveiling in Charlotte, but I kept up the pretense that I didn't know he'd been there. I had a feeling there was a softer side under that hard exterior, but he wasn't about to let anyone see it. As long as there were no more taco food fights, I figured things were probably all right.

"Mornin', y'all," Cassidy said as she walked in. She was dressed in street clothes, rather than her deputy uniform, and her dirty blond hair was down. As always, her sister June was with her. June's darker blond hair was pulled back in a ponytail. They both took off their coats and hung them on the backs of two chairs.

"Mornin', Cass," Scarlett said. "And how are two of my favorite girls on this fine Saturday?"

"Can't complain," Cassidy said.

Scarlett's lips curled in a mischievous grin. "Any plans tonight? Hot date, maybe?"

I glanced at Bowie, but he kept his eyes on his sangria.

"Nope," Cassidy said. "Not unless you count a night at home in my pajamas watchin' old movies a hot date."

"If it was with someone, I would," Scarlett said.

Cassidy just smiled and shook her head. "Men are impossible. No offense to those of the male persuasion at this table."

267

"None taken," Devlin said.

Gibson shrugged. "Nah, you're right, we are."

"Least you're honest," Cassidy said.

I caught June's eye. "How's your fantasy football team doing this year?"

"I'm winning," June said, her voice flat.

"Good for you," I said.

"It shouldn't come as a surprise to my competitors," June said. "I win every year."

"That is a fact," Jameson said. "And the reason none of us play in Juney's league anymore."

June didn't seem fazed by that. But June never seemed fazed by anything.

Jonah came in, pocketing his phone. "Sorry about that. My mom called."

"How's your mama doin'?" Scarlett asked.

"She's fine, I suppose." Jonah took a seat and poured himself a drink.

"You look like you need that," Devlin said.

Jonah took a long sip. "She's just… unhappy with my life choices at the moment."

Devlin raised his glass. "I feel your pain, brother."

They clinked glasses.

"I made the mistake of telling her I need to move out of Jameson's place," Jonah said. "She thinks I'm homeless or something."

Jameson had asked me to move in with him, and of course I'd said yes. I'd practically been living there already, but I was thrilled to make it official. We'd told Jonah he was welcome to stay—and really, I wouldn't have minded a bit—but he'd decided it was time to find a new place to live.

"You could move in with me," Bowie said. "I have an extra room that's not being used."

"You sure?" Jonah asked.

"Yeah, why not?" Bowie said. "I have the space. Besides, I hear you're a good cook."

Jonah laughed. "I hear that, too. All right, it's a deal, then."

They shook hands to make it official.

"How are the wedding plans coming, Leah Mae?" Scarlett asked.

"It's going to be so nice," I said. My dad had asked Betsy Stirling to marry him and I was helping Betsy plan the wedding for next summer. "Simple, but sweet. Y'all are invited, so I hope you'll come."

"Of course we will," Scarlett said. "Wouldn't miss it."

June had randomly put her finger on her nose. She had a magazine sitting out and she quietly thumbed through the pages, the index finger of her left hand sitting on the tip of her nose.

"What's that for, June Bug?" Jameson asked, tapping his own nose.

"I'm not it," she said.

"Not it for what?" Jameson asked. "No one said anything."

"The pitcher of sangria is low, so I estimate the probability of our waitress asking if we want another in the next several minutes at ninety-seven percent. That will inevitably lead to a rush to decide who's buying the next pitcher. I'm planning ahead."

Jameson laughed. "All right, then."

The waitress walked up and smiled. "Are y'all ready to order? Or can I get you another pitcher of sangria first?"

"Not it," June said without looking up.

The rest of us touched our noses, a chorus of *not it* sounding around the table.

"Damn it," Devlin said. He'd been last. "All right, another pitcher. This one's on me. I don't know how you're all so fast."

"Years of practice," Scarlett said, patting his cheek.

We all had a few drinks and ate an enormous breakfast. By the time we were finished, I was so full I thought I might burst. Jameson and I decided to take a stroll around town to walk off some of the food and sangria. He held my coat for me while I slipped my arms in, and put his hand on the small of my back as he led me outside.

The October air was crisp, the warmth of summer long gone. Clouds hung low in the sky, but it was dry. Probably not cold enough to snow, but it wouldn't be long and Bootleg Springs would be blanketed in white. I couldn't wait.

We walked down Bathtub Gin Alley to the corner of Lake Street and I stopped.

"Something wrong?" Jameson asked.

"No. I want to show you something."

I took his hand and led him down Lake Street to an empty storefront. It had once been a novelty shop, but the owners had closed it down some time ago, and it had been sitting ever since. I'd passed it a hundred times and an idea had been forming in my mind. I hadn't told anyone yet, and just the thought of saying it out loud made my tummy tingle with nerves.

We stopped in front of the store. It had a big *for rent* sign in the window.

"I've been thinking," I said and tucked my hair behind my ear. "Maybe this is crazy, and if it is, I want you to tell me the truth. But I think I want to open my own boutique. I could sell some of my own pieces, but also clothes and accessories from other designers that fit the style I'm going for. It would be totally unique, a mix of country and trendy fashion. I think it could be a big hit, especially during the tourist season."

Jameson glanced between me and the store a few times. "Leah Mae, this is genius."

I bit my bottom lip. "Really?"

"Absolutely. I love this idea. You have a great sense of style. All the girls think so."

"I don't know a lot about owning a business, but I could learn," I said. "I've been looking into some online business classes to start."

Jameson smiled, making my heart squeeze. He cupped my face in his strong hands and kissed me. "I am so proud of you."

"Thank you," I said. "I have to see if I have enough savings to get it started. I should be close."

"Well, if not, we should talk to June."

"June? Why?"

"She's something of an investor here in Bootleg," he said. "She helped Lula open the spa, and gave Clarabell and Whit a loan to do some updates to Moonshine."

"That's amazing," I said. "You think she'd help me open my boutique?"

"I reckon she would. We'll need a solid business plan. Juney likes numbers. But she can even help with that. She's great at it."

"Wow. How does she have money to invest in all these businesses?"

He shrugged. "She works for a big company out of Annapolis. Smart as she is, I reckon she makes a good living. She likes to invest that money in small businesses, especially here in Bootleg. Even I worked with her a few years back."

"So I could really do this." I reached out and touched the glass window. I'd been so afraid to say it out loud—afraid it would sound like a terrible idea.

"Darlin', not only can you do this, you will," Jameson said. "I'll have your back every step of the way."

He took me in his arms and kissed me again, deep and slow. The cool air tingled my skin but Jameson's warmth spread through me.

"I love you, Jameson Bodine."

"I love you, too. To the stars and back."

He put his arm around me and we stood in front of the store for a long moment. I could already see it. The sign out front. The window displays. I had a lot of work to do before I could open, but I could do it. I was building a future here, in Bootleg Springs, one step at a time. A future where I had a place. A home.

Most importantly, a future with Jameson. And I couldn't imagine anything better.

Epilogue
Jameson

My angel was no doubt free from her cage.

Leah Mae stood chatting with Cassidy over by the cake table. Her long lavender dress looked like a dream on her, showing all the lines of her willowy body. I'd been staring at her for hours and trying to keep my hands in appropriate places. We were at a wedding, after all. But it wasn't easy.

The day had finally come for Clay Larkin and Betsy Stirling to get hitched. And they'd done so, on a warm July evening in true Bootleg Springs style. The ceremony had been here, at Gin Rickey Park, right out in the sunshine and fresh air. Afterward, they'd served moonshine and sweet tea in mason jars, along with a table full of food that could have fed an entire town—which was a good thing, because the entire town was here.

Leah Mae drifted through the reception with a beautiful smile on her face. Her honey-lemon skin glowed in the sun, her blond hair shining like spun gold. Those red lips were almost more than I could resist.

What could I say. I loved my girl.

She'd been working hard since the fall when we'd started putting plans for her boutique in motion. June had helped her work the numbers and had been thrilled to invest in her little venture. 'Thrilled' being a relative term. It was hard to tell with June Bug, but I was pretty sure she'd been excited. Leah Mae had spent her time taking business classes online and working out the details of her boutique—everything from the decor to the items she'd sell.

Scarlett and my brothers had helped us renovate the store. Leah Mae had done the ordering, focusing on other small up-and-coming designers who fit her style. The whole place was fun and kinda funky—what Leah Mae called *Vogue with a country twist*. She'd named it Boots & Lace. It suited her perfectly.

Her mom and stepdad had come out to visit in the spring. I reckoned they hadn't been too sure about Leah Mae settling down in Bootleg. But after seeing the store, and spending a few days with her, it seemed to have changed their minds.

I'd been happy to meet them and sent them on back to Florida with a small sculpture I'd made. It was a rose made out of thin sheets of metal, meant to remind them of their daughter. Leah Mae's mom had gotten a bit teary when I'd given it to them.

The grand opening of the store had been a smashing success. Locals loved it, and tourists were already discovering it. Leah Mae's Instagram following had helped some, and people had come from hundreds of miles just to shop in her store.

I was so damn proud of her, I hardly knew what to do with myself.

I'd been just as busy. Since my installation in Charlotte last fall, demand for my work had gone right crazy. My smaller pieces sold out in days, and I was still booked solid for the next year with larger commissions. Dee was thrilled, I was doing what I loved, and making a damn good living. Couldn't ask for much more.

Well, I could. And I was fixin' to.

"Come on, Jame," Bowie said, sneaking up next to me. He took a quick look around, like he was afraid of being caught. "It's time."

I grinned and nodded. We crept away from the reception, heading toward the lake. Devlin, Gibson, and Jonah were already there, standing around Gibson's Charger.

Devlin glanced around. "Tell me again what we're doing?"

"Proper send off," Bowie said. "For Clay and Betsy."

Gibson popped the trunk and we pulled out some bags and a wooden platform.

"You sure this is everything?" I asked.

"Should be," Gibson said. "Let's get this set up."

"Yeah, before Scarlett notices I'm gone," Devlin said.

"She knows already," Bowie said. "It's not Scarlett we need to worry about."

Devlin put his hands on his hips. "This is illegal, isn't it?"

"Only if we get caught," Gibson said, and started pulling fireworks out of the bags.

"That's not how the law works," Devlin said, but laughed when he said it.

I didn't worry about Devlin's reluctance. Just reached into my inside pocket and pulled out the diagram. Gibson closed the trunk, and I spread out the paper so we could all see it.

"Here's how it all goes together," I said. "The order is important, so don't mess it up."

"You sure this is going to work?" Jonah asked.

"Yeah," I said, although I wasn't positive. "I reckon it'll be a sight regardless."

We all got to work, sorting the fireworks into the right order and fastening the mortar tubes to the platform. Gibson was in charge of the sparklers, and he wound them up in a tight bundle with electrical tape. Jonah double checked the placement of everything, consulting the diagram I'd drawn.

"This looks good," Jonah said.

Bowie looked over his shoulder. "Yep. I think we got it."

I tied fuses together and added the starter fuse that would

make the whole thing work. When it was finished, we all stepped back and looked at our handiwork.

"Let's get her lit and launched," I said.

We put the platform in the water. I checked the line of fuses one last time, then lit the end. Gibson and I pushed it off, letting it float out in to the dark waters of the lake.

"Go," I said, waving everyone off. I'd made the fuse long so we had time, but we needed to scatter before this thing blew.

I stuffed my hands in the pockets of my dress pants and walked quickly back to the park.

"There you are." Leah Mae walked over to meet me. "Where'd you run off to?"

I slipped my hands around her waist and kissed her nose. "Nowhere."

She grabbed my hand and tugged. "Dad and Betsy are leaving. We need to go see them off."

The wedding guests had all gathered under strings of white twinkle lights. Jimmy Bob Prosser waited in his big Ford pickup. The bed was decked out with quilts, and the back had a big *Just Married* sign. Strings of beer cans hung from the back bumper.

Clay and Betsy walked through, carrying a wicker basket between them with a red and white checkered napkin. People clapped and congratulated them. Some put baked goods and mason jars filled with moonshine or canned preserves into their basket. A little Bootleg send-off to start their honeymoon.

I glanced over at Gibson and caught his eye. He tipped his chin. Should be any second now. I slipped my arms around Leah Mae and pulled her close.

"What's—"

Whatever she was going to say was lost in the first loud boom over the lake. A spray of green sparks burst in the air, followed by blue. Then white. A fountain of silver and gold lit up the sky. The wedding guests clapped and cheered. Clay put his arm around Betsy as they watched the little show.

The last firework went off in a burst of color. After a second of quiet, the crowd started clapping and cheering again. I cleared my throat and moved my hands up to cover Leah Mae's ears.

The sparkler bomb went off with an enormous boom and the wedding guests went wild. Fists rose into the air, cheers went up, and Clay Larkin laughed, hugging his bride.

Leah Mae turned her face toward me and spoke quietly into my ear. "Did you have something to do with all that?"

"I have no idea what you're talking about."

We watched Clay and Betsy get up into the back of Jimmy Bob Prosser's truck. They waved at their guests, all smiles. Clay blew a kiss at Leah Mae. She put her hands across her heart, smiling like the sun, with tears glistening in her eyes. The cans clanked and rattled as they drove off into the darkness, ready for the first night of their new life together.

A wave of nervousness swept through me. Lighting a bunch of illegal fireworks didn't get my heart rate up. But this? I patted my suit pocket. This was enough to tie me up in knots.

With the guests of honor gone, the reception started to break up. Leah Mae made the rounds, thanking people for coming. Shaking hands, having her cheeks kissed. I drifted back toward the cake table. There was still cake to be had, and although I'd already had a piece, it wasn't right to let such a fine confection go to waste.

I took the little box I'd been carrying out of the inside pocket of my suit and felt the shape of it in my hand. Wasn't sure I'd be using it tonight. I'd been carrying Leah Mae's engagement ring around with me for a solid week, wondering how I was going to ask her. I hadn't wanted to compete with her daddy's wedding, so I'd waited. Held onto it, hoping I'd know when the time was right. Now that her dad was off with his new bride, the ring felt like it weighed a million pounds. It was begging me to give it to her.

But I was nervous as all hell about it. I didn't know the first thing about proposing to a woman. I wanted to do it right— Leah Mae deserved a perfect moment—but I was afraid I'd get tongue-tied and mess it up.

I must have been so lost in thought, I wasn't watching where I was going. I bumped right into my sister, just before I reached the cake table.

The box tumbled out of my hand and landed on the ground.

Scarlett reached for the box. I bent down and snatched it away, shoving it back in my pocket, but it was too late. She'd seen it. She knew.

Her eyes widened. "Is that a—"

"No."

"Yes it is, that's a—"

"Okay, yes." I stepped closer. "Keep your damn voice down."

She opened her mouth and by the breath she took, I knew whatever she said next was going to be neither quiet, nor subtle. I clapped my hand over her mouth before she could ruin my life.

"Scarlett Rose, don't you say a word. If you tell a soul I have this, I swear I'll tell everyone…" I paused, because that wasn't the threat it had seemed when I'd first started saying it. Scarlett wasn't exactly the secretive sort. I slowly released her.

"You'll tell everyone what?" she asked, an amused sparkle in her eye.

"Well… I reckon I don't know. Damn you for not having any secrets I can use for blackmail."

She laughed. "Jameson, I'm insulted. You think you can't trust me to keep this quiet?"

"You were about to yell something about me having a ring in my pocket."

"I was not." She put her hands on her hips.

"You were, too." I glanced around to make sure no one else was near. "Just please promise me you'll keep this between us."

"Of course I will," she said. "When are you askin' her? Tonight?"

I rubbed the back of my neck. "I don't know."

"You don't know? Don't you have a plan?"

"Am I supposed to have a plan?"

Scarlett rolled her eyes and groaned. "Yes, you're supposed to have a plan. How are you going to ask?"

"You know… get down on one knee and all that."

"Okay, that's a start," she said, tapping her finger against her lips. "Have you talked to Clay already?"

"Of course."

I'd gone to see Clay Larkin to tell him my intentions before I'd bought the ring. That had been a nerve-wracking conversation. In true Bootleg father fashion, he'd put me through the ringer a bit. Stood with his arms crossed and eyed me with suspicion. But I'd faced him like a man, with my head held high. Wasn't nothing going to keep me from loving his daughter for the rest of my life.

I'd spoken true—said what I needed to say—and he'd smiled. Shook my hand and said it would be an honor to see his daughter marry me. Choked me up a bit, if I was being honest.

"Good, at least you did that much already," she said. "Do you want me to make an announcement? You could bring her up front and ask her in front of everyone."

"No." I almost put my hand over her mouth again. "No, I don't want to ask her in front of everyone."

"I'm just sayin', it looks like that ring is burning a hole in your pocket. We need to get this locked down."

"Says the girl who won't get engaged until she's thirty."

"Don't start with me, Jameson Bodine. Do you want my help or not?"

"No, I don't want your help."

She grinned at me. "Of course you do."

I glared at her. "Don't make a scene. I'm just nervous is all."

Scarlett put her hand on my arm and smiled. Not a smile full of sass and mischief. A sweet smile, with a little hint of sympathy. "Don't be nervous. You love her, and she loves you, and that's all that matters. You'll know when the moment is right."

"Thanks, Scar."

She punched my arm. "Love you, Jame. Go get your girl."

I rubbed my arm where she'd hit me—Scarlett hit hard—and watched her walk off toward Devlin.

"I think everyone's going down to the lake," Leah Mae said behind me.

I jumped and spun around.

"Sorry," she said with a soft laugh. "I didn't mean to startle you."

I ran my hand down her bare arm. "It's okay. Do you want to join 'em?"

"Yeah. I think your brothers are already building a bonfire."

"Let's go, then."

Leah Mae took off her heels and let them dangle from her hand. I put my arm around her and we walked down to the beach. My brothers had wasted no time in getting a good blaze going. A few people backed in their pickups and put down the tailgates. Took out coolers. Someone turned up the music and the party continued in the moonlight next to the water.

The ring was in my pants pocket, so I took off my suit jacket and draped it over the back of Gibson's car. Leah Mae loosened my tie and slid it out from the shirt collar, then unbuttoned my top button. I grinned at her.

"I like you undressin' me."

She smiled and slid her finger down the rest of the buttons. "You looked great tonight."

"Thanks. You look beautiful all the time, but tonight? Darlin', you're stunning. You shouldn't look so pretty at a wedding. Ain't fair to the bride. Although I reckon Betsy didn't mind."

"Betsy was beautiful."

"She and your dad looked mighty happy." I put my hands around her waist and we started swaying to the music. "You threw them a very nice wedding."

"It was lovely, wasn't it?"

The light of the fire reflected in her eyes and her skin glowed. It reminded me of the bonfire at Scarlett's place last summer. That was a year ago, now. I'd gazed at Leah Mae that night, wishing things had been different. Wishing she could have been my girl.

Now she was. And I was ready to make that a permanent arrangement.

My anxiety melted away as I looked at my beautiful girl. And I knew it was time. I brushed her hair back from her face and my mouth turned up in a smile.

"Why are you giving me your little boy smile?" she asked.

"Little boy smile? I didn't know I had one."

"You do." She slid her fingertips across my lips. "It's my favorite of your smiles."

"I reckon there's a reason."

"What's that?"

"Darlin', I'm about to get down on one knee. And when I do, I'm going to ask you to marry me."

She gasped, but I touched her lips with my fingertips and drew her closer.

"When I do, everyone's going to look. It's going to get all quiet and all those eyes will be on us. And I'd wait until we have a chance to be alone, but honey, this ring is singing to me and it won't stop. I need to see it on your finger, and I need that now. So here's what I'm fixin' to do."

She bit her lip and nodded.

"I'm going to ask you here first, right now. Real quiet, so no one can hear me—so it's just for us. And when that's finished, I'll do it right, on my knee like a man should."

Her eyes shone with tears. "Okay."

I looked deep into her gorgeous green eyes and leaned closer so our noses touched. "Will you marry me?"

She shifted even closer, letting her lips brush against mine. "Yes."

I kissed her sweet lips while I slipped my hand in my pocket. When we separated, I slowly lowered. I heard gasps and murmurs as I got down to my knee and looked up at her, holding the ring.

The noise around us quieted and I knew all eyes were on

me. But I didn't worry so much about that anymore. She was what mattered.

"Leah Mae Larkin, will you do the honor of being my wife?"

Her face glowed in the firelight, the flames reflecting off her smooth skin. "Yes, Jameson Bodine. I will."

I took out the ring and slipped it on her finger. Everyone around us exploded with cheers. Whoops and hollers. Her smile was like the sun. I stood and picked her up, lifting her feet from the ground. She wrapped her arms around my shoulders as I twirled her in a circle, then set her down.

Keeping my arms around her, I kissed her again. Tasted her sweet lips. Those lips I was going to keep kissing, until the two of us were old and gray.

I held her close and kept right on kissin' her. Because damn it, I loved this woman with everything I had. Maybe I wouldn't always know what I was doing, but I knew one thing: I was going to spend the rest of my life loving her and letting her love me right back.

Author's Note

Dear Reader,

Can we all just pack up and live in Bootleg Springs? Who's with me?

I can't even tell you how much I've loved working on this series with Lucy. Okay, I can, and I'm going to try. We've had so much fun planning this out, creating these characters, and plotting (maniacally? never) the mystery.

Jameson had a special place in my heart from the beginning. I knew he was quiet and unassuming, but there was a world inside of him. He's a little damaged, but he feels things very deeply. He just needed the right woman to bring it out in him, and make him believe opening up to someone was worth the risk to his heart.

Leah Mae thought she was living her dream. We don't see a lot of her life before she comes home to Bootleg, but it was full of jet-setting around the world. Walking in fashion shows. Starring in photo shoots. It was what she'd always wanted. But sometimes childhood dreams don't turn out to be so great once you're living them.

Bootleg Springs has a special magic, and it brought these two childhood friends back together. And they realized there was a whole lot more.

I enjoyed writing Jameson and Leah Mae's story so much. Since I was following Lucy's book, Whiskey Chaser, I felt like I had to really up my game. Lucy is an amazing writer, and her world building, dialogue, and comedy are so fantastic. I had to stretch myself as a writer to hopefully meet the very high standards she set in book one. But it was a good challenge, and one that's helped me grow as a writer.

I hope you enjoyed this second installment in the Bootleg Springs series! There's definitely more to come. This will be a six book series, and the mystery of Callie Kendall will span all six books. Yes, you'll find out the truth, and yes, there will be more clues along the way.

But no, I won't tell you the secrets now.

If you want to keep in touch, join my newsletter, or come hang out in my Facebook reader group, Alpha Ever After.

Thanks for reading!
CK

Ready for more from Bootleg Springs?

Moonshine Kiss

BOOK #3 BY LUCY SCORE
WITH CLAIRE KINGSLEY!

Continue for an excerpt from *Moonshine Kiss*.

Chapter One

Cassidy

Eight years ago...

I don't feel so good, Cass." My best friend and perpetual partner in crime, Scarlett Bodine, looked up from her hands and knees. She wiped her mouth on the sleeve of her t-shirt.

I stripped the just-in-case hair tie off my wrist and fashioned her long, dark hair into a sloppy knot. "That's 'cause you puked up half a bottle of Jack and a couple of beers, Scar," I reminded her. "You shouldn't have taken Zirkel's bet."

Wade Zirkel had stupidly bet Scarlett he could outdrink her. He was still passed out in the dirt back at the bonfire.

"I'm hungry," she moaned. "Wait, no. More puke."

As Scarlett heaved up her dinner of cheese sticks and coffee into our old Sunday school teacher Mrs. Morganson's hedgerow, I patted her shoulder and drunk dialed my choice of designated drivers.

Bowie picked up, his voice husky. "Y'all need a ride, don't you?"

Just a couple of words and I swear my heart did a swan dive into my belly full of Jack Daniels.

"Maybe I'm calling to listen to your pretty voice." My super sexy flirting was ruined by a hiccup.

"You owe me $10."

It wasn't the fee for the ride. It was the bet we'd made not four hours ago when I'd picked up Scarlett. I was home for the summer fresh off my first year of college, eager to show off my sophomore self to my best friend in the world. And maybe her older brothers. One in particular.

Bowie Bodine.

I'd been doodling that man's name on my notebooks since elementary school. My crush on him was woven into the fabric of my childhood. In kindergarten, when I'd learned to write my own name, I'd insisted on the spot that my teacher show me how to write Bowie's, too. In junior high, I'd developed an obsessive interest in the high school baseball team thanks entirely to their all-star pitcher, Bowie.

"I got your damn ten dollars, mercenary. Now, get your ass down to Mrs. Morganson's before your sister poisons her boxwoods with regurgitated bourbon."

"Ah, hell. Be there in five. I'm holding you personally responsible if Scar tosses up in my back seat again, Cass." He hung up.

I smiled and undid one extra button on my shirt.

"Fix your hair," Scarlett instructed from the ground. "Can't land a man with drunk hair."

Scarlett was aware of my friendly feelings toward her brother. We had a plan. I was going to entrap Bowie with my feminine wiles, marry the man, and then Scarlett and I would be real-life sisters.

I was calculating with a stubborn streak wider than ten miles, at least, according to my mom. With Scarlett's take-action-without-minding-the-consequences attitude in my corner, Bowie didn't stand a chance against my long game.

I'd switched up my strategy from the hand painted

sign-carrying preteen at every home game to the leggy, cleavage-displaying, ambivalent college girl. I flirted lightly as if it were mere habit and pretended that I had handsomer fish to fry than Mr. Bodine.

I didn't. There was not a handsomer fish in all the water in all the world than Bowie. And I had a good feeling about this summer. I was bourbon-confident.

By the time Bowie pulled up in his SUV, I'd managed to drag Scarlett to her feet and wiped her face.

He climbed out in well-worn jeans and a clean polo. My stomach did a weird slosh. It was his casual, first-date outfit. It either hadn't gone well or I'd interrupted. Either way, he was here, and I was happy.

I'd gotten used to watching the man of my dreams date other women. Hell, *I* dated and had a damn good time doing it.

But I was confident that *someday* Bowie and I would end up together. My confidence was telling me that this summer might be that someday.

He shook his head and grinned his crooked grin that he'd been smiling at me for our entire lives as he took in our drunk and disheveled selves. "Looks like you girls are havin' a good night." He opened the back door. "Throw her on back here."

"Bow, I want pancakes!" Scarlett said, throwing her arms around her older brother's shoulders.

"Jesus, Scar. You smell like puke and hot dogs."

"Cheese sticks," I corrected, shoving Scarlett into the back seat and rolling her window all the way down. Bowie and I spent some quality time together over Christmas break cleaning Scarlett's last puke fest out of his door pocket.

"I had a corndog, too," Scarlett sang. "Junior was makin' some in the microwave."

"That's probably why you just destroyed Mrs. Morganson's shrubbery," Bowie observed.

Scarlett thought that was hilarious and laughed until she hiccupped.

"Where to, trouble?" Bowie asked, settling behind the wheel as I buckled myself into the passenger seat. Trouble was his pet name for me. It was meant ironically since I was never in trouble. I'd never be calling someone for bail money on dollar shot night at The Lookout. Not with my dad presiding as sheriff over our sweet little slice of West Virginia. I was the good girl. The smart girl. The criminal justice major who planned to come back here and serve my town. I was the best friend who got Scarlett out of her messes of trouble.

Bowie was like me. Practically a choir boy. Secretly, I thought maybe he was doing his best to make up for his parents while I was living up to mine.

Scarlett warbled a little song in the back seat.

"Let's get some food in her," I suggested, leaning back in the seat and sighing.

Bowie nodded at the waters he'd thoughtfully stashed in the cupholders. "You know the drill."

"Hydration," I twanged. I opened Scarlett's bottle for her and handed it back. "Drink up, buttercup."

Bowie opened mine for me, and I drank deeply. I wasn't much of a heavy drinker. I had better things to do than go around getting shitfaced all the time. But Scarlett sure could be persuasive when she got started.

But the fact was, I was always there to hold Scarlett's hair.

I always called Bowie, and he always came.

It was who we were.

Chapter Two

Cassidy

The 24-Hour Eats Diner was our go-to place to shove fried foods down to soak up the varieties of alcohol underage drinkers were inclined to ingest. It was far enough out of town that we didn't have to worry about running into any Sunday school teachers or father sheriffs. Best of all, it was completely empty.

I slid into the booth and was surprised when Bowie shoved in next to me, leaving Scarlett the whole other side to herself.

My heart did that familiar tap dance when he was close to me. No matter how many boys I dated, none of them ever made me feel that cocktail of nerves and anticipation that he served up for me. It was almost embarrassing how eager my body was just to be close to his.

I opened my menu and pretended to study it. In my peripheral, I gave Bowie the once-over. What was it exactly about him that got me? Was it habit? Had I just loved him for so long there was no other way to feel about him?

He was tall like his brothers but leaner. Gibs and Jame were two sides of the same lumberjack coin. Flannels and facial hair. But Bowie was a little more stylish with his haircut and his clothes. Dark hair, gray eyes. That nice, almost-straight nose that had the slightest kink in it from a baseball knocked back at him after the pitch. He'd made the catch, got the out, and earned two black eyes for it.

He was leanly muscled everywhere from the line of shoulders to the tapered waist. I knew, from up close visual inspection, that he had those abs that were all the rage in Misty Lynn's mama's collection of *Playgirl* magazines that she'd charged us a buck a piece to look at in seventh grade.

But Bowie was more than a sexy-as-hell body. There was so much going on behind those sterling silver eyes. When he looked at me, I felt like he was trying to decode my DNA. Like he wanted to know *everything*. It left me breathless and the exact opposite of the apathetic, available woman I was trying to be.

He was smart. He was kind. He was quiet. He was steady. He was good. Deep down, movie star hero quality good. I'd be stupid not to love him.

I just didn't know if he loved me.

The signs pointed to a strong maybe. I'd been keeping a running tally for about three years now, every look, every comment, every stray physical contact. My instincts were telling me that the man had feelings. But I preferred a black and white, definitive answer.

"I'm havin' pancakes *and* waffles," Scarlett decided. She was lying down on the booth bench, holding her menu aloft over her face.

"You want coffee?" I asked her as our usual late-night waitress approached.

"Yes, please," Scarlett called.

"What'll it be?" Carla the rockabilly poster girl asked, peering at us through her purple cat-eye glasses. We were in here, drunk and a little disorderly at least once a quarter, yet she'd never shown us the slightest bit of recognition, forcing us to increase the percentage of her tip to astronomical realms.

We'd left her fifty percent last time. I thought that would at least get a "the usual?" out of her.

"Coffee, water, pancakes, and waffles, please," Scarlett ordered from her repose.

"Water and the veggie omelet," I decided. I didn't need caffeine coursing through my system when Bowie's arm was resting on the back of the booth an inch from my shoulders.

He ordered his eggs and sausage and coffee while I tried not to think about how close that arm was to touching me.

Carla wandered off in no hurry to plug our order into the system.

"Y'all have fun tonight?" Bowie asked me.

Let's see, I'd done shots with Scarlett and three summertimers—what Bootleggers called the outsiders who flocked to our hot springs and lake every summer. Then I'd picked the cutest summertimer and showed him a two-step by the fire that had both our heads spinning. I'd gotten into a debate about recidivism with a fellow criminal justice major. And now I was sitting here with Bowie Bodine's arm almost around me.

"Yeah. It was all right," I told him. "You have a date tonight?"

He gave me one of those long, quiet looks. "Yeah."

"Have fun?" I asked, blasé as you please. *Cassidy Tucker couldn't be bothered to care about his date, no sir.*

"It was all right." He echoed my own words with a slow grin.

He shifted, taking up more space in the booth. When his knee brushed mine, I considered swooning and then decided against it. It should take more than the accidental brush of denim to impress me, I decided.

Scarlett snort-laughed at something that was only funny to her in her alcohol-addled mind, and Bowie and I shared an amused look. I was finally an adult. Nineteen years old. I'd long clung to the idea that Bowie had never made a move on me because I was too young.

It was either that or he was physically repulsed by me.

But I was pretty sure that wasn't it. I was no big-boobed, bleached-blonde Misty Lynn Prosser. I had my own long-legged, freckled-nose appeal. It was a damn shame it was taking Bowie so long to realize it.

Our food arrived, and Bowie's arm disappeared from the back of the booth. I was a little relieved seeing as how the "will he or won't he touch me" debate would have raged in my head until I'd bitten through my tongue or lip. It'd happened before. There'd come a day when I'd probably choke to death on something because I was too distracted by his presence to chew my dang food. As a safety precaution, I'd taken to eating less around Bowie.

Scarlett popped back up on the other side of the booth and gave Bowie a ten-minute, breakfast carb mouthful rundown of our evening. "Cassidy, what was that guy's name that you were dancin' with?"

Even drunk, my Scarlett was a schemer. She said it as innocent as you please, but I saw her eyes skim Bowie's face, looking for a reaction.

I reached for my water. "Blake." I was almost sure of it. Or maybe it was Nate? Hell, his name wasn't Bowie and that was that.

"Looked like you two were gettin' real cozy," she purred. My best friend was a tiny little fireball with an evil, calculating mind. I loved her to bits and pieces.

I lifted a shoulder as if my own dating exploits were too boring for comment.

Bowie was suddenly very interested in his plate of food. I didn't know what that meant, but Scarlett was grinning like a jack-o'-lantern on Halloween.

Acknowledgments

To Lucy, for joining me on this crazy moonshiney adventure. Cheers, my friend! *clinks glasses from across the country.

To Elayne, for cleaning up my words.

To Nikki and Jodi, for taking time out of your busy schedules to beta read this crazy book and make sure I didn't do anything stupid.

To David, for not making fun of me too much when I started saying y'all. And for always making me coffee and giving me chocolate.

To all our readers, you lovely people are the absolute best and I hope we can both continue to share the crazy, fun, sexy, and sometimes wild musings of our brains with you.

About the Author

Claire Kingsley is a #1 Amazon bestselling author of heartwarming, sexy romance, including contemporary romance, romantic comedies, and small-town romantic suspense. She writes fun, quirky heroines, swoony heroes who love big, romantic happily-ever-afters, and lots of big feels.

She can't imagine life without coffee, great books, and all the crazy characters who inhabit her imagination. She lives in the inland Pacific Northwest with her three kids.

Website: clairekingsleybooks.com
Facebook: Claire Kingsley
Instagram/TikTok: @clairekingsleybooks

Printed in the USA
CPSIA information can be obtained
at www.ICGtesting.com
LVHW040010041124
795605LV00007B/255